'Your *valet*?'

Cassandra was incredulous. 'You want me to pretend to be your valet?'

'I don't *want* you to pretend to be anything. I want you to be twenty-five miles away in Hertfordshire under your father's eye. But you're not, are you? You're here in my bedroom.' Nicholas crossed his arms across his chest and leant against the bedpost, ignoring her blushes. 'And if Aunt Augusta walked in here now and found you, I'd be marrying you.' He grinned at her. 'I don't think either of us would thank her for that!'

Dear Reader

Bonfire Night lights up the November sky, and this month we have books which create their own fireworks! Francesca Shaw is back with a frothy Regency, MISS WESTON'S MASQUERADE, and in MAIDEN COURT Laura Cassidy follows up on Bess and Harry's marriage from her first novel THE BLACK PEARL. Our American offerings are the second part of the Ferguson brothers duo, THE HELL RAISER by Dorothy Glenn, and then we have ROSE RED, ROSE WHITE by Marianne Willman, set in the days of Edward IV. Enjoy!

The Editor

Francesca Shaw is not one but two authors, working together under the same name. Both are librarians by profession, working in Hertfordshire, but living within walking distance of each other in Bedfordshire. They first began writing ten years ago under a tree in a Burgundian vineyard, but, although they have published other romances, they have only recently come to historical novels. Their shared interests include travel, good food, reading and, of course, writing.

Recent titles by the same author:

MASTER OF WINTERBOURNE

MISS WESTON'S MASQUERADE

Francesca Shaw

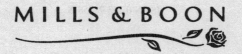

MILLS & BOON

MILLS & BOON LIMITED
ETON HOUSE, 18–24 PARADISE ROAD
RICHMOND, SURREY, TW9 1SR

MILLS & BOON, the Rose Device and LEGACY OF LOVE are trademarks of the publisher.

First published in Great Britain 1994
by Mills & Boon Limited

© Francesca Shaw 1994

Australian copyright 1994   Philippine copyright 1994
This edition 1994

ISBN 0 263 78858 X

Set in 10½ on 12 pt Linotron Times
04-9411-76368

Typeset in Great Britain by Centracet, Cambridge
Printed in Great Britain by
BPC Paperbacks Ltd

CHAPTER ONE

THE Audley Street Chapel clock struck nine, echoed by others more distant, their chimes carrying clearly on the still morning air. Cassandra Weston emerged with caution from the shelter of a dusty laurel bush and stood brushing down her cloak as she surveyed the Square.

There were people abroad, but only servants and tradesmen hurrying about their masters' business: mercifully none of the Quality who might pose a danger to her. At home in Hertfordshire she and Papa would have already breakfasted; the workers at Home Farm would have finished the milking and the streets of Ware would be bustling with market-goers by now.

A small cart rumbled past over the cobbles, causing her to draw back into shelter. Now it was full light, Cassandra felt even more conscious of the awkwardness of her situation, but nothing would be gained by hesitating. She ran her hands through her disarrayed chestnut hair, swallowed hard and picked her way across the cobbles to the steps of number 6, Grosvenor Square.

The knocker was heavy and cold in her hands but still she hesitated before letting it fall. It was five years since she had last seen her Godmama: what if she had miscalculated, presumed too much on the lasting affection of her mother's best friend? Perhaps Lady Lydford would take one look at her and

pack her straight back to Hertfordshire and Papa.
And if she did that, what recourse would be left to
her? She thought of the oily, sliding waters of the
Thames and shuddered, letting the knocker fall
from her fingers with a resounding thud.

The door swung open with startling suddenness
to reveal not the expected footman, but the stately
figure of the family butler whose eyebrows rose at
the sight on the doorstep.

'The tradesman's entrance is at the rear.'

The door was already closing before Cassandra
found her voice. 'Wait, please, Peacock. It is
Peacock, isn't it?'

The butler hesitated and looked more closely at
the small dishevelled figure. 'And what if it is?' he
asked cautiously, obviously puzzled by the contrast
between the sight before him and an educated voice.

'I must see Lady Lydford.'

'The Dowager Countess is not at home.'

'Then I will wait,' Cassandra said more firmly.

'I did not mean that her ladyship is not At Home,
I mean that her ladyship is not at home. She is, in
fact, not even in the country: a fact that any of her
ladyship's acquaintances well know.' Peacock began
to close the door again.

'Out of the country?' In her desperation she had
never considered the possibility that her godmother
would not be in London. Shock, compounded by
hunger and fatigue sent her head reeling. Her knees
gave way and she sank onto the cold stone steps,
whispering 'Godmama not here. . .?'

The butler, who had stooped to seize her arm
roughly, froze, his eyes suddenly alert, scanning her
face. 'You cannot remain here on the steps. Come

inside.' He cast a rapid glance across the Square, but the only people in sight were a milkmaid emerging from Brook Street, pails suspended from the yoke across her shoulders, a street sweeper and a hurrying page boy.

Breathless, Cassandra found herself standing in the hall, an expanse of black and white marble. The light from the central lantern gleamed richly on the balustrade of the curving staircase and the few pieces of elegantly arranged furniture.

A footman slipped silently from an anteroom to disappear through a door under the stairs. Peacock sighed almost imperceptibly, his eyes on the man's back. 'I think it best you should see his lordship and not wait where the other servants can see you.'

'The Earl is at home?' For some reason she had assumed that with her Godmama away, all members of the family would be absent.

'For the present. He leaves for the Continent today.' Perhaps regretting his impulse to admit her, Peacock gestured abruptly to her to follow. A slight figure in the dusty cloak, Cassandra followed the butler's disapproving bulk, trying not to let her ill-fitting shoes clatter on the polished stair treads.

With a glance behind him to ensure the unwelcome and embarrassing visitor was still there, Mr Peacock halted on the second floor landing and scratched lightly on the door in front of him.

As it opened, Cassandra craned her neck, but could glimpse only a portion of the room past Peacock's square shoulders and nothing at all of the man inside who was speaking.

'. . .how the Devil would I know how many neck-cloths I will need before we reach Paris? Does it matter? Do they not manufacture such articles on the Continent?'

Nicholas Anthony St John Cheney, Seventh Earl of Lydford, was evidently out of humour. Cassandra fought down an urge to turn and run down the staircase, across the chequerboard hall, out into the morning-quiet street beyond, and stood her ground.

'None of the quality we would accept my lord.' The valet coughed softly. 'Mr Peacock is at the door, my lord.'

'I am aware of that, Franklin. Well, Peacock? Have you come to announce some further disaster to overset my plans?'

'I could not say, my lord. There is a young. . . person to see you.'

'What makes you think I would wish to interview a young person — or, indeed, anyone else — at this hour in the morning?' A flash of vivid crimson brocade was intermittently visible: the Earl was obviously pacing impatiently.

'I believe you will wish to see *this* one.' The butler spoke with a curious emphasis, stepping aside as he did so to reveal the shrinking figure behind him to the irritable gaze of a tall gentleman wearing a dressing gown shrugged carelessly over shirtsleeves and breeches.

'Have you been at the port, Peacock? Why should I wish to see this scrubby boy?'

'The young person was asking for the Dowager Countess, my lord.' Peacock was very much on his dignity. 'In view of her ladyship's absence, I thought it best to escort the young. . .'

'Will you stop referring to this boy as a Young Person! Here — you boy, come in, stop skulking in the shadows. Have you performed some service for my mother which requires recompense?' He turned impatiently to the butler. 'I do feel, Peacock, that you could have dealt with this.'

'Perhaps, my lord, if you were to enquire the young person's name. . . Meanwhile, there is a matter which requires Franklin's urgent attention in the laundry room.'

The valet grimaced as he slipped out onto the landing. 'Got out of bed the wrong side and three hours too early,' he muttered *sotto voce* as he passed them.

Peacock propelled the cloaked figure into the bedchamber and shut the door. Cassandra's heart sank at the disappearance of her only ally, however reluctant.

Lord Nicholas stood regarding her unfavourably, arms folded across his chest. The bright sunshine streaming in through the long casements caused him to narrow his green eyes assessingly. To Cassandra, quaking in her borrowed clothes, he resembled, with his aquiline features and high cheekbones, nothing more than a sparrowhawk who had sighted an insignificant but tasty mouse.

'Should I know you?' A hint of puzzlement touched the assured voice.

Pushing aside the folds of cloak, she stepped forward into the sunlight, which shone on the boards behind her. 'Yes, although it must be nearly ten years since we last met.' Cassandra was aware she was blushing. She had not expected to find herself in a gentleman's bedchamber, least of all that of the man who had been her hero since she was eight years old. 'I. . . I was hoping to see Godmama.'

'Your Godmama! My mother, you mean? Then you must be. . .' He looked her up and down, frankly incredulous.

'Cassandra Weston.' She let the heavy wool fall to the floor revealing the jerkin, breeches, coarse woollen stockings and the ill-fitting shoes she had borrowed from the stableboy in yesterday's urgent flight.

'Little Cassie? Good G. . .' He checked the oath and walked slowly round her, his expression halfway between amusement and exasperation. 'What prank are you engaged on? You shouldn't be jauntering around London in those clothes: where is your maid?'

'I don't have one.'

'No, I suppose not, at your age.' He came to a halt in front of her, hands on hips, amusement winning out over irritation. 'How old are you? Twelve?'

'Certainly not!' She was about to tell him she was all of eighteen, then some instinct made her hold her tongue. Let him believe she was still a child, at least until they were in more proper surroundings with a maid as chaperone.

'Well, fifteen, then, you cannot be much more! You look the most complete urchin — what have you done to your hair?' The Earl leaned forward and lifted a strand between fastidious fingers. 'It appears to have been cut with shears and it's full of cobwebs.'

'Embroidery scissors; they were all I could find,' Cassandra replied bleakly. The loss of her mass of chestnut curls had seemed a small sacrifice at the time; now, seeing herself through his critical eyes, she regretted it. 'And I had to hide in the gardens of the Square. The stage arrived at ten last night and it took me so long to find the house, I thought it too late to knock.'

'If we retire before two in this household we consider it a dull night, but I suppose in the wilds of Hertfordshire all activity ceases as the sun goes down.' He was watching her face as he teased her. She saw his eyes narrow. 'You're as white as a shirt under that dirt, child. When did you last eat?'

'At noon yesterday.' And she could not tell him that after her father's ultimatum she had run from the dining-room and been violently sick.

The Earl tugged the silken bellpull beside the hearth and gestured her into a chair with its back to the door. When a footman brought chocolate, ham, bread and sweet rolls, he watched her eat hungrily for a few moments before pouring himself a cup of chocolate.

'Would you care for some ham?' Cassandra suddenly remembered her manners.

'Not at this unearthly hour of the morning!' he gave a snort of amusement at her expression.

'But it is almost ten o'clock! Surely you would not still be abed?' Her father was always railing against the laxity and dissipation of London life: perhaps he was right.

'Indeed I would if I were not taking the Dover road this afternoon. But never mind that: what mischief are you about? Your father is not going to be pleased to receive you home looking like that.'

Cassandra jumped to her feet, heedlessly overturning the plate of rolls in her agitation. 'I am not going back! He mustn't know I am here!'

'You've run away?' All the amusement was gone from his face. 'This is not some prank hatched in the schoolroom, then? Have you no concern for your reputation?' He read the answer in her desolate face. After a moment, he got to his feet and began to pace in thought, hands thrust deep into the pockets of his dressing gown. 'You really could not have chosen a more inconvenient time to quarrel with your father. . .'

'It is more than a quarrel,' Cassandra cried.

She realised the Earl was not taking any notice of her, his brow furrowed in thought. Eventually he announced: 'If you stay here with Mrs Mitchell, the housekeeper, and write to your father, then no harm will be done. With the family away, no-one of consequence will visit us here. You must stay in your room, of course, until your father comes to take you home. . .'

'I will not go home.' Cassandra grasped one brocade sleeve with frantic hands. 'If you try and make me, I will throw myself in the Thames.'

There was a short silence while he freed her fingers from his sleeve and smoothed out the rich fabric. 'What melodrama are you playing out?' His voice — and face — were cold. 'You ridiculous child, you are not between the pages of a novel.'

'Papa does not permit me to read novels,' Cassandra said stiffly. 'I am not a child, pray do not treat me as one. Oh, if only Godmama were here — I cannot expect you to understand, you are a man!'

'That I cannot deny,' he said drily, recovering some of his humour. 'Sit down and tell me the story from the beginning.' The clock on the mantel chimed ten. 'But without embroidery. I am in no mood for a melodrama: time is pressing, we must resolve this before I leave London.'

'I doubt you can help me,' Cassandra stated despairingly. 'Only Godmama could do that. . .'

She broke off as the valet slipped into the room with an apologetic murmur. 'The luggage my lord?'

'Take the dressing case, the rest can wait — for a few minutes.'

The Earl's obvious impatience to be gone spurred Cassandra to blurt out the truth as soon as they were once more alone. 'My father insists I marry Lord Offley.'

'*Lord Offley*?' He was every bit as outraged as she could have hoped. 'That disgusting rake? Why, he must be thrice your age! He's no fit husband for any decent woman, let alone a young girl of your sheltered upbringing. Are you sure you have the name right? I cannot believe your father would have anything in common with such a man.'

'Nor has he. Father has not left home this last decade since Mama died, except for a few visits to the London booksellers. In Hatchards last year, he chanced to meet this widow, Lord Offley's sister, and now he is besotted with her. . .'

'Bella Mainwaring?' The Earl grimaced. 'Bella Mainwaring and your father! She has been on the catch for a complaisant husband these last six years, but I cannot imagine a man of your father's. . . habits being attracted to such as she.'

'Please do not attempt to be polite about Papa's character,' Cassandra interjected bitterly. 'He is a mean, reclusive, tyrannical, selfish. . .'

'Quite. Although I doubt a dutiful daughter should say so.'

'Since my mother died I have been his companion, I have kept house for him on a pittance. I have been loyal and dutiful and obedient.' And very, very lonely, she thought to herself, but could not voice it aloud. 'And now he wants to marry this woman. He is infatuated with her. But she will not countenance it while I am still in the house. She knows I see her for what she is: a fortune seeking female, who will see my father in his grave as swiftly as she saw her first two husbands into theirs.'

'You are well-born and no doubt well dowered.' Nicholas leaned back in his chair regarding her critically. 'You are young, but not impossibly so. And presumably, when correctly dressed, passably presentable. Why does he not permit you to have a Season next year and find an eligible husband you can accept?'

Cassandra chose to ignore his unflattering description of her looks and prospects. 'The Season costs money and requires planning. He will spend neither time nor money on me, although I am his only child.' She knew she was sounding bitter, but was beyond caring. 'Yesterday at luncheon, he told me if I did not agree to marry Lord Offley, I would be shut in my room until I acquiesced, however long that took.' She shuddered. 'Have you met Lord Offley? He has a wet mouth, and he keeps wanting to touch. . .'

She had all the Earl's attention; his mobile mouth was drawn into a thin line of distaste. 'I know him only too well, although he is not of my circle. Your instincts about him are quite correct: there are tales I could not possibly tell an innocent girl.' He got to his feet and walked to the window, pulling back one of the drapes to stare out over the Square.

Cassandra could not read his mood, but she felt reassured by his anger on her behalf. When she was eight years old he had come to visit with his mother. He had rescued her kitten from a tree and she had thought him the most wonderful youth in the world. Now, regarding his broad shoulders, she felt the same security she had experienced when he had swung down from the tall oak clutching the terrified cat.

'My lord,' she began as the silence stretched on.

'Nicholas, call me Nicholas,' he said absently. 'We are almost cousins. I must think what to do for the best. . .' He was interrupted by a loud crash and the sounds of splintering wood.

'What the Devil!' Nicholas wrenched open the chamber door, Cassandra at his heels. Leaning over the landing balustrade, they had a birdseye view of the hall below. Franklin, the valet, was flat on his back on the marble floor, one leg twisted beneath him. Mr Peacock was directing two footmen to lift a valise from his body. Shirts cascaded from the split leather and neckcloths fluttered on the splintered ends of the banisters.

'Is he all right?' Nicholas called down.

The butler raised his face to his employer. 'I think not my lord. He is unconscious and I fear his right leg is broken.'

'Send for the surgeon.'

'At once, my lord. We will carry him through to the anteroom sofa.'

The Earl thrust Cassandra back into his room. 'Wait there.'

As she wandered round the chamber, a fresh cup of chocolate in her hand, Cassandra felt her spirits lighten despite her concern for the unfortunate Franklin. She had no idea what was to become of her, unchaperoned in this great house with a nobleman who was about to leave the country, but she had an irrational confidence that Nicholas would take her side, would not allow this marriage to take place.

Behind a small screen she found a ewer and basin. One glance in the glass hanging on the wall sent her flying to pour water and wash her hands and face, but even dragging a comb through her hair did nothing to tame it. Experimentally, she dipped the comb in the water and wetted her hair, smoothing it closer to her head and back off her face.

Critically she examined the result: really, she thought, she made a very passable boy. Her lashes were rather long over her blue eyes, but she had dark, definite brows, high cheekbones and a firm mouth. Cassandra was accustomed to being told she was a passably handsome girl, a description she had taken to mean she would never be pretty. Now that seemed an advantage.

By the time Nicholas returned, a furrow of worry between his brows, she had brushed down her clothes and straightened her necktie. 'Has the surgeon been?'

'He has,' replied Nicholas shortly. 'Franklin will be going nowhere for at least a month; his leg is badly broken. There is no hope now of finding a valet willing to travel in time. Well, there's the end of it, I shall have to postpone my departure, I cannot possibly travel without my manservant.'

'You do not seem very concerned about Franklin.' Cassandra was slightly shocked, and disappointed her hero seemed so unsympathetic.

Nicholas's brows rose haughtily. 'He is being attended by an excellent surgeon, he has a comfortable bed and has nothing to do but lie in idleness at my expense until his leg knits.'

'You make it sound as if the man has done it on purpose in order to inconvenience you!'

'You have to admit, Cassie, I have had my full share of inconveniences today,' he said wryly. 'Now what are we going to do with you?'

The question went unanswered. Distantly, from the stairs, Peacock's voice could be heard raised in what even Cassandra realised was untypical agitation. '. . .his lordship is not yet out of his chamber, my lady. He is not receiving visitors yet. . .'

'Nonsense, Peacock, my nephew will see me.' A forceful female voice overrode his protests.

'Oh, my God!' Nicholas sprang out of his chair, dragging Cassandra to her feet and thrust her behind the screen. 'Aunt Augusta!'

Outside the chamber door, Peacock was making a despairing last effort. 'I believe his lordship is not yet dressed. . .'

'Well, he should be, idle young hound.' The door swung open as Peacock gave up the struggle. 'Lady Augusta Armitage, my lord.'

'So you are up, after all, Lydford.' Through the crack in the screen, Cassandra could see a formidable matron wearing a crimson mantle and an alarming turban. At the look on the Earl's face, Cassandra was hard pressed to suppress a giggle.

'Good morning, Aunt. To what do I owe the pleasure?'

'Why are you not properly dressed? I do not hold with the habit you young men have of lolling about until all hours. Wait until you are married, all this will stop!'

'I am sure it will, Aunt. Won't you take a seat? Let me ring for fresh chocolate.' While his aunt arranged her gown, Nicholas whipped Cassandra's cup and saucer off the tray and hid them behind his back. His aunt had eyes like a hawk and a nose for scandal second to none. If she knew he had a girl in the house, let alone his room, they'd be married by lunchtime. He shuddered at the thought.

'That would be very refreshing, Lydford, thank you. And now, to the purpose of my visit. Sit down, stop fidgeting, why don't you.'

Cassandra had to stuff her sleeve in her mouth to stifle her laughter as Nicholas sat down cautiously, manoeuvring the cup under the chair.

'Of course, I am always delighted to see you Aunt, but you say you have a particular purpose for your visit today. . .?'

'I certainly have — to bring you to some sense of your duty, since your poor mama seems unable to. I know you are about to set off on some wild escapade round the Continent. . .'

'A series of cultural visits only, I assure you, Aunt. Now we are at peace with France again, the opportunity presents itself. . .'

'It is to be hoped the Corsican Monster is safely caged this time.' Lady Augusta paused long enough to allow him to pour her chocolate. 'I shudder every time I think of that upstart Napoleon. However, I did not come here to speak of politics. It is time you were married, Lydford. I met my dear friend Lady Hare at a reception yesterday evening. Her niece was with her, a charming girl, eminently suitable. I have asked them both to stay next week at Woodham Park and I want you to postpone your departure and join us there.'

Cassandra realised from the hunted look on Nicholas's face that this was a familiar theme. 'Aunt, grateful as I am for your invitation, what you suggest is impossible. I have a boat to catch tomorrow morning.'

'Not without your valet, you won't,' his aunt retorted triumphantly. 'I have heard of this morning's accident. Do not try and gull me! You, of all men, will not leave without someone to look after your linen.'

The look on Nicholas's face was so comic, Cassandra stepped back quickly before laughter got the better of her. Unfortunately she backed into a small table, sending an ornament tumbling.

'Nicholas! What is that? Is there someone in the room?'

Desperately Cassandra seized a pile of freshly pressed shirts and scurried head down from behind the screen towards the door.

As she pulled it closed behind her, she heard the formidable voice demanding 'Who was that?' Controlling her breathing with an effort, Cassandra pressed her ear to the panels.

'Why, my new valet, of course, Aunt.'

'That scrubby boy? Are you out of your senses?'

'It's Franklin's nephew. He will do until I reach Paris. Beggars can't be choosers.' Even through the oak, Cassandra could hear the enjoyment in Nicholas's voice. She suspected he rarely had the advantage over this formidable lady and was relishing it now. Abandoning her post, she tiptoed down the landing and let herself into the next room.

She realised she was in Nicholas's bedchamber: through the linking door to the dressing room she could hear Nicholas's voice and the more strident tones of his aunt. Goodness knew how long Lady Augusta would stay, she may as well make herself comfortable.

The bed looked inviting, freshly made. Cassandra put the shirts carefully on a dresser, kicked off her shoes and sat on the edge of the bed. It was wide and soft with a mountain of white pillows. Surely it would do no harm to settle down here for a few minutes?

'So that's where you've got to.' Cassandra struggled back to consciousness to find Nicholas standing at the end of the bed regarding her. 'You can come out now—she's gone.'

'Are you going to Woodham Park to stay as she asks?' Cassandra sat up, rubbing the sleep from her eyes.

'And abandon my trip for a week of hideous embarrassment while she throws the simpering niece of Lady Hare at my head? I think not.'

Cassandra saw a wicked gleam in his eyes. 'Your aunt will be very displeased.'

'All the more reason for not being here.' Nicholas riposted. 'Hurry, get up. I have had an idea. We have a lot to do—finding you clothes that fit for a beginning.'

'Why, you are running away from her! I do believe you are frightened of her!'

Nicholas's mouth twisted humorously. 'There is not a man in Christendom who isn't! Her late husband was terrified of her. But we will not be here to experience her wrath.'

Cassandra pricked up her ears at the 'we'. It sounded as though, whatever the plan, he did not intend leaving her with the housekeeper after all.

'You have a scheme for me?' She looked into his face eagerly, but he was not attending to her. His expression was preoccupied.

'I must do something about trimming your hair,' he began. 'And I think I can find you some clothes to fit.'

'But Nicholas,' Cassandra shook his arm to gain his attention. 'What are you going to do with me if you're going to France? And how can you go to France without a valet?'

He looked down at her, a slow, mischievous smile curling his lips. 'But I have a valet. I'm looking at him—or rather, at her.'

CHAPTER TWO

'Your *valet*?' Cassandra said incredulously, as Nicholas's words sank in. 'You want me to pretend to be your valet?'

'I don't *want* you to pretend to be anything. I want you to be twenty-five miles away in Hertfordshire under your father's eye. But you're not, are you? You're here in my bedroom.' He crossed his arms across his chest and leant against the bedpost, ignoring her blushes. 'And if Aunt Augusta walked in now and found you, I'd be marrying you, not Emily Hare.' He grinned at her. 'I don't think either of us would thank her for that! Well? Do you have any better ideas?'

'I. . .why cannot I stay here with your house-keeper until Godmama returns?' Under the coarse neckcloth, Cassandra could feel the rising heat of embarrassment. Marry Nicholas! He had been her idol for so long, a wonderful 'big brother', she could never think of him in *that* way. He was jesting, of course, believing her to be so young. And, of course, he was making it quite evident how unthinkable the idea was.

She pulled herself together, realising he was still talking. '. . .there is no saying when my mother will return. After all, she is her own mistress with no-one to please but herself. My aunt, on the other hand, will not give up organising my life so easily: she must not find you here.'

'But surely she'll think the house is empty. . .'

'All the more reason for frequent visits to supervise the servants. You cannot hope to remain here undetected and, I can assure you, my aunt is of the old school: if your father says you must marry Lord Offley, then marry him you will. She would have no truck with disobedience.'

Cassandra could well imagine Lady Augusta's reaction if she discovered an unmarried girl who had run away from home and taken refuge in a gentleman's chambers! She would have to marry Lord Offley or Nicholas or be ruined in the eyes of Society.

She was conscious of Nicholas's silence: he had made a suggestion, now it was up to her to decide. Go with him and take the risk of public exposure and ruin, or go back and face a marriage she abhorred. She shivered, remembering Lord Offley's lascivious gaze. She may have led a sheltered life, but she knew exactly what was in his mind when he looked at her like that.

She raised her eyes to meet those of the very different man who was offering her the chance of escape.

'Cassandra,' Nicholas prompted gently. 'I realise I have given you an impossible choice: you are between the Devil and the deep sea, but we have no time to waste. You must decide now.'

An impossible choice! What seemed impossible was to hide her elation from him, make him think she was the frightened, vulnerable child he believed her to be, not the determined eighteen year old she was. Cassandra could think of nothing she would rather do in the entire world. To journey abroad—

to Paris! And with Nicholas, whom she had idolised since she was eight years old! Hastily she cast her eyes down before he could see the welling excitement there.

'Yes, Nicholas.' She managed to sound demurely obedient and trustful. 'If you think it would work. . .'

'All we have to do is to get you to Paris. Mama will know what to do with you. No doubt she will announce that she invited you to stay and invent a suitable chaperone for the journey. And, this way, at least I catch tomorrow's boat.'

And escape Aunt Augusta's schemes, Cassandra thought wryly, although she did not voice it aloud. Life with Papa had taught her that men needed their dignity preserving, however ridiculous they could be.

'Do you trust me to look after your linen?' she enquired with mock seriousness, eyeing the careless elegance of his attire. The dressing gown had gone, to be replaced by a dark blue double breasted coat, a snowy cravat and shining Hessians over buff breeches.

'Looking at the way you are turned out, I have the deepest misgivings.' He eyed her dubiously. 'Where did you get those garments? The stableboy?'

'Yes, as it happens. They are his Sunday best.'

'But hardly suitable for the valet of an Earl. I'll see what I can do with your hair, meanwhile. . .' He tugged the bellpull. 'Come back into the dressing room.'

Cassandra hopped off the bed with alacrity, glad to escape from the bedchamber. Not that she felt threatened in any way: naturally she had no experience of how a man *should* react to finding a girl in his bed, but it seemed to her that Nicholas was unflatteringly unmoved.

In the dressing room, she submitted meekly to being swathed in a towel while he dragged a comb ruthlessly through what remained of her curls. 'This will have to be a severe crop if you're not to look as though the moth's been at it.' He snipped quickly and deftly, the fine hair falling on to her face and making her sneeze. Nicholas brushed it off her cheeks with surprising gentleness.

Peacock entered the room silently, a suit of dark clothing over his arm, disapproval etched on every feature. 'The underfootman's church clothes, my lord,' he announced frostily. 'An undersized youth. They should fit Miss Weston.' He departed stiff-backed.

'He knows who I am?'

'He has been with the family twenty years, he certainly knows who my mother's godchild is.' Nicholas tossed aside the towel impatiently. 'Hurry up and get dressed, it will soon be noon. We will eat on the road at the first change of horses.' He paused with one hand on the doorknob. 'If you need anything, ring for Peacock. Don't be seen outside these rooms — and hurry,' he urged as the clock chimed once more.

The underfootman's Sunday best was a good fit. Cassandra tucked the ends of the neckcloth into the black cloth waistcoat and straightened a wrinkle in one of her stockings before examining herself in the long glass. The waistcoat was rather tight, but that was a good thing, she reflected. It served to flatten her small breasts; when she shrugged on the coat, the effect was complete. No-one would guess she was not a boy, she assured herself.

Ten minutes later, Nicholas's keen scrutiny confirmed what she had seen in the glass. 'Passable, in fact, more than passable. It's a good thing you're not pretty. Just remember to stride when you walk, stand up straight, and don't say anything unless you have to.' He seemed oblivious to the hurt look Cassandra gave him. She knew she wasn't pretty, but he might at least have said she made a good looking boy! 'That's good: scowl like that,' he added, blithely piling insult on injury.

Cassandra followed him down the curving staircase to the hall where Peacock handed him into his caped driving cloak. 'Is the luggage stowed, Peacock?'

'It is, my lord, and the heavy baggage should have reached Dover this morning. Your gloves and hat, my lord.'

Ignorning the butler's disapproving glance, Cassandra ran blithely down the steps to where the curricle waited, a diminutive Tiger holding the heads of four matched bays. 'I shan't be needing you, Jem.' The Earl swung up onto the box, gathering the reins in his gloved hand and steadying the team.

'What, m'lud? Not taking me? Who'll sort the 'orses out?'

'I think I'm capable of giving simple instructions to ostlers, Jem. You can follow tomorrow and bring the team back from the *Shoulder of Mutton* at Dartford. Get up, er. . . Cass.'

Cassandra scrambled up to sit beside him.

'Cross your arms and sit up straight,' Nicholas

hissed out of the corner of his mouth. 'Let them go, Jem!'

The team was fresh and enough of a handful to occupy his lordship's attention for the first ten minutes as he negotiated the thronged streets leading to Piccadilly and Green Park. Sitting up straight as she'd been bid, Cassandra hardly knew where to look first. The quiet streets had been transformed into bustling life, so crowded she wondered that the traffic was moving at all.

Carriages of all kinds wove their way around tradesmen with barrows, a man driving pigs, a broken down hackney carriage with the wheel off while two coachmen quarrelled over who had caused the accident. . .

'Look at that beautiful lady, Nicholas.' She uncrossed her arms to tug at his sleeve. 'Oh, I wish I had a dress like that!'

Nicholas glanced in the direction she was pointing and snapped, 'Sit still and cross your arms! And don't gawp. . .'

'But I've never seen a dress like that, so daring. How does she make it cling so?'

'Never you mind,' Nicholas said grimly, swearing under his breath as a coalman shot a load of coal noisily down a cellar chute making the wheelers shy. He was beginning to think that a fresh team and Miss Cassandra Weston were more than any man should have to deal with at once. 'No woman walking the streets unaccompanied is any better than she should be!'

'Oh, Nicholas, is that the Banqueting Hall?' Cassandra was quite uncrushed by his irritation. 'Slow down, please, I want to look at it.' She was swept up by the exhilaration of being driven through London, seeing before her eyes all the sights she had read about.

'Perhaps you would like me to stop and buy you a guidebook?' he enquired politely.

'I wish you would.' His sarcasm was lost on her; she had almost forgotten why they were there, who she was with. 'Papa has Mr Pennant's *London*. If I had thought, I would have brought it with me, for Papa swears by it as a guide.'

'Cassandra, I have no intention of sightseeing, gawping at streetwalkers, visiting bonnet shops, calling on the Prince Regent or any of the other diversions you seem to have in mind! Now, you tiresome child, you will sit still and be quiet, or I will set you down on Westminster Bridge and you may throw yourself in the Thames or walk home to Ware as you wish.'

They both subsided into smouldering silence. Cassandra waited until Nicholas had turned the team onto the bridge, then asked in a small voice, 'Do you regret bringing me?'

'I must have been mad.' He spoke grimly. Cassandra realised he was looking at her and sniffed defiantly: she would not let him see she wanted to cry. It wasn't her fault it was all so new and exciting.

'Don't sniff, child. I don't allow Jem to sniff — and besides, your nose is getting pink.' The Earl smiled at her, his irritation suddenly gone, as they passed the new obelisk in St George's Circus. 'If you want to sightsee, how about that magnificent building on our left?'

'What is it?' Cassandra enquired eagerly, craning to look.

'The King's Bench Prison.'

Cassandra shuddered and averted her gaze from the grim walls, her appetite for sights disappearing. Soon the wide streets of Southwark were behind them; Greenwich and Blackheath with their palace and parkland passed and the horses were breasting the long pull of Shooters Hill at a steady trot.

'Are there highwaymen?' she asked apprehensively, gazing at the thick wood which grew right down to the road edge and inching closer to Nicholas.

'Probably. There are horse pistols in the holster beside you. If we're attacked, it's the groom's job to fire them.' He glanced at her pale face. 'Don't worry, I'm teasing you, we're safe enough in daylight and there are other travellers on the road. Besides, the Mail is a far more tempting target. If you look out at the crossroads, you might see a corpse on the gibbet,' he added slyly.

Mercifully Cassandra was spared the sight. It was nearly two o'clock before they arrived at the *Shoulder of Mutton* in Dartford. Cassandra's stomach grumbled as she climbed down from the high seat and stood quietly to one side like a good servant, while Nicholas gave orders to the ostlers for the return of his team and looked over the horses which were to replace them for the next stage to Chatham.

This was another side to him she had not seen before: the cool assumption of authority, the way the inn staff jumped to his every order. No wonder he was so confident, he was used to receiving compliance everywhere he turned. Not for the first time Cassandra realised how much easier life would have been if she'd been born a boy. Meanwhile, she was going to enjoy pretending—all the way to Paris.

'There's time for some bread and cheese and ale.' Nicholas shouldered his way into the inn and found them a corner table. 'I should get a private parlour with you here, but this will be good practice for you. Just remember to act like a boy—and drink your ale, don't sip it.'

Cassandra copied the way he lifted his tankard and drank deeply, shuddering as the bitter liquid ran down her throat. 'It's disgusting! How can men drink this for pleasure?' But Nicholas not was listening. He had turned, one long arm across the back of the settle, and was watching the arrival of the Dover coach which had just clattered into the yard and was disgorging its noisy cargo. 'What's the matter?' His watchfulness made her suddenly uneasy.

'Nothing, I hope, so long as no-one who knows me is on board and stops to talk. Drink up, we'd better get on our way.'

They pushed their way back through the group, an ill-assorted collection of all social classes from young blades to plain-dressed artisans, all stretching to relieve the stiffness caused by the coach's rattling progress.

Cassandra let her breath out in a sigh of relief as they regained the road without anyone hailing Nicholas. So caught up was she in her own predicament, she was only now beginning to realise what an embarrassment she might be to him. He seemed unruffled, but his broad shoulders relaxed as he drove the new team well up to their bits down the old Roman road to Rochester.

The green countryside with its rows of neatly kept hops marching up the slopes and the groups of oasthouses was pleasant enough to distract her thoughts until Rochester. She hoped they would change horses there: perhaps find time to look at the castle and the ships lying at anchor on the wide Medway, but Nicholas pushed the tired team on to Chatham for the next change.

They made good time, but still it was well past five before they entered Canterbury and even Cassandra's enthusiasm for sightseeing was blunted by tiredness. She passed the cathedral with scarcely more than a glance at the twin towers soaring over the narrow streets. They changed horses for the last time at Bridge.

The good weather that had favoured them all day mellowed into a still, warm June evening and their shadows were lengthening on the road before them as they drove, at last, down the long hill into Dover.

The castle crouched on the clifftop, dominating the port straggling down the valley to the sea's edge. Cassandra sat up, straightening her weary shoulders and crossing her arms like the perfect servant. She ached in every limb from the joltings of the road, yet all she had done was sit alongside Nicholas.

He had driven the strange horses for mile after mile, negotiated potholes and tollgates, avoided village urchins and stray dogs, and yet he looked as fresh as when they had set out from Grosvenor Square. Only the crinkles of tiredness at the corners of his eyes betrayed any sign of fatigue. Cassandra watched his hands, sure and strong on the reins, the long flexible fingers sending almost imperceptible signals to the leaders.

The curricle was bowling down to a wide esplanade and, suddenly, there was the sea sparkling grey in the evening light, the salt tang filling the air — and filling Cassandra with a strange exaltation.

'Stop bouncing,' Nicholas chided, but he was grinning. 'You really are the most irrepressible child! Have you never seen the sea before?'

'No! I've imagined it, of course. . .but it's so big, so. . .'

'Wet?' Nicholas supplied wryly. 'Now behave yourself, we're nearly at the *Ship Inn*.'

'Oh.' Cassandra said flatly, noticing for the first time the abundance of inns and lodging houses that lined the street, all of them disreputable and dirty.

'Don't worry, it's not one of these. You'll find the *Ship* comfortable enough. And the bedlinen is at least clean.' As he spoke, he wheeled the team into a cobbled yard under a gaudily painted sign of a galleon in full sail, which swung so low that Cassandra ducked instinctively.

The yard was bustling with other sporting carriages, like their own, and a number of chaises with piles of luggage strapped high behind. 'Now you see why I was so eager to leave on time: we would have lost the accommodation otherwise.'

Cassandra climbed down stiffly, pleased to see the yard was freshly strewn with clean straw and that neatly dressed grooms hurried forward to take the horses.

She stared in awe at one of the passengers alighting from a closed carriage on the arm of a foppishly dressed gentleman. The lady was wearing a Spanish pelisse in a dove grey sarsenet trimmed with Chinese binding. Her delicate hands and feet were both gloved in dainty lemon kid: Cassandra watched open-mouthed as this vision stepped down onto the cobbles without a thought for her exquisite footwear.

She was jolted out of her study by Nicholas stepping forward and raising his hat. 'Lady Broome. What a pleasure to see you here: are you making the crossing?'

'My dear Earl!' The lady fluttered forward, extending her gloved hand. 'You know my brother George?' The gentlemen exchanged nods. 'Nothing would prevail upon me to brave the Channel, not even for a glimpse of Paris fashions before they reach Town. I am here to meet my sister-in-law. And you?' She raised a coquettish brow, laying one hand on the Earl's sleeve and turning towards the inn door.

'Alas, the perils of the ocean for me — and without your presence to stiffen my resolution. . . Cass! Don't stand there with your mouth open, boy, bring my dressing case!'

Resentfully Cassandra tugged at the leather straps securing the bags. Mouth open, indeed! The heavy case fell off the top of the pile wrenching her arms.

'Need a hand with those, lad?' One of the grooms was beside her. 'Amazing what these nobs put into their cases, feels like a load of bricks, don't it?' The man swung the remaining pieces down and took them into the *Ship*, Cassandra following behind, trying to manage the heavy case and stride manfully at the same time.

The Earl was leaning easily against the mantel-piece in the coffee room. Seeing Cassandra, he hailed a passing waiter. 'Show my man to my chamber with the luggage. Cass, check the heavy luggage has arrived and unpack my evening dress: I shall dine with Lady Broome and Sir George this evening.'

Cassandra opened her mouth indignantly, then closed it again with a snap. After all, what else did she expect? She'd freely entered the charade, she couldn't complain when she was asked to act the part. But Nicholas didn't have to act his with such relish!

The room was a good one with a bow window overlooking the main street and affording a glimpse of the sea beyond. A maidservant was mending the fire and the heavy luggage was piled high in one corner. With a nod at the girl, Cassandra began unpacking the dressing case, laying out the silver backed brushes and shaving gear.

Poking into the various valises, she found what seemed appropriate evening wear and clean linen. She was laying a nightshirt on the bed when a thought struck her: where was she to sleep? Where did servants sleep in establishments like this? And more immediately, where was she to eat?

What time was it—and when would Nicholas require warm water? How little she knew! It was all very well to have to act like a boy. That was easy, compared with learning to act like a valet!

'Oh, hang the man!' Cassandra stamped her foot, angry that Nicholas had abandoned her in this strange place and, suddenly, not a little frightened.

'Language, infant!' Nicholas was leaning against the door jamb. He seemed lazily amused, his eyes narrowed as he watched her.

'I am not an infant! How could you leave me

without giving me some idea what to do with all this!' She gestured wildly at the pile of cases, irrationally more angry now he was there than she had been before.

'What did you expect me to do?' he enquired, strolling into the room. 'Invite you to take tea with Lady Broome?' He shrugged off his coat and handed it to her. 'Brush this will you, it's dusty from the journey.'

'Brush it yourself!' Her chin came up and she threw the coat onto the bed. 'You just go off with that *woman* and leave me. . .'

'Calm down, Cassandra—and don't treat my coats like that! I'm sorry I left you, brat. To tell you the truth, I keep forgetting you're not a boy, you're so good at it.'

He straightened and strolled across to look down at her, his eyes warm with amusement. One long finger tilted her chin up, forcing her gaze to meet his. 'Stop sulking, Cassie. I couldn't just leave Lady Broome, it would have looked most odd. Besides,' he smiled reminiscently, 'what better way to kill an hour than in the company of a beautiful woman? Moreover, you seem to have managed well enough. Have you ordered hot water?'

Cassandra bit her lip, acknowledging to herself that her real complaint was Nicholas's preference for Lady Broome's company over her own. 'No. I didn't know what time you wanted it. I'll get it now.' She paused, her hand on the door knob, 'Nicholas. . .where am I to sleep tonight?'

He paused, arrested, his cravat half undone. 'Lord, I hadn't thought of that. Go for the water, I'll think of something.'

Cassandra returned with a steaming ewer to find Nicholas pulling a battered screen across one corner of the room. 'What are you doing?' She set the jug down on the dressing table and came to peer round the edge. 'Where did you get that from?' A low truckle bed was set behind the screen.

'It was under the bed. I'll take this, you have the bed.'

'I can't do that, Nicholas,' she protested, scandalised. 'I cannot sleep in the same room as you! It's. . .'

'. . .the only thing we can do,' he finished for her. 'What would you prefer? To share with the male inn servants?' He looked at her pink face and added ruefully, 'You're as compromised as you're ever going to be, Cassie. By running away with me dressed as a boy, you burned your boats, child: a night in my company can make it no worse.'

Cassandra knew her blush was deepening; her tongue felt too clumsy to get round the words. 'But we. . . I never thought. . .'

'I don't believe you thought from the moment you left home! But then, neither did I — at least, not about this.' He hesitated, 'Look, Cassie, I'll pull the screen across. It'll be almost as if we're in two separate chambers.'

Cassandra cast round for other reasons not to share the room. It wasn't as though she didn't trust Nicholas. . .it was just that the big bed was strangely disturbing. Her eyes fell on the shortness of the pallet. 'Your feet will stick out of the end. You won't be able to walk tomorrow. I'm much shorter, I'll sleep in it.'

'You are in my care, Cassandra, and you will do

as I tell you.' The Earl's tone brooked no argument. 'You're my mother's godchild and I must see you safely delivered to her. It's bad enough that you're jauntering around in boy's clothing, unchaperoned, without sleeping in a servant's bed in an inn!'

Cassandra knew when she was beaten. 'Thank you, Nicholas.' She gestured to the jug. 'Your water will be cooling.'

Her capitulation appeared to surprise him. With a slight shrug, he moved the screen round the dressing table and disappeared behind it. Cassandra dithered in the centre of the room. She had begun to feel more comfortable in the valet-master role, now Nicholas had turned it on its head by treating her as a girl, if not a lady.

However, it seemed now the question of the bed was settled, he had no further qualms. A shirt came sailing over the top of the screen followed by a crumpled neckcloth. 'Pass me a clean shirt, please.'

Cassandra handed one round the screen and busied herself with brushing down the corbeau blue coat and cream kerseymere breeches. 'Which waistcoat do you want? The sage green or the white?'

'Green. Can you pass me my, er. . .' For once Nicholas seemed at a loss.

Silently Cassandra handed the unmentionable nether garments round the screen. It was a good thing he couldn't see the smile on her face. Really! Did he think she was *such* an innocent? Who did he think sewed on her father's buttons?

By the time the Earl emerged, smoothing down his cuffs, Cassandra had her face under control. She had polished his quizzing glass and found a fine cambric handkerchief. 'Cologne, my lord?'

'Naturally.' He wasn't rising to the bait, although Cassandra saw his mouth twitch briefly, as if in amusement. 'Now, for your supper, go down to the kitchen and bring something back up here. I don't want you eating in the Inn—it would be hazardous as well as unseemly.'

'Yes, my lord,' said Cassandra demurely.

'Cassandra. . .'

'Yes, my lord?'

He paused at the door, a tall, lean figure in the severe evening dress, the candlelight honing his features into an unfamiliar austerity. 'Go to bed early like a good girl, we've a long journey tomorrow. And stop calling me "my lord", you are beginning to sound like Peacock.'

The door shut behind him with a distinct click. As sounding like the butler had been Cassandra's aim, she was rather pleased with the rebuke. Nicholas was inclined to treat her like a child and while that had its advantages it was beginning, for some reason, to gall her. Teasing him—very gently—was the only way she could assert her character without alarming him with her femininity.

She began to tidy the room, gathering up discarded clothing and straightening the dressing table, her mind on this man who had unexpectedly taken control of her life.

Revealing her true age would not matter once they were on the other side of the Channel; Nicholas would hardly abandon her on the road to Paris. And yet. . . Cassandra paused, her arms full of the opulent folds of his dressing gown. Something told her that he would not be pleased when he discovered how she had deceived him, fooled him into thinking she was a child.

But that was still days away, now she was starving. She would see what the kitchen had to offer.

The cook had been too busy in her steamy kitchen to pay much heed to one undersized valet and Cassandra had secured a plate of mutton stew and bread and a mug of ale without drawing attention to herself. But in trying to find the back stair in the gloom of the labyrinthine corridors of the *Ship* she took a wrong turning. Light streamed through a door which stood ajar in front of her; through the gap came the chink of glass, the scrape of cutlery and the sound of voices.

Her curiosity got the better of her: by dint of flattening herself against the wall, Cassandra could see a wedge of the dining-room. It was warm, full of light and bustle and infinitely more enticing than the prospect of her own room. Besides, the plate of stew was cooling fast. Quietly she moved a stool closer to the door, perched on it and began to eat.

The room was crowded with diners of the Quality. Cassandra chewed absently, her eyes and mind full of the shifting colours of the women's gowns, the richness of the men's attire. She wanted to be there, part of it. Her father had denied her the chance to join even the provincial social life that Ware had to offer. If dinner in a Dover inn was this glamorous, how much more wonderful was Paris going to be!

She was almost lost in a reverie of elegant gowns and charming men when the party sitting nearest her door rose to reveal Nicholas and Lady Broome sitting alone at a table. Of Sir George, there was no sign.

Cassandra gasped as her eyes took in Lady Broome's gown cut so low it scarcely contained the full swell of her breasts. What fabric was showing was silver gauze over deep rose silk. Her dark hair was cropped dashingly short in the latest mode, its only adornment a silver filet threaded through with its loose ends fluttering at her cheek.

It was only then that Cassandra noticed her companion: Nicholas was lifting his glass to toast her, a lazy smile curving his lips as their eyes met and held. Lady Broome leaned towards him to touch her glass to his. The two dark heads almost touched before Nicholas leaned back, still holding the look.

Cassandra drew in her breath with a sharp hiss. This was a very different Nicholas to the safe elder brother who had teased and bullied her all day. Not, of course, that she wanted him to look at her like that. . .

Absently, she took a sip of ale. Lady Broome was speaking now, her rippling laugh cutting across the hubbub of the room to reach Cassandra in her dark corner. She had obviously put a question to the Earl, who was shaking his head, a look of regret evident on his face. His fingers caressed the delicate filigree of silver on her cheek as his lips moved with soft words.

'Silly goose!' Cassandra exclaimed crossly, unsure which of them she was referrring to. Couldn't he see how blatantly she was flirting, playing with him? Of course he could—and he was enjoying every moment of it. . .

When Cassandra regained the bedchamber, she still felt nettled and vaguely disappointed in Nicholas for being so easily beguiled. She unbuttoned her waistcoat, taking a deep breath: boy's clothing gave considerable freedom, but it pinched in unexpected places. She sat on the bed and peeled off her stockings, then realised she had no nightgown to put on. She held Nicholas's up against herself, but it was far too long. Casting about to find something to put on she padded barefoot across the boards to a valise and tugged out a shirt. Pulled over her head it brushed the top of her knees: not quite seemly, but then she had little alternative.

The bed was high and deep with an old fashioned feather mattress which closed round her as she climbed in. Cassandra looked guiltily at the truckle bed, then hardened her heart. Nicholas had ordered her to take this bed, and after all he had enjoyed *his* evening! *He* hadn't had to sit in the dark eating greasy stew while other people dined and flirted.

She snuggled down into the pillows, stretched her aching legs and waited for sleep to overtake her. But, despite all that had happened over the past twenty four hours and her lack of rest the night before, her eyes refused to close.

She supposed she ought to be worrying about what her father would be doing. Somehow she doubted he would have gone to the expense of hiring a Bow Street Runner to pursue her. Now she was out of the house, Bella Mainwaring would agree to marry him, and provided Cassandra's flight caused no local scandal, he wouldn't care if he never saw her again. Cassandra knew she was undutiful in thinking like this, but their relationship had never been characterised by affection and she had long since given up hope of his changing.

No, what was keeping her awake was the enigma of Nicholas. Enough lingered of her old hero worship to make her trust him implicitly, but she could not deceive herself that he had taken her with him for any other reason than his own convenience, and his desire to avoid delay. But the Earl of Lydford was used to getting his own way under all circumstances: Cassandra had a sinking feeling that with her in tow, and no valet to smooth their path, things were not going to go with the ease which he had come to expect. This was hardly likely to improve his uncertain temper.

Not that he was out of temper this evening, far from it. Cassandra replayed the scene in the diningroom, Lady Broome's curls bent close to the Earl as she fluttered both fan and eyelashes. She remembered Nicholas's gaze lingering on the vivacious face and creamy throat before him.

Cassandra let her mind drift into fantasies of how she would look in evening gowns of silk and gauze; of feathers and jewels; of kid gloves with innumerable pearl buttons and fragile slippers. In clothes like that, no gentleman would call her 'brat' or 'infant' or think her a child.

She had just reached this gratifying conclusion when the door opened cautiously and Nicholas slipped in, his hand cupped round the flame of his candle. 'Asleep, infant?' he whispered, flattening Cassandra's fantasy most effectively.

'No,' she said baldly.

'Why not? Did you get some supper?' He was keeping his distance from the big bed. In the flick-

ering candlelight his face was underlit, expression-
less, the face of a stranger.

'Mutton stew.'

'That's all right, then.' He turned towards the
screen.

'Is it? I would rather have had guinea fowl and
Dover sole and claret.'

'You must have hung around the kitchen a long
time. Wasn't that rather tempting fate?' He
shrugged off his coat.

'It wasn't in the kitchen,' Cassandra began, then
realised she was getting onto dangerous ground.

'Where then?' Nicholas turned and faced her.
'Have you been prowling around the inn?'

'I saw you in the dining-room with that woman,'
she burst out.

He sauntered over to the bed and looked down at
her. In the semi-darkness his shirt was very white,
his face inscrutable. He seemed to loom above her.

Cassandra scrambled up against the pillows,
clutching the quilt to her throat. The silence
stretched on, then he said slowly, 'There are
moments, brat, when you seem a lot older than your
tender years. Goodnight.'

Cassandra held her breath until he was safely
behind the screen. There was a clatter as he tossed
his shoes into a corner and rustlings as he shed his
clothes, then the truckle bed creaked and the light
was blown out.

She found it impossible to give herself up to sleep.
She had never shared a bedroom with anyone, let
alone a man! There were several minutes of creaking and tossing while Nicholas adjusted his long

frame to the narrow bed, then the only sound in the room was his breathing, regular and slow.

Her last thought as she finally drifted off was that innocent though this night was, she was now, in the eyes of Society, ruined beyond redemption. The surprising thing was, somehow she didn't care.

CHAPTER THREE

'NICHOLAS.' Cassandra tugged his sleeve as he stood in the stern surveying the port of Dover as it receded slowly into the early morning mist. 'That sailor says that with this breeze we're only going to be four hours reaching France.'

'Thank heaven for that,' his lordship remarked absently, then focused sharply on his charge's eager face. 'And what the devil are you about, talking to common sailors?'

Cassandra blinked at his vehemence. 'He's a very nice man, and his wife lives in Dover with their three small sons and they all want to be sailors, too. . . I know why you're so mumpish!' She broke off and studied his frosty profile. 'You're feeling seasick.'

'And you, I suppose, are not?' He could not doubt it, looking at her shining eyes and wind blown hair. She was licking the salt from her lips with relish and the sea breeze had whipped colour into her cheeks.

'Not in the slightest, I wish we could sail all day.' She looked closely at Nicholas's set face. 'If you are feeling unwell, you must not go below. It is too close and full of others being sick. The smell is disgusting.'

'Thank you for your advice,' Nicholas said stiffly. 'There is nothing amiss with me save the effects of trying to sleep in a bed several sizes smaller than I.'

He buttoned his greatcoat firmly to the neck and set off to stride up and down in the small deck space not occupied by roped piles of barrels and boxes destined for the Continent.

Cassandra grinned to herself and settled on a barrel in a sheltered corner to watch the sailors coiling the maze of ropes cast off when the ship left port. Well, she had offered to sleep in the truckle bed. . .

One of the deckhands passed her, saying with a wink, 'You're faring better than your master, lad! Having trouble with his breakfast, is he?'

'I think he's feeling sick — not that he'll admit it.' Cassandra felt a prick of guilt at discussing Nicholas with this sailor. She had never seen Nicholas other than in complete command of himself: it seemd her idol had, if not feet, then one toe of clay. 'Is there a cure?'

'Well. . .' The seaman scratched his grizzled head under the knitted cap. 'I doubt he'll relish it, but what you need is a nice piece of fat bacon. Tie it on a long thread, swallow it down and jiggle the thread up and down. . .'

'Yes, thank you very much!' Cassandra interjected hastily, her stomach rising in sympathy with Nicholas's. The sailor grinned amiably and moved on down the deck with the rapid rolling gait they all shared.

Her nest among the barrels was snug and yet afforded her an uninterrupted vista of the grey Channel waters widening behind them as England slowly receded. She had expected the sea to be a great lonely expanse, but it was not. In the brightening morning light, coastal scows paralleled the shore; the fishing fleet was returning to harbour accompanied by a wheeling cloud of gulls clamouring raucously for scraps. And in elegant contrast, a sleek private yacht, its sails snowy, glided past headed for Newhaven.

She was so absorbed it was some time before she realised the Earl was standing at her shoulder. 'Enjoying yourself, brat?' he asked softly.

'You startled me!' Cassandra's heart thumped unaccountably in her chest, then she glared at him indignantly as he ruffled her hair with a careless hand.

He was smiling, the colour once more back in his cheeks. 'Aren't you afraid of all this deep, cold water? I presume you cannot swim? What will you do if you fall in?'

'You'd save me,' Cassandra said confidently. Her hero seemed himself once more. 'Are you feeling better? One of the sailors told me a certain remedy. . .'

Nicholas held up his hand hastily. 'If it's the one with the piece of fat bacon, I don't need it repeating.'

All too quickly for Cassandra the coast of France filled the horizon, the cliffs dipping down to long sandy beaches. The hundled roofs of the small port of Calais grew steadily closer, then unaccountably the boat hove to and dropped anchor. Nicholas hailed a passing crewman.

'You there! What's going on? Why are we not entering harbour?'

'Can't, sir. It's low water. Look, boats are coming out already to take you and your baggage off. Cost you a guinea, sir.'

'A guinea!' exclaimed Cassandra, her housewifely instincts revolted. 'But we've already paid to cross, why must we pay again?'

'Quiet, Cass, don't draw attention to yourself,' Nicholas commanded. 'Those rogues have the upper hand. If we want to land on French soil, we must pay French prices!'

They hung over the rail together, watching as the swarm of flat-bottomed rowing boats hove up. They were crewed by men and boys wearing rags no better than beggars, their feet in wooden sabots.

There was a chaotic period while negotiations took place to secure a boat for each party, then they and their luggage were roughly loaded. Cassandra was dangled dizzily over the edge of the packet boat by her wrists before being seized by the men in the craft below and dropped among the bags. She noticed a momentary look of concern on Nicholas's face as she was manhandled, then relief as the crew seemed to sense nothing amiss.

On the quayside their luggage was seized and carried away by a gang of brawny females, their skirts kilted up to show bare, muscular calves.

Jostled by the crowd, Cassandra struggled to keep an eye on their things. 'Nich. . . My lord! Where are they taking the baggage?'

'The Custom House. Follow me and keep your mouth shut.'

Nicholas strode off in pursuit of their porters, Cassandra scuttling to keep up through the press of touts all shouting the names of various inns.

In the Custom Hall officials searched their bags with an insolence that shocked Cassandra. 'Why do you not protest?' she whispered, scandalised as dirty hands rummaged through the fine linen.

'Quiet, or they will deny us a passport.'

'But you have one.'

'An English passport will not serve here, we need a French one for the onward journey.'

Cassandra jumped in alarm as a hand was thrust into her pocket. The searcher tossed her pocket handkerchief onto the bench, then turned with obvious attention of searching the rest of her clothing.

She felt the man's fingers touch the breast of her coat, then Nicholas's hand whipped out and clamped onto the official's wrist.

'*Un moment, mon ami*! I think this is what you are looking for.' There was a glint of gold coin and the man turned away, waving them through the throng to the row of desks where clerks were writing passports.

Cassandra stood swaying, hardly conscious of what was going on around her until the Earl's firm hand under her elbow guided her out into the fresh air.

'Cassie? Are you unwell?' His face was close as he bent over her. Cassandra blinked, forcing herself to concentrate on him; for the first time she noticed brown flecks in his green eyes and the way one brow slanted up fractionally more than the other.

'Cassandra!' Nicholas's voice was preremptory. 'You can't faint here, pull yourself together. We're going to an inn now, you need food.'

Obediently she stumbled over the cobbles beside him, following the handcart loaded with their luggage. She was hungry, yes, but it wasn't that that had made her feel faint. It was the thought of those dirty rough hands pawing her body, the reek of garlic and sweat in the Hall and the land seeming to move under her feet.

By the time their porter delivered the bags to the doors of the *Hotel d'Angleterre*, Cassandra was feeling more herself and able to look around at the scurrying servants and throng of well-dressed guests. The air was full of noisy English voices raised in demands for food and wine, and the shouts of ostlers backing horses between the shafts of travelling carriages.

Eyeing the hubbub, Nicholas remarked, 'It's as well I reserved a private parlour. This place has regained all its popularity with the Grand Tourists after the war: they say the owners have made a fortune here.'

They dined alone in their private parlour, ignoring the waiter's raised eyebrows at the Earl's latitude in permitting his valet to share his table.

'Won't they think it odd?' Cassandra asked as the door closed behind the man.

'It's of no matter, they think the English are mad, anyway,' Nicholas shrugged. 'Pass the buttered crab, I believe it is the speciality of the house.'

Drowsy with food and sea air, Cassandra fell asleep as soon as her head touched the pillow in the tiny chamber Nicholas secured for her.

Next morning she tumbled downstairs rubbing the sleep from her eyes to find him already up and dressed, impatiently tapping his foot on the cobbles as he watched the first carriages leaving the inn yard.

'Hurry up, Cass, if you want any breakfast,' he

ordered. 'And, for heaven's sake, do something about that neckcloth, you look more like a scarecrow than a valet.'

She was becoming accustomed to his uncertain temper first thing in the morning. By the time they settled themselves in the carriage hired from the inn, the Earl's mood was positively cheerful. Cassandra gathered he approved of the horses they had obtained and that even the French postillion passed muster.

After the dismal streets of Calais the wide open countryside with its fields of green corn and red poppies came as a surprise and a pleasure. There were no hills or deep valleys to slow the horses, only a rolling greenness which pleased the eye until interrupted by small, squalid villages, or collections of tumbledown farm buildings.

'Bored?' enquired the Earl, sometime later, as she settled herself back against the cushions with a deep sigh.

'I expected it to be so different: but it could be Hertfordshire.'

'What did you expect?' Nicholas grinned at her, his teeth flashing white with amusement. 'Dragons or strange costumes? This is France, not Cathay.'

'But after the sea crossing, everything seems so ordinary,' Cassandra lamented.

'Can you play cards?' Nicholas produced a pack and started to shuffle them. 'No? I'll teach you to play picquet.'

By the time they passed through the gate of Amiens that evening, Cassandra had won several sixpences. 'Are all card games this simple?' she enquired disingenuously, as Nicholas put away the pack.

'I am learning a little about you, Cassie. Under that country girl exterior beats the heart of a gamester.' He regarded her wryly. 'My mother will not be pleased with me, teaching you to gamble.'

Despite the warmth of the cheerfully lit inn, Cassandra felt strangely chilled as she carried the dressing case inside. For a time she had forgotten how close the end of their journey was. Her adventure was almost at its close. Nicholas would leave her in Paris — with relief, that much was evident — and she must learn to be a young lady again.

The Earl sensed her mood. Poor child, she had borne up far better than he could have expected. Most delicately raised young women of his acquaintance would have had the vapours inside five minutes: but then, he was forgetting just what a child she was. He patted her arm. 'Bear up, Cassandra, we're nearly there. By this time tomorrow you'll be safe with Mama.'

'And you?' She raised her eyes to his face, hoping to see some hint of regret that she would not be with him.

'Ah, well. . .' He paused in the act of tying a clean neckcloth, a slight smile curving his lips. 'I intend enjoying Paris to the full. I think I deserve a little diversion after playing the governess.'

Stung, Cassandra bit out, 'Have I been such a burden then? After all, it was your idea to bring me!'

'You ungrateful brat!' He swung round, fists on hips, to regard her coldly. 'I would have left you on the doorstep if you hadn't threatened to throw yourself in the Thames.'

'It wasn't that at all,' she flared. 'After your valet broke his leg, it simply suited your convenience to bring me with you. But, of course,' she added sarcastically, 'I should have realised, you're regretting not going to stay with Aunt Augusta and meeting the eligible Miss Hare!'

'If nothing else, Miss Hare would be more amenable!'

'And such a suitable match!'

'You provoking brat. . .' he seized her by the shoulders and gave her a little shake. 'You ungrateful, ungracious. . .'

'You needed a valet.' Cassandra struggled, but only succeeded in making him tighten the hold. 'If I hadn't come with you, you wouldn't be here now! So don't try to pretend you did it out of the goodness of your heart — it suited your purposes, that's all!'

His eyes narrowed as he studied the flushed, angry face raised to his. 'How old did you say you were, Cassandra?'

Hastily she struggled to remember what she'd told him. 'Fifteen,' she stammered.

'So I thought.' He dropped his hands and stepped back. 'I suggest you curb your temper in future dealings with gentlemen. Some might take it as a provocation.'

'And you wouldn't?' Some devil tempted Cassandra to persist.

'All you provoke me to, brat, is an urge to paddle your britches! Come on, I need my dinner.'

* * *

The next day's journey from Amiens to Paris was accomplished in an atmosphere of cool politeness. Both Cassandra and the Earl suspected they had gone too far, but neither was prepared to admit it and apologise.

If they had thought the formalities at Calais irksome, they were much worse at the gates of Paris, where officials of the *Bureau du Roi* examined the carriage and its contents at tiresome length.

'Why don't you bribe them?' Cassandra enquired irritably, tired of being jostled by the importuning crowd of touts and trinket sellers who had descended on the travellers.

'I am more inclined to hire a new valet from amongst those offering their services,' the Earl remarked, gesticulating at the crowd of smartly dressed young men who noisily proferred references from previous employers.

'They're wearing earrings,' Cassandra observed censoriously.

'But no doubt they can tie a cravat.'

Her smouldering silence lasted just as long as her first glimpse of the Seine and the sight of the fashionable quarters where the great houses of the nobility still existed despite the Revolution. At first, Cassandra was enthralled, but she soon turned to Nicholas, her nose wrinkled with disgust.

'It's filthy! The mud! And there are no pavements — look at that lady there.' She pointed to an elegantly dressed woman hopping from one stepping stone to another, her gown gathered up. 'And it's so noisy and crowded.'

'I believe it to be the most populous city in Europe,' Nicholas remarked. 'But there are compensations. When my mother begins to take you about, you will enjoy the gardens and the shops, no doubt.' He spoke absently. Cassandra was convinced he had all but forgotten her now they were almost at his uncle's house and he could be rid of her.

'And what will you do?'

'Meet with friends, play cards, go to the opera. . .' he replied airily, twisting in his seat to admire a handsome young woman promenading slowly along the edge of the Tuileries gardens.

Cassandra ran her hand through her tumbled curls and twitched her neckcloth into some sort of order, ready to meet her godmama. What a pity it was, she thought, that a nice boy who rescued kittens from trees should grow up to be frivolous, bad tempered, arrogant. . .

'Why are you glaring, Cassie? And try at least to stop sulking. We're here. If you look like that my mother will pack you straight back to your father.'

The postillion wheeled his horses to swing through the elaborate ironwork gates of the *porte cochère* of a great *hôtel*. Immediately servants ran into the wide cobbled courtyard to fling open the carriage doors and let down the steps.

Cassandra climbed down and stood looking around her, mouth half open at the magnificence of the classical pilasters and the regular ranks of many-paned windows. 'Does your uncle own this?' she whispered, awed.

'No, he hires, like everyone else who visits. He is never here long enough to warrant a permanent establishment.' He broke off to acknowledge the bow of the Steward who stood at the head of the steps to greet him. '*Bonjour*, Gaston. Is my uncle at home?'

'I fear not, milord. Sir Marcus has been recalled to Vienna. *Helas*! He will be *desolé* at missing your lordship—but, *c'est la vie*, these are the inconveniences of the life of the diplomat.'

Cassandra felt a wave of relief. She had not relished the thought of being introduced to Sir Marcus Camberley, who could not help but disapprove of her actions. Now she would have Godmama to herself and could explain it all. Feminine company and sympathy; a woman to talk to who would understand her dilemma. . .

Gaston was ushering the Earl across the wide marble entrance hall, bowing him into the salon when his eye fell on Cassandra following behind. With a snap of his fingers he summoned a footman, 'Take his lordship's valet to his suite.'

'No, Gaston, I want him with me.' Ignoring the Steward's raised eyebrows, he enquired, 'Is the Countess at home?'

'*Pardon*, milord, I have not made myself clear, *Madame la Comtesse* has accompanied *Monsieur* her brother to Vienna. She acts as his hostess this Season, you understand.'

If Cassandra had not been so distressed herself, the look on Nicholas's face would have been almost comical. 'Not here?' He pushed his hands through his hair, then sat down in the nearest chair, his long legs thrust out in front of him. For a long moment he looked from Cassandra to the Steward and back again. The silence stretched on, then he came to a decision.

'The brandy, Gaston. Bring it yourself and close the door. I need to consult with you.'

'*Certainment*, milord.'

Cassandra sat numbly on the edge of a brocade covered sofa. She hadn't thought beyond Paris, beyond the sanctuary Godmama would provide. Now her mind seemed blank, all she could do was wait, watching while Nicholas warmed the brandy glass between his palms, apparently lost in thought. The Steward waited patiently, his intelligent dark eyes flicking from the Earl to the young lad.

'This person, Gaston, is not my valet. It is Mademoiselle Weston, the god-daughter of my mother.'

'Indeed, milord.'

'Indeed. She has had to leave the shelter of her home for reasons I do not propose to enter into, and finding my mother away from home has accompanied me here. For purposes of discretion and propriety she has been dressed as you see her. Now I find *Madame la Comtesse* is not here to take charge of her. You see my predicament, Gaston?'

'Indeed, milord,' the Steward repeated. 'A situation of some delicacy.'

'You have had experience of many delicate matters in your years with my uncle. Does any solution present itself to you now?'

The Steward hesitated only briefly. 'If I may suggest, milord: the housekeeper, Madame Robert, is a woman of intelligence and refinement. She would be an excellent chaperone for the young lady until *Madame la Comtesse* returns. I presume there is no question of Mademoiselle Weston going out into Society until then?'

'Certainly not! That will do admirably.' Nicholas finished the brandy and began to get up. He'd known Gaston would come up with a solution to his problem. A respectable housekeeper was just the person to take charge of the child. His duty as her godmother's son was quit.

'Do I have no say in the matter?' Cassandra enquired frostily. The play of emotions on Nicholas's face was all too plain; he'd rid himself of an inconvenience, now he could get on with enjoying himself.

Nicholas eyed her sharply. 'No.'

'So I am to be a prisoner in this house, bored to tears, with no diversion. . .'

'There is no alternative, unless you want me to pack you straight home again, you ungrateful br. . .' He stopped suddenly, aware of the Steward's presence. 'I shall do my best to make sure you are not bored. If I arrange a small allowance for you, you may engage a dressmaker. Tomorrow I will find you a dancing master, a French master and a drawing master. That way your days will be filled, and by the time my mother returns, you may be fit to go about with her, perhaps even attend young people's parties.'

Cassandra felt a rush of contrition. She was acting like the child he thought her. Nicholas was trying to do his best for her under the most difficult of circumstances. The suspicion that he would have done almost anything to get rid of her was unworthy.

'Thank you, Nicholas, that is very kind of you,' she said meekly.

'That is settled, then.' He shot her a suspicious

glance, as if he had expected some resistance. 'Go with Gaston, then, he will take you to Madame Robert. And behave yourself, child.'

He kept calling her 'child'. It galled, but it served her purpose.

The sharp-eyed Frenchwoman to whom Gaston handed her with an explanation in rapid French was not so easily fooled.

'I thought Monsieur Gaston said you were fifteen,' she commented an hour later, handing Cassandra a towel as she climbed out of the bath.

'I. . .' Cassandra was within an inch of confirming the lie when she looked up and met the other woman's beady regard. The dark eyes were not unkind, but they were shrewd. 'I am eighteen,' she confessed. 'But the Earl believes me to be younger.'

'And you thought it wise not to set him right,' the housekeeper said drily. 'I see.'

'You do, *madame*?' Cassandra was surprised.

'But, yes. You have to leave home—an *affaire* of the heart, no doubt?—the Earl is your only friend. Why embarrass him with the truth?'

Cassandra smiled to herself, but said only, 'You speak excellent English, *madame*.'

'My late husband was a wine merchant. For many years we lived in Bristol. When he died I returned to France: the English climate does not suit me.'

She bustled around gathering up the discarded boy's clothes. 'When you are dressed *à la jeune femme*, we will engage for you a lady's maid. Until then, we must be discreet, I will look after you.' She held up a peignoir borrowed from the Countess's wardrobe. 'Put this on and I will fetch you a little supper. Tomorrow we will find you a few simple dresses. While the Earl is here, it is best you remain fifteen.' Her lips quirked in amusement.

Cassandra relaxed, curled up in an armchair before the fire. The warmth of the day had turned to evening cool in the high-ceilinged mansion. Despite everything, she felt happy. She was in Paris, her father would never find her here, and Madame Robert was a wonderful ally. She was going to enjoy herself, and when Nicholas returned from his Grand Tour, he was going to find a young lady of quality and accomplishment staying with his mother. He would never call her brat again.

'*Bonjour, ma petite.*' Madame Robert swept the curtains open with a rustle of taffeta. The sunlight streamed in across the parquet floor, striking colour from the rich Turkey rug.

'*Bonjour, madame.* What time is it?' Cassandra sat up in the big bed, hugging her knees and gazed round. She'd been too exhausted the night before to take in all the details, the magnificence of the room. Now she looked wide-eyed at the crystal chandelier, the Chinese wall-paper and the ormulu furniture.

'Almost noon. I have ordered you a light *repas.*' As she spoke, there was a tap on the door. *Madame* took a tray from the servant and put it across Cassandra's knees. The inviting smell of sweet rolls and hot chocolate filled the room and Cassandra ate hungrily while the housekeeper bustled around the room.

'Where is Lord Nicholas?'

Madame Robert arranged the silver-backed brushes on the dressing table to her satisfaction, then came to stand at the foot of the bed. 'He has gone out. Many people have left cards in anticipation of his arrival; he is a gentleman who moves in the very best circles.' It was evident that this was a source of pride to the staff.

'But what about me?' Cassandra asked indignantly. 'I thought he was going to find me a dancing master.'

'And so he will,' *madame* soothed. 'He asked me to tell you he will take supper with you. No doubt he will tell you all the arrangements he has made then. Meanwhile, the dressmaker will arrive at two; I have sent orders already for a few simple gowns. I trust she will have something suitable to hand so that you can leave this room. Until then you must remain in this chamber, as his lordship ordered.'

Cassandra could not dispute the wisdom of this: it would be indiscreet to be seen in the valet's clothes and she could hardly leave the chamber dressed in Godmama's peignoir. Her breakfast finished, she made her toilette, amusing herself for almost an hour trying to coax her ruthlessly cropped curls into something resembling a coiffure and failing dismally.

At two o'clock promptly, Madame Robert appeared with the dressmaker, who had brought half a dozen ready made gowns and her sewing basket with her. She fussed around Cassandra, pinching and tweaking fabric, pinning and tucking until three of the gowns, a sprigged muslin, a twilled sarsenet and a printed poplin, could be made to fit Cassie's slight figure. While the dressmaker whipped seams and let down hems, Madame Robert sorted through muslin fichus and collars to ensure the shoulders and necklines of the new dresses were suitably modest.

'Ah, *charmante*,' the dressmaker murmured, as Cassandra tried on the sprigged muslin again. 'It is a pity English girls have no figure and are so tall, but *mademoiselle* has a certain something in her *deportement* that is most attractive.'

'These dresses will do very well indeed,' Madame Robert was saying, while Cassandra viewed herself in the pier glass. 'Now *mademoiselle* will need at least two walking costumes. . .'

The two women lapsed into rapid French which Cassandra made no attempt to follow. She looked critically at herself in the mirror: she may not have much of a figure, but what she had was certainly improved by the clever cut of the simple gown with its high waist and neatly draped skirts. She twisted and turned to get a view of the back, pleased to see how slender and feminine she looked after several days in boy's clothes. Would Nicholas still call her 'brat' dressed like this?

The novelty of her new dresses and her restricted surroundings soon wore off as the afternoon dragged on. The few dreary tomes by French philosophers which the bookcase held were of no interest to her. Outside there was sunlight and movement and voices carrying over the high wall from the city streets beyond.

Somewhere out there was Nicholas, visiting friends, enjoying himself, flirting, no doubt, with an army of desirable, elegantly dressed women. She crossed to the glass again, uncertain now that the dress was as grown-up and flattering as she'd first thought. When she compared its modest, pale lemon fabric with the heavy luxury of the silk peignoir, she felt positively dowdy.

By supper time there was still no sign of Nicholas. Eventually she ate alone in her room, bored almost to tears with her own company after being used to Nicholas's for the past few days. She wanted to show him her new gown, hear about his day, gossip of Paris, this wonderful city she'd only glimpsed. And she wanted to hear when her lessons could start and how soon she could go about with Madame Robert. . .

It was almost midnight and Cassandra was in bed when she heard the noise of carriage wheels on the cobbled courtyard beneath her window. She leapt out of bed and ran barefoot to the long casement. Below her, Nicholas was getting out of the carriage, but he was not alone. Another carriage pulled up behind and men and women in evening attire alighted from both.

Cassandra could not see them properly from above, but she could hear their laughter as they passed between the flickering *torchérès* into the house. The beast! Cassandra stamped her foot with fury. He'd promised to meet her at supper and instead he'd been out carousing with these people. . .he'd probably forgotten she existed. She'd spent all day by herself waiting for him to come home. . .

Angrily she wrenched open the door, careless of the fact she was wearing only the silk peignoir. Gaston was ushering the party into one of the drawing-rooms as she peered over the banister. They must have come on from the theatre, the three women in the group were bejewelled, gems flashing on the milky expanses of *décolletages*.

'Make yourselves at home, *mes amis*,' Nicholas called over his shoulder. 'I will be with you in a moment.' He began to run up the staircase, his opera cloak flung over one shoulder. Hastily Cassandra retreated to her room, her heart beating hard.

Well, at least he was coming up to apologise for missing supper with her! She sat on the edge of the bed and fluffed her hair up. Several minutes passed, but no knock came at the door.

He'd gone to his room without a thought for her! Furious, Cassandra swept her skirts around her and marched out of her room and down the corridor. Nicholas's door was ajar: she stood silently outside watching him.

In the candlelight, the black and white of his evening clothes were in stark relief. He had tossed aside the cloak and was adjusting his cravat before the glass. Cassandra moved slightly and the change in light must have caught his eye for he turned and saw her.

For a long moment Nicholas did not recognise the figure in the doorway. The brighter light from the landing cast a halo round tumbled dark curls and gleamed on the rich emerald silk which pooled around the pale bare feet which peeped provocatively from the folds. One white shoulder showed where the fabric had slipped with the woman's agitated breathing.

Instinctively he stepped forward, drawn by the sensuality of the still, silent figure. Then he saw who it was.

'Cassandra!' He stopped, scandalised as much by his own arousal as her appearance. With an effort he got his reactions under control. 'What are you doing out of your room — and dressed like that?'

'How else should I be dressed?' she demanded. 'It *is* bedtime, after all!' Her chin came up defiantly. Strangely, seeing him made her even angrier, although she could not have said why. 'You promised you'd be home for supper. . .' She could hear the childish whine in her voice even as she said it — and so did Nicholas. His expression changed from one she could not read to one of annoyance.

'You stupid child! Get back to bed this instant. If anyone were to see you. . .'

Her eyes sparked and she shrugged dismissively, sending the gown slithering down the other white shoulder. 'They'd only wonder who that child was — who should have been in bed hours ago.'

'Not dressed like that, they won't.' Before she could move, he had taken one rapid step forward, seized her by the shoulders and brought his mouth hard down on hers.

Nicholas held her crushed hard against him as he deepened the kiss with an erotic expertise that made her dizzy. Fireworks exploded behind her closed lids, her bare skin where the gown had slipped from her shoulders seemed to burn against the fabric of his shirt and his hands on her back moulded her body to his insistently.

Cassandra was beyond rational thought, surprise or any idea of resistance. Of their own volition, her fingers sought the crisp curls at his nape, twining and inciting with a quite instinctive knowledge.

A little moan of wanting began in her throat and he freed her as sharply as he had taken her. Bewildered, she staggered, her eyes on his face, trying to understand this new Nicholas, trying to fathom why he had broken the embrace so brutally.

'Nicholas?' The timid whisper appeared to goad him to fury.

'Let that be a lesson to you.' His voice was as harsh as his face. 'You must learn that if you provoke gentlemen, they will respond to what you have offered.'

'I was not provoking. . .' Her eyes were huge in her white face, the hurt in them shaming him even more than he felt already.

'What do you call that?' His fingers pulled up the silken ruffles to cover her bare shoulders. 'If you come into a man's room dressed like a whore, you must expect to be treated like one. I taught you a lesson for your own good. Now go to bed.'

He strode past her and out of the room. From the foot of the stairs his voice drifted back to her, light and careless. 'Have you drinks, *mes amis*? Dice or cards?'

CHAPTER FOUR

CASSANDRA threw herself across her bed and pummelled the pillows until her clenched fists ached and the memory of Nicholas's contemptuous face faded.

'Pig! Pig!' she sobbed into the coverlet. How could he treat her like that! Gradually her fury subsided, leaving her feeling sick with humiliation at the way Nicholas had used her — the way she had responded to him. She hadn't intended to provoke him, she told herself, then felt her cheeks burn at the way she'd responded to that kiss and the strength of his arms as he'd crushed her body to his.

Cassandra had had no experience of men, but she knew now that this was exactly what she'd been wanting him to do ever since she'd walked into his bedchamber in Grosvenor Square. She lifted her hot face from the pillow, scrubbed the tears off her cheeks and sat up. Well, however attracted she felt to Nicholas, his cold dismissal proved he felt nothing for her. As far as he was concerned, she was an embarrassing child and tonight's incident would only make him more determined to leave her safely chaperoned in Paris while he continued his Grand Tour unencumbered.

The sound of laughter from the salon below sent her to the open casement. Light streamed from the long windows across the paved courtyard painting the shadows of the miniature orange trees against the walls of the *hôtel*.

'It's not fair!' Cassandra fumed to her reflection in the panes. All along Nicholas had misunderstood her, had treated her like a boy even when she didn't have to act the part, then when all she'd wanted was to be noticed, he'd treated her like a. . . She remembered what he'd called her and couldn't say it.

She was just another possession as far as he was concerned, like his servants and his house and his carriages—something he didn't notice until it discommoded him. Well, it was about time the Earl of Lydford did notice her!

Cassandra looked at herself again, but this time with more calculation. The shock had left her pinched and white about the face, her hair damp and flattened on her head. The soft femininity of the afternoon had gone: the boy Cass stared back at her with reddened eyes.

Ten minutes later Cass peered silently through the balusters as a footman deposited a tray of glasses on a side table in the hall. Before he could return, she sped swiftly down the stairs and picked up the salver. Her heart was thudding against her ribs, but no-one looked up as she slipped through the door into the salon.

Four men were lounging around a card table throwing dice. Beside them, flushed with excitement and wine, four women were egging them on with sharp little cries of encouragement. The light from the mass of candles glinted off jewels and bullion lace, cut crystal and silverware.

Cass's hands shook, setting the wine glasses tinkling and she put the tray down hastily just as the footman brought in the decanters. His eyes widened at the sight of her, but she took them from him, shutting the door in his startled face.

The gamesters still paid her no attention. The women were laughing, teasing one of the men whose luck seemed to be out.

'Throw a double six, my dear Comte, and I will give you the rose from my bosom,' the redhead said throatily, leaning towards him to show off the prize nestling between her scarcely covered breasts.

The Count, a dark, sardonic man with a beak of a nose smiled lazily at her. 'I shall want more than the rose if I score high, my dear Juliette.'

His voice, as warm as honey, did nothing to disguise his meaning, even from Cassandra. Her small gasp of outrage was audible. Several heads turned towards the dark suited figure but Nicholas, without looking up, ordered, 'Pour the wine and go. We will serve ourselves.'

Cassandra lifted the heavy decanter with both hands and began to pour the red wine gingerly, one eye on Nicholas's dark head. This wasn't what she'd planned when she'd scrambled into the valet's clothes. She'd wanted to give him the shock of his life by appearing as a boy, pay him back by forcing him to play act in front of his sophisticated friends.

She'd only meant to appear for a minute, give him a fright. Now she was trapped — and he hadn't even looked up from the dice, or noticed it was her.

The woman perching like a bird of paradise on the arm of the Earl's chair was running her fingernails absently through the crisp curls at his nape. Cassandra met the woman's eyes and registered with shock that she must be a good ten years older than Nicholas, although her beautifully painted complexion belied it.

'Nicholas, my darling,' she drawled, 'where did you find such a delicious boy? I declare, he is positively edible — and so young! Why, look, we shock him!' The fingers were still on Nicholas's neck, all her attention was fixed in that gaze.

Cass could feel the scalding blush flood up from her neckcloth as the woman sauntered over and touched one cheek with a long finger. '*Regardez, mesdames*, his cheek is smooth like a peach.'

Nicholas turned, his expression of mild irritation freezing into a mask of disbelief at the sight of Cassandra dressed in the dark suit he'd given her in London.

Juliette, the redhead, laughed. 'Oh, Mariette! Even for you, he's a little young. And so innocent. . .how could you think of bespoiling it?'

The tip of Mariette's tongue touched her upper lip fleetingly. 'Just watch me. . .'

'Leave the lad alone!' Nicholas spoke quietly but with an underlying edge of menace. 'It is his first time out of England and I don't want his head turning, or he'll never be any use to me.'

Mariette turned from Cassandra with a flounce of bad temper. 'You are so high minded, milord! All this concern over a lackey.' She snapped her fingers, 'Wine, boy!'

Cassandra moved round the table proferring the salver, her head giddy with relief at her close escape. It had never occurred to her that anyone would take her seriously as a boy — in *that* way!

She kept her eyes averted as Nicholas leaned over to take his glass: she sensed he was too angry to risk a meeting of eyes. She came to the Count last. He lounged back in his chair, a malicious smile playing on his lips at Mariette's discomfiture. As Cassandra served him, he gave her a conspiratorial wink. Grateful, she smiled warmly at him and failed to see his eyes narrow with sudden speculation.

'That will be all, Cass,' Nicholas ordered. 'Get to your bed.'

Thankfully, Cassandra put down the tray, bowed and left as quickly as she could. The cool of the deserted marble hall was delicious after the over-heated atmosphere of the salon. She sank wearily onto the bottom stair, pushed her sticky hair off her temples and drew a long, shuddering breath.

Of all the stupid, foolhardy things to do — to risk exposure in that way and at the hands of a rapacious female like Mariette! Cassandra shuddered and dropped her hot forehead into her hands. Goodness knew what Nicholas would do in the morning! Throw her out onto the streets of Paris probably — and who could blame him?

'Oh, no. . .this is the *end*,' Cassandra moaned. How could she have provoked Nicholas like that?

'Come, come, *ma petite*, things cannot be so bad.'

Cassandra started to her feet at the sound of the warm, sympathetic voice, then realised, as she found herself staring into the deep brown eyes of the Count, that he had addressed her in the feminine form.

'What. . . Sir. . .?' she stammered. 'I think you must be mistaken. I am. . .'

'A young woman and a very pretty one at that.' His gaze travelled slowly from the top of her cropped head to her small feet in the buckled shoes.

His eyes were knowing, yet somehow compassion-
ate. 'We have a little *mystère* here, I think. I love a
mystery; life is too predictable.'

Cassandra's eyes flew to the door, expecting at
any moment someone to come in search of him.

'Do not fear.' He seemed to understand her
apprehension. 'They know I dislike the dice — they
are not easy to manipulate, unlike cards and
women.' The laughter lines creased at the corners
of his eyes and Cassandra found herself smiling
back: the Count seemed to be something of a rogue,
but a likeable one for all that. 'They will think I
have gone into the library. We can talk there.'

'But I don't want to. . .' Cassandra found herself
being propelled firmly into the booklined room and
the doors were closed behind her.

'And I think you need to talk to someone, *ma
petite*.'

Cassandra's mind raced. She did need someone
to talk to: could she trust this man, about whom she
knew nothing, not even his name? No, she dare not
tell him anything. Nicholas would never forgive her
if she compromised him so.

Warm hands cupped her chin and gently tipped it
up, forcing her to meet his eyes. 'We will have a
glass of Madeira, my little one, you are shivering.
Then you will tell me what is troubling you, and
why a well-bred young lady is involved in some
masquerade that necessitates these garments.'

Cassandra found herself sitting meekly, watching
his long, beringed fingers flicking dismissively at her
fustian jacket. 'But I know nothing of you, not even
your name.' Despite herself, she felt her guard
slipping in the face of his charm.

'That is easily remedied. I am Guy de Montpensier, Comte de Courcelles, at your service, *mademoiselle*.' He swept her an elaborate bow before subsiding elegantly into the chair opposite. He raised an interrogative brow then sipped his wine, apparently entirely happy to wait until she was ready to confide in him.

Cassandra knew she should not be in this position, alone in a room at night with a strange man—a Frenchman to boot! She watched him from beneath her lashes as he lounged in the wing chair. He was not as tall as Nicholas, nor as muscled. No, the Count was altogether more languid and almost a dandy in his dress.

The big nose dominated his face. He should have been ugly, but for the charm of his wry smile and the warmth in his brown eyes. All of a sudden the urge to tell someone everything was overwhelming.

'It began when my father announced he was marrying again,' she blurted and soon the whole sorry tale was tumbling out. The Count sat sipping his wine, nodding occasionally when she faltered.

'. . .and he said I looked like a. . .like a. . .' Words failed her at last.

'And so you decided to pay him back? Very understandable. And that is how we find ourselves having this talk, *n'est pas*?'

Cassandra took a gulp of Madeira, feeling it warming its way down her throat. She shouldn't have told him, but she was glad she had.

The silence stretched on. The Count had finished his wine and sat, apparently deep in thought, his fingers steepled.

'Monsieur le Comte. . .'

'Guy.'

'Guy. . .what am I to do?'

'*Malheureusement*, little one, I can offer no better solution than the one you have already before you. Wait here until your *marraine* returns from Vienna.'

'But Nicholas will be so angry, he will throw me onto the streets!' Cassandra wailed.

Guy leaned forward and took both her hands in a warm clasp. 'Nonsense, he is too much the English gentleman! He will be very angry, *sans doubte*,' he shrugged. 'But you will feel braver in the morning.'

'But. . .'

'Should that happen. . .' he was saying as the door opened.

'Cass, what are you doing in here?' Nicholas sounded more mildly irritated than the anger she expected.

Cassandra shot out of the chair, knowing her face must be a picture of guilt. 'Nicholas, I was just going to my room. . .'

'Indeed, you are,' he said levelly. His eyes, resting on the Count, were cold. 'Really, Guy, one never knows where you will turn up next.'

The Frenchman swept him an ironic bow, but his expression was wary. 'Miss Weston and I were merely discussing her impressions of France.'

'Miss Weston? So, Cassandra, you have been confiding in my friend here? A pity, he is known as one of the worst gossips in Paris.'

'You do me an injustice, *mon brave*—surely you mean the best!' His insouciance did not quite disguise the edge of tension in the room.

'A warning, *monsieur*. Miss Weston's predicament is not a subject for one of your witty stories.'

'But Nicholas, *mon ami*, it is so *piquant*. . .so irresistible!' Guy spread his hands, 'With the names changed, of course. . .'

'Indeed. And how irresistible will you find it if I send my seconds to wait on you?' Nicholas enquired amiably.

There was a long silence. Cassandra looked from man to man, unable to read how serious Nicholas was.

'Nicholas,' she said imploringly. 'Please stop talking about duels, you're frightening me!'

'*Cherie*,' the Count remarked with a grimace, 'you are not alone! He frightens me, too.'

Suddenly she realised the two men were grinning at each other and that her alarm was quite misplaced. The realisation made her angry. 'Men!' She stamped her small foot and flounced out of the room, carefully not slamming the door behind her.

Through the crack she heard the clink of glasses and Nicholas's short laugh. 'I do declare, Guy, the child is more trouble than a barrel-load of monkeys. Thank heaven, I do not have a daughter.'

'Not one you know of, at any rate, *mon brave*.'

Cassandra stamped upstairs, their laughter ringing in her ear. Men! They were all as bad as each other.

The Earl was no less infuriating the next day, nor more inclined to forgive her.

Madame Robert was just attempting to arrange Cassandra's cropped locks into a more feminine style when Nicholas swept into the chamber.

'Milord!' The housekeeper cast a scandalised eye over his shirtsleeves and crimson dressing gown.

'You may leave us, *madame*. I wish to speak to my ward alone.'

Madame Robert dropped a curtsey and left stiff-backed.

'I am not your ward.' For some reason, she preferred to be called 'cousin'.

'I wish to blazes you were not my anything!' He had obviously had very little sleep. It had done nothing for his temper but, Cassandra thought wistfully, it had not marred his looks. 'Unfortunately you have made yourself my responsibility and after last night. . .'

Cassandra blushed deeply, remembering the heat of his body crushed against hers. 'How could you be so unkind as to talk about that?'

'After you confided the truth to one of the worst rakes in Paris, we need to talk!' They were obviously at cross-purposes: her indiscretion with the Count was obviously more important than the encounter in his bedroom. 'Guy will never be able to resist the joke, it will be all over the City.'

'Is he a rake?' Cassandra enquired, momentarily distracted. 'I've always been warned about them, of course, but I never thought I'd ever meet one.'

'Cassandra, of course, he's a rake and a gamester to boot! Not that he'd have believed a word of your story, of course. He assumes you're my mistress, I've no doubt.'

Cassandra gasped in horror. 'Nicholas! Why would he assume that? Didn't you tell him how old I was?'

'I doubt if it would have made any difference what I told him after you'd sat there batting your eyelashes at him and holding his hands. He's quite well aware you are only fifteen. You are so naive, Cassandra! You make me feel forty.' He ran his hands through his hair and broke off to pace around the room.

Cassandra sat nervously fingering the muslin of her gown, wondering what was going on in his head as he paced about like a caged panther. With a sinking heart, she recognised how foolish she'd been. Nicholas's whole plan had depended on her staying quietly in the house so no whiff of scandal leaked out. Now she had compromised both of them, and possibly her beloved Godmama, too. She could hardly be expected to give countenance to a girl widely believed to be her son's mistress.

'Nicholas?'

'What?' He came to a halt before her, green eyes serious on her face and she realised how much she was going to miss him.

'I must go home, mustn't I?'

'Impossible. I refuse to send you home to Offley's tender mercies. No, there is only one solution. You must go to Vienna.'

'Vienna? To Godmama?' Cassandra leapt from the chair with excitement. She took two steps towards him, ready to throw her arms round him, then thought better of it. 'Oh, Nicholas, thank you, it's more than I deserve, I know.'

'Indeed, it is,' he observed tartly. 'Now sit down and stop prattling, I must think.'

'I wasn't. . .' Cassandra began, then subsided into silence, her eyes on his thoughtful face. Vienna! Godmama would bring her out and there'd be balls and receptions and beautiful gowns — and Nicholas would have to admit she was no child.

'Mama's travelling carriage is in the stables, which is fortunate. Gaston will know of a reliable courier to take charge of the journey and Madame Robert will be able to recommend a firm duenna to look after you.' He was jotting notes on a set of tablets. 'Four fully armed outriders, I think, better to be safe than sorry. . .'

'But Nicholas — aren't you coming, too?'

'Why should I?'

'But I thought you were going to Vienna next.'

'No of course not, that was never my plan.' His eyebrows shot up. 'I never intended to follow the direct route which you will now take. Once I leave here — sooner than I'd intended, thanks to your foolishness — I am meeting an old acquaintance in Marseilles. And then I have my papers to travel into Italy. . .' He broke off at the sight of her disappointed face. 'Cassandra! You did not believe I was about to change my plans in order to escort you personally to Vienna? Heaven help me, child — haven't you caused me enough trouble already?'

'But Godmama would expect. . .'

'Mama would have expected me to have boxed your ears back in London and packed you off to your father! Never have I done anything I regret more than bringing you here.'

'That I doubt,' Cassandra responded waspishly.

'Meaning?'

Cassandra recognised his rising temper, but was too angry to heed it. 'What's done is done, and you are responsible for me, you said so yourself. I don't want to go by myself with some hatchet-faced female. And it will be dangerous: you shouldn't abandon me.'

'I am flattered you should think I could protect you where four armed outriders could not. What you are really afraid of is being forced to behave yourself for a change.'

They were glaring at each other now. Nicholas slipped the tablets into his pockets and stood up. 'You will do as you are told while you are under my protection. I have a cultural itinerary planned and I intend to follow it.'

He had turned towards the door, dismissing her. 'Cultural activities like last night, I suppose?' she jibed. 'Intellectual conversation with half-naked women? A philosophical study of games of chance? I can imagine what an exhausting time you will have. No wonder you won't come to Vienna with me — it might stop you enriching yourself culturally.'

'You are your father's daughter, Cassandra Weston.' Nicholas swivelled slowly to face her, anger etched in his features. 'You are a shrew, sharp-tongued, devoid of feminine graces and intolerant to boot. Well, I capitulate. You have your victory.'

Cassandra swallowed her resentment at his insults. 'You will accompany me, then?'

'On the contrary, Miss. You will accompany *me*. You can see what pleasure there is to be had in travelling on rough roads, sleeping in flea-infested inns and eating disgusting food. And, of course, I shall rely on you to draw my attention to all the cultural sights along the way.'

He was exaggerating the difficulties to frighten her, of course. Cassandra turned sparkling eyes on his face. 'Oh, thank you, Nicholas. I knew you wouldn't have been so unkind as to have left me!

Marseilles and the Mediterranean and Italy! Will we cross the Alps?'

'I sincerely hope not. I despair of you, Cassandra: this is not a treat, this is a punishment. Now, get ready and pack your bags. We will leave after luncheon, before the Count has spread the news of your presence round every gossip in Paris.'

'Shall I travel as your daughter or your niece?' Cassandra smoothed her muslin gown. 'We had better decide for the passports.'

'Daughter?' Nicholas grinned wickedly, showing a gleam of white teeth. 'Oh, no, Cassandra. I have no intention of dragging a lady's maid across Europe to lend you countenance. I brought you here as my valet, and my valet you will remain.'

'I will say this for you, Cassie, you don't sulk.' Nicholas leaned back against the brocade squabs of his uncle's travelling carriage and eyed her with more favour than he had for several days.

They had been handed back their documents duly stamped at the *Porte d'Italie* and Cassandra was folding them carefully back into the leather satchel on the seat beside her.

'There's never been much point in sulking,' she observed, with a last regretful look out of the window as Paris receded behind them. 'When you spend all your time alone, nobody notices.'

'Poor brat. What a very dull life you must have led. No wonder you wanted an adventure.' Nicholas closed his eyes and settled his shoulders more comfortably. 'Wake me up if anything interesting happens.'

Cassandra sighed and gazed out of the window. It

was as if the three days in Paris hadn't happened: perhaps she'd dreamt it. Her fingers came up involuntarily to brush her lips. No, that embrace had been no dream. She shivered with mixed pleasure and apprehension. It was foolish to dwell so on her first kiss. It hadn't meant a thing to Nicholas, that was plain. And now she must settle back into the master-servant relationship when they were among people. When they were alone she must be careful: if she continued to provoke and tease him, he would soon realise she wasn't the child she pretended.

Or did he realise, anyway? The Earl of Lydford was no fool. Perhaps he was pretending to believe her for her own sake. If the truth came out into the open, he would have no choice but to send her off to his mother and hope she wasn't ruined irretrievably.

On the other hand, his taste in women seemed to run to the older, elegant, experienced and, no doubt, married ladies like Lady Broome. He wouldn't notice well-scrubbed, innocent country girls. The carriage lurched on the rutted surface of the dry road and Cassandra grabbed a hanging strap to steady herself, wishing she'd brought a book with her. An Italian one would have served to polish up the reading she'd already done in her father's library.

Nicholas dozed on, seemingly unaffected by the jolting. Cassandra sighed. This was about as exciting as driving to Ware market on a Wednesday: perhaps foreign travel wasn't as stimulating as all the books said.

CHAPTER FIVE

AFTER four long, dusty, uncomfortable days on the road, Cassandra was rueing ever challenging Nicholas to take her with him. The roads East would have been no better, it was true, but at least she would have been treated as a young lady, with all the status of travelling as the ward of the Earl of Lydford.

Instead, at the end of the interminable roads, mercifully shaded with the poplars Napoleon had had planted to shelter his marching troops, all she could look forward to was a hard truckle bed behind a screen in the corner of Nicholas's chamber.

The inn at Briare had been acceptable, but the food at Nevers had been every bit as bad as Nicholas had threatened; swimming with grease and heavy with garlic.

As the coach swung out of Macon, bouncing over the cobbles behind a fresh team, Nicholas caught her eye and asked, 'Comfortable?'

'Perfectly, thank you.' Cassandra had vowed not to complain, to give him no excuse to say 'I told you so'. Instead, she smiled back, tried hard not to scratch the additional flea bites she had acquired the night before in the inn, and distracted herself with catching glimpses of the river traffic on the Saône.

'Not much more of this,' Nicholas remarked, studying the post road map he had bought in Paris. 'We should reach Lyons this afternoon.'

'I'm quite all right. At least your uncle's carriage is well-sprung and clean, unlike those filthy hired coaches. Or the diligences,' she added, as they swung out to overtake one of the public coaches with its creaking wicker sides and piles of luggage, lumbering along at four miles an hour.

'Well, you might be all right, but I'm as stiff as a post.' Nicholas stretched his long legs as far as he could, then put his hands behind his neck to rub the sore muscles. 'I need some exercise and a change of scene from these squalid hovels and dusty verges.'

'I have to admit the scenery has been disappointing, although the river's interesting.' Cassandra knelt up on the seat to look out over the wide river, glittering grey in the sunlight. 'Everyone seems so poor,' she added, her eyes following a group of ragged children waiting to beseige the diligence with outstretched palms.

'The women are handsome, though.' Nicholas was admiring a slender young woman, her skirts kirtled up to show strong tanned calves. Catching his eye as the coach slowed to negotiate the herd of pigs she was driving, the woman smiled, exposing a few blackened teeth. 'Perhaps not,' he added quickly, withdrawing back into the coach.

'None of them seem to have many teeth left,' Cassandra observed. 'The guidebook says it's caused by the frequent fogs, but I can't see how, can you?'

'No, but it is a powerful aid to virtue. Come, let's play cards.' He pulled out a pack from one of the numerous pockets lining the doors of the coach and began to deal. 'Your picquet is becoming passable.'

Cassandra even managed to win a hand, feeling

decidedly in charity with her companion for a change. He was so nice, she thought wistfully, while he was like this, just like an older brother, not the arrogant Earl of Lydford. Those older women weren't good for him, she decided censoriously, they encouraged him to be hard and frivolous.

'A penny for your thoughts or can't you decide what to do with that hand?'

Hastily Cassandra discarded a red three and answered honestly. 'I was thinking how nice you were being.'

'You make me sound like an ogre. Of course I'm being nice, you're behaving yourself.' He grinned, 'And that was a very foolish discard. My point.'

Cassandra swung one buckled shoe back and forth, fighting the urge to kick him on the ankle. Aggravating man! At least he was still treating her like a child which, all things considered, was safest.

The Saône and Rhône met at Lyons, cutting their way through a ridge of hills down which the city tumbled to the quaysides. After the succession of squalid villages and provincial towns through which they'd passed, Lyons seemed almost as splendid as Paris.

The postillions turned the carriage in to the yard of the *Dauphin*, one of the best inns in the city. The tired horses stood steaming in the traces as Cassandra climbed down and began giving instructions in rapid French to the porters, while Nicholas was greated by the *patron*, effusive in his greetings to the English milord.

'We are in luck tonight,' Nicholas commented, as the innkeeper bowed them through the front door.

'I have secured two bedchambers and a private dining-room.'

'Yes, I overheard.'

Nicholas arched a laconic eyebrow. 'You are turning into an passable valet, Cass. The state of my linen is improving—although I cannot say the same for my boots—and your French is excellent.'

'Your lordship is too kind,' Cassandra murmured, sketching a bow as she stood aside for him to enter the room.

'Impertinent brat,' Nicholas murmured in return. 'Wine and biscuits, my good man. And send hot water and two baths. I dislike dirty servants,' he added, catching the innkeeper's surprised look at such consideration for a valet.

The luxury of soaking in hot water, after days of surreptitious dabbing with a rag and cold water, was blissful. Cassandra emerged pink and glowing to rummage in the medicine chest for the salve to dab on her flea bites. The jar was almost empty, obviously Nicholas was similarly afflicted. She put on her one remaining clean shirt, buttoned her waistcoat firmly over her breasts, checked with a sideways glance in the mirror for betraying curves and, satisfied, tapped on Nicholas's door.

He was sitting, feet up, in the window seat, languidly paring his nails and watching the street below.

'We need to go shopping,' Cassandra remarked. 'I need a shirt and you need neckcloths and we both need flea salve. I don't believe oil of lavender does *anything* to keep them away.'

'And you need another haircut.' Nicholas was looking at her critically. 'Those wispy little curls are really quite fetching. . .' His green eyes were suddenly warm on her face and Cassandra felt the blood rush to her cheeks. '. . .but not on a valet. Come here, I'll do it now while I have the scissors out.'

Reluctantly, Cassandra came and perched on the edge of the window seat. 'Look down so I can do the back.' His fingers seemed to burn on the skin at the nape of her neck as he lifted and snipped each curl. 'Stop wriggling,' he ordered, dropping one hand to her shoulder to hold her steady as he trimmed around her ear.

Cassandra could feel the heat of his body, warm from the bath as hers was, his breath feathering her ear, the coldness of the metal as he rested the scissors on her cheekbone for a second. Her breath came short, and under the constricting waistcoat she felt her nipples harden against the fine linen shirt. Instinctively she turned her face to his, her lips slightly parted and found him watching her, the scissors still in his fingers.

There was a long silence, heavy in the hot room. The only movement was the motes of dust dancing in the sunlight. Nicholas bent towards her, his eyes fixed on her parted lips. The scissors dropped from his heedless fingers and skidded across the polished boards with a clatter; it was enough to jerk both of them back to reality.

Cassandra leapt to her feet. 'Where's the clothes brush? I've got hair all over my waistcoat.' She was almost gabbling, avoiding his eyes as she rummaged in the dressing case for the brush.

A tap on the door and a waiter bringing in a tray of wine and almond biscuits was a merciful distraction. Nicholas seemed quite relaxed as he sipped the wine, but Cassandra still could not bring herself to meet his eyes.

Nicholas had once more made himself comfortable in the window seat, thumbing through the guidebook for references to Lyons. 'At least the shops here are recommended, both for clothes and for luxuries. It's getting cooler, shall we go now and eat when we return?'

'Er. . .yes.' Cassandra shrugged her coat on. He seemed quite calm, she must have imagined he had been about to kiss her again. It was extremely immodest of her to feel like this, to *want* him to kiss her, she told herself severely, trying to look as masculine as possible by matching his long stride as they crossed the yard.

The streets were bustling, the crowds jostling in the *traboules*, the narrow alleys which threaded their way between the medieval houses to the river quays. The *Lyonnais* were noisier, more lively than the northern French. They were darker, more voluble and their French was alarmingly fast to Cassandra, trying to catch phrases as she walked.

When they reached the shopping quarter, Cassandra found an apothecary's shop, its window full of jars of vipers in oil and even a stuffed crocodile. She purchased a large jar of unguent, guaranteed to repel even the most virile flea, more oil of lavender and a good supply of olive oil soap in angular brown lumps.

There was no shortage of linen drapers and, acting the good servant, Cassandra was soon loaded with parcels of shirts, neckcloths and body linen. Nicholas was striding on ahead when she caught a glimpse of sunlight on vivid colours and he found her, nose pressed against the glass, gazing longingly at a display of the most exquisite painted silk fans. There were flower patterns, roses, Chinese scenes, lovers in arbors. Small fans and large fans and fans with feathers and beads.

'Cass, come on, I want my dinner.' Cassandra turned to find him laughing at her. 'Valets do not stand lusting after fans! You are being stared at.'

'I don't care, Nicholas,' she breathed. 'They are beautiful. Look at that one at the back with the classical scene. It's Arcadia, I think, see the nymphs and fauns.'

'Wait there.' He left her standing on the pavement and went inside, shaking his head ruefully. When he emerged, he had a flat package tucked under his arm, silk ribbons streaming.

'What's that?' Cassandra demanded, tripping over her feet as she tried to keep up with him, while looking over her shoulder at the shop window.

'Never you mind. You gave me an idea. It's a present for a lady I know.'

Cassandra glared at the blue broadcloth stretched taut across his shoulders. So that was it, a trinket for one of his married mistresses when he got home to England.

However, it seemed the lady was nearer at hand. As the waiter brought food into their private dining-room, Nicholas strode in, fastening his cloak over his evening attire.

'You're not going out?' she demanded.

'I certainly am. I've ordered you an excellent dinner, you'll be quite comfortable here with no need to go out. And don't wait up,' he added as the door closed behind him.

Cassandra tore a roll apart and spread butter on it with a lavish hand. He obviously wasn't going out for dinner — he could have had a perfectly good dinner here with her, even if that was a fricassee of frogs' legs she could see at the end of the table. And she very much doubted if an evening of cultural activity was what the Earl had in mind, although she suspected the theatre would feature in his plans. Cassandra had heard about opera dancers, who apparently provided much of the entertainment for gentlemen bored with the play.

Cassandra was still wide awake as the clocks were chiming two and the door to the adjoining chamber creaked open. About time! He was so inconsiderate — there was she, lying imagining him with his throat cut by pickpockets in some darkened alley. . .

No, it wasn't that keeping slumber at bay, she admitted to herself. It was the thought of Nicholas in the arms of the lady for whom the fan was intended, of her gratitude for the pretty gift.

Candlelight showed under her door and footsteps crossed the floor. To her surprise, her door opened slowly, and Nicholas tiptoed in. Cassandra froze, her fingers grasping the coverlet. What was he doing in her room? Even when she'd had to sleep behind a screen in his chamber, he had never once entered that private space.

She half closed her eyes, trying to feign sleep, certain he would hear the sound of her racing pulse in the silent room. Under her lashes she watched him move towards her bed and bend down.

Cassandra closed her eyes and almost stopped breathing: she knew he shouldn't be there, knew she should cry out, but she could not — she didn't want to. She felt him gently place something on the foot of the bed, then he tiptoed out again.

Gradually she relaxed her fingers as the door closed behind him and sounds made it obvious Nicholas was preparing for bed. The candle next door was snuffed. Cautiously Cassandra sat up and peered down at the foot of the bed. In the moonlight she was able to discern the shape of an oblong package with a tangle of ribbon. He had given her the fan.

When she woke in the morning the package was clutched in her arms like a child's doll, the ribbons crushed. Eagerly she pulled off the paper to examine the prize in the daylight. Gold leaf gleamed around the edge, the ivory sticks were smooth as butter under her fingers. Slowly she opened it up, tracing the delicate painted figures with a fingertip.

The door of Nicholas's chamber banged, startling her out of her reverie. What time was it? Judging by the bustle in the street below and the strength of the light flooding through the windows, she had overslept. Nicholas must have gone out without her.

Cassandra balanced on one foot, tugging on her other shoe, worrying about oversleeping. Usually she was up well before Nicholas and had his hot water, clean linen and breakfast all organised before he shouted for the first cup of coffee.

In his room, yesterday's shirt was tossed on the floor and in their private parlour, the remains of rolls and an almost empty coffee pot showed he had eaten before leaving. Cassandra rang for chocolate and rolls for herself and began tidying the bedchamber.

Should she pack their valises or not? Nicholas had not said how long he intended to stay, nor what their route from here would be.

When the chocolate came, she curled up in the window seat, the opened fan propped up at her feet, sipping the hot drink. Beneath her the street was thronged with tradesmen making deliveries both to the inn and to the private houses on either side. There were few carriages abroad at this hour and few gentry on the street: Nicholas ought to be easy to sight when he returned.

Warm in the sunlight bathing the window seat, Cassandra wriggled comfortably against the cushions and realised to her surprise that she was happier than she had ever been in her life. Despite the fleabites, the boy's clothes, the bumpy roads and Nicholas's uncertain temper she felt alive, vital — free. For nearly eighteen years she'd been her father's silent companion. Showing emotion was frowned upon, as were high spirits, or any display of temperament.

At best, her father had treated her as a rather unintelligent housekeeper. Now she was discovering that she could live off her wits. Rubbing shoulders with all classes, speaking French, pretending to be a boy, were all new experiences. A few weeks ago she would never have believed this could happen. When she'd run away from home she was only seeking sanctuary, not this new world of experiences.

But the most unexpected boon was this companionship she and Nicholas had achieved. If that was what it was. . . Cassandra looked at the fan again, biting her lip with indecision. If only she knew what he felt about her, what his reasons were for giving her the fan.

She'd missed Nicholas in the street below: the door behind her opened and he strolled in whistling, hands in pockets.

'You sound very cheerful,' Cassandra remarked, wondering who was responsible for putting the twinkle in his eye and the spring in his step.

'The sun is shining and not every young woman in Lyons is toothless.' He tossed his cane and gloves to one side. 'So, you decided to get up at last. Are we packed?'

'No! You didn't tell me we were going.' Cassandra scrambled off the seat, then remembered the fan. 'Thank you for the er. . .' She could feel herself blushing and blundered on. 'The fan. . .it's very beautiful.' She gazed at the buckles on her shoes, wondering why it was so difficult to thank him.

'Oh, it's nothing. You've been a good child, and I couldn't resist the look on your face, like an infant in a toyshop.' He flicked open the top of the chocolate pot to see if any remained, then threw himself down in a winged chair. 'You can put it somewhere safe until you're grown up.'

A good child! Cassandra burned with indignation, within an ace of telling him just how old she was, then bit back the words. What would he do if he realised she was eighteen? Pack her off to Vienna with a respectable widow—or give in to the instincts that had brought them so close to a kiss yesterday?

Cassandra couldn't decide which would be worse:

all she wanted was to stay with Nicholas on this long route to Vienna, to build on the friendship that was growing between them. Anything else was too complicated.

'Cassandra?' Nicholas had obviously been speaking to her for a few moments. 'Do wake up! The cases need to be packed: see to it while I talk to the postillions. We've got a boat to catch.'

A boat? Cassandra was still asking questions when they arrived on the quayside. The postillions unhitched the horses, were paid off by Nicholas and clattered away, leaving the carriage stranded on the cobbles.

'But where's the boat? And we can't leave the carriage here. . .'

'Stop tugging at my coat tails and watch.'

A group of men swung a crude wooden crane over the carriage and heaved until it dangled precariously in the air. The wheels were removed and handed over the quayside into a large, flat-bottomed boat where they were laid in the bottom, half submerged by dirty bilge water. To Cassandra's horror, the body of the carriage was swung over and down until it rested upon them.

'We can't go in that,' she protested looking at the crude boat rocking on the swift flowing River Rhône. 'It's nothing but a giant punt!'

'That giant punt is costing me seven guineas. Would you rather jolt over miles more road? Or perhaps crowd onto the public boat? We can stop at night, there are inns all along the banks.'

Cassandra looked dubiously at the vicious swirl of the current and felt her stomach contract. 'I can't swim, Nicholas. . .'

'Nonsense, nobody's going to fall in. And look how much you enjoyed crossing the Channel.'

She wouldn't let him see how afraid she was. Cassandra watched the four boatmen making ready their long poles and sorting ropes. A rather more practical problem asserted itself.

'Nicholas.'

'Um?' He was watching them make the carriage secure with a lashing of cords.

'Will we be on the boat all day? I mean. . .they're all men and I. . .'

Nicholas grinned at her discomfiture. 'Don't worry, infant. The very latest in travelling commodes is in the carriage which, as you know, is equipped with curtains.'

'Oh, thank you! I didn't think it would occur to you.'

'It didn't, but it's suggested in the guidebook. Now climb down and let's be off.'

Once the moorings were let go, the boat was pulled swiftly into the current. Two of the boatmen pulled on the primitive rudder, a long oar protruding through a hole cut in the stern; the others fended off with poles on either side.

'Cass, what are you doing? Get in.' Nicholas was already in the carriage, but Cassandra perched on one of the thwarts keeping her feet out of the bilge water with difficulty.

'I'm staying here,' she stated flatly. 'If this thing goes down, I'm not going to be stuck in the carriage.'

The wind was stronger on the water. Cropped as Cassandra's hair was, it was whipped into her eyes making them weep. Gradually the novelty of being on the river overcame her nervousness and she started to enjoy herself.

The tall houses and warehouses began to diminish as they left the city behind them, but the river was surprisingly busy with traffic crossing from bank to bank, or boats like their own laden with every cargo from sheep to bales.

The men had to work hard to keep a straight line down the Rhône, using their poles as brakes and steering oars. Other boatmen waved or shouted comments, some of them obscene enough to bring a blush to Cassandra's cheeks. Unsteadily she stood up and spoke to Nicholas. 'They all seem very rough. Are they reliable?'

'This was the most respectable crew I could find.' Nicholas seemed relaxed, but Cassandra noticed the coach pistols were out of their holsters and very much to hand. 'This is hardly a pleasure trip on the River Thames. When the boat reaches Arles, it will be broken up for firewood and the men will have to make their own way back upstream. They need to be tough.'

The banks seemed to fly past: Nicholas speculated they must be travelling at six miles an hour. The bridges were the most perilous to negotiate and at most of them, Nicholas and Cassandra disembarked and walked round to wait for the men to pole the boat between the piers.

'You are looking rather pale, Cass. Are you feeling sick?' Nicholas climbed down from the carriage, carefully picking his way to keep his feet dry.

'Not sick — hungry. It seems ages since we had breakfast.'

'They will pull into the bank at that village at the

next bend.' Nicholas pointed and Cassandra could see a straggle of houses with one rather more respectable building on the water side with its own jetty into the river.

The crew had a struggle to pull the boat out of the mainstream current into the quieter water that lapped the grassy banks. A man came down from the inn to catch the mooring rope and a scrubby boy was dispatched to warn the *patron* that guests were on their way. Cassandra's legs felt as wobbly as when she'd crossed the Channel, and the quiet inn with its dabbling ducks at the waterside was very welcome.

The inn was surprisingly clean and the food wholesome, although all that was provided was the simple *ordinaire*: cheese, olives and crusty bread with rough red wine to wash it down.

Cassandra made excuses to avoid reboarding the boat until Nicholas got quite short with her, pointing out that they would not reach Vienne for their night's lodgings if she tarried any longer.

'What *is* the matter with you?' he demanded, exasperated.

Cassandra shrugged and climbed reluctantly aboard. The fact that one of the men was baling out did nothing to soothe her fears, but they made a safe landfall at Vienne as the sun was setting and the air was cooling.

By the third day, as they re-embarked after a night in Montelimar, Cassandra was beginning to feel quite confident; able to make her way from one end of the boat to the other without mishap, and even exchanging badinage with the crew. Nicholas was in despair at the development of her vocabulary, but Cassandra pointed out that a few choice curses all helped her masculine disguise.

By mid-morning the weather had changed: the sky turned grey, a cold wind began to cut at their backs and the water, already turbulent, was whipped up into choppy wavelets.

Nicholas spoke to the boatmen, who shrugged their shoulders and muttered about the cruel winds of the Rhône. They were aiming to leave the boat at Arles, but the men seemed doubtful they would reach it that day, especially as the weather would make the difficult bridge at Pont St Esprit even more dangerous than usual to negotiate.

The crew seemed edgy and joked and sang less as they swept downstream. Nicholas showed Cassandra the map: Pont St Esprit was just below the junction of the Rhône with the Ardeche. The smaller river came tumbling down from the mountains swollen with snow-water.

'*Messieurs*!' The chief of the crew hailed them. 'We will put into the bank soon to let you off. You will have to walk to the other side of the bridge. It is not safe for you to remain on board.'

The boat was already tossing uncomfortably, the murky water sucking at the sides as the men struggled against the vicious current to turn into the bank. Cassandra could see an inn at the waterside and a group of people on the jetty watching the men's exertions. She felt nervous, but after almost three days afloat, she had trust in the skills and strength of the men.

They were within hailing distance of the shore when there was a loud crack. One of the side oars had snapped under the strain and, with a despairing wail, the crewman toppled into the water. The other men were powerless to assist him. Nicholas threw a rope from the stern, but the man had already disappeared below the choppy water.

In the confusion, and with only three oars, the boat had already spun back into the main current.

'Hold tight, *messieurs*!' the steersman shouted. 'We must all shoot the bridge together!'

The stone arches with their sharp prows slicing the current loomed large ahead of them. As they hurtled towards the piers, the bridge seemed to grow larger and larger, while the gap through which they had to pass appeared to Cassandra's terrified gaze to narrow.

Nicholas scrambled to her side, crushing her to the side of the coach and holding on for grim life as they sped inexorably towards the smooth slide of water under the central arch.

For a moment it seemed they would slip safely through, then an eddy caught the prow and sent it crashing against the stonework. Cassandra was aware of a great rending of wood, then the world turned upside down. She was wrenched from Nicholas's arms and thrown into the chilly, dirty water of the Rhône.

There was no light, only a thick green darkness which filled her eyes, ears and nostrils. She was going down and someone seemed to be beating her all over with sticks.

Desperately she kicked off her shoes, and felt a sudden relief as her coat was dragged off by the force of water. Surely any moment she must come up, but a great hand seemed to be holding her down, pushing her towards the muddy depths.

Her mind called 'Nicholas!', but her mouth was full of water, spilling down her throat. She was going to die. She had time to realise that, to wonder if Nicholas had made it to the shore, to start to say a prayer. Then everything went black.

Treading water in a patch of still water mercifully clear of the current, Nicholas scanned the surface feverishly for any sign of Cassandra. The water was opaque, too thick to see. It was pointless to dive, he could only pray the undertow would throw her clear.

The onlookers had launched boats: he could see two of the boatmen pulled out safely. If he did not see Cassandra soon, he too would have to swim for shore. His legs felt like lead with the weight of the water and the insistent pull of the current. He had almost given up when a sudden flash of white that could have been a fish broke the surface downstream. It was a hand.

Nicholas struck out strongly towards it, promising in his mind anything in the world if it was Cassandra, if he could reach her before she sank again. The whiteness was only a glimmer under the surface when he reached it, his fingers clamping around the wrist.

As soon as he touched the narrow bones, he knew it was Cassandra. Desperately he pulled her up, encircling her ribcage with his arm and striking out backwards for the shore. There was a warning shout behind him, the back of his head grazed painfully on the wood of a rowing boat and arms dragged them both into the sanctuary of the craft.

Nicholas hung over the side of the boat retching, suddenly too sick to help either of them until his lungs cleared. The next thing he knew, they were

on the river bank, the grass feeling wonderful under
his grasping fingers.

'The boy is dead, *monsieur*.' Someone was touching his shoulder in clumsy consolation. Nicholas
shrugged the man off and staggered to where
Cassandra was lying, her mud-streaked face colour-
less, her lips pinched and blue.

He lifted her shoulders, but there was no sign of
life, no answering flutter of the eyelids as he shouted
her name.

CHAPTER SIX

'CASSANDRA!' Nicholas couldn't, wouldn't, believe she was dead. He lifted her shoulders, but there was no sign of life, no answering flutter of the eyelids as he shouted her name again.

She hadn't wanted to come on the boat, had been afraid, however well she'd hidden it, and he'd ignored her fears. Because it had suited him, he had treated her like the boy she was not. . .and now she was lying lifeless in his arms.

'*Monsieur*, leave him, you can do nothing. The priest is coming down. . .' One of the boatmen was tugging at his shoulder.

'Damn you, no!' Nicholas snarled, too angry to respond in French. He would not accept it, not admit she was dead. His rage at himself cleared his mind: he remembered a man being dragged from the village pond when he was a child and the blacksmith turning him over and beating the water out of him until he came back to coughing life again.

Ruthlessly he tipped Cassandra's limp body over his knee and with his clenched fist struck her hard between her shoulder blades repeatedly. Under his fingers there was a fluttering pulse, then a sudden cough, a retch and she was violently sick.

Cassandra struggled feebly against the rough hands that were beating her. It was bad enough to be dead without being struck. Perhaps she was

already in Hell, which seemed unfair, so she said
so.

'Not fair. . .' it was only a croak, but the hands
stopped pummelling her and turned her over gently.
Someone was cradling her, stroking away whatever
was clogging her eyes and nostrils; it felt as though
lips were grazing her cheek, her temples, her closed
eyes.

The world beyond her eyelids was no longer green
and she could feel the sun on her face. Someone
was saying repeatedly, 'Thank God!' Perhaps it
wasn't Hell, after all, but Heaven. A voice she knew
said 'Cassandra, Cassie, open your eyes. . .please,
look at me.' It sounded like Nicholas, but the
imploring tone was one she had never heard on his
lips before.

Clean, cool water was splashing over her face and
she managed to open her eyes. Above her,
Nicholas's face, white and out of focus, swam close.

'I told you I couldn't swim,' she managed to
croak.

'And I told you I'd save you, you ungrateful brat,'
he replied, but his voice broke on the last word.

Cassandra's body convulsed in a violent shudder
and her eyes closed despite herself. There were
voices on the fringes of her consciousness. 'A blanket, monsieur. . .wrap the boy warmly. . .the
Veuve Aubrac sends to say there are beds ready.
Hurry, *monsieur*, before an ague sets in. . .'

Strong arms lifted her from the muddy bank and
Cassandra knew she was being carried. With an
effort of will, she forced her eyes open and saw
Nicholas's face, set with effort, as he picked his way
over the rough ground.

'Lie still, brat, don't wriggle,' he ordered, his breath coming short. 'There's a good inn here and you will shortly be safe in bed.'

There was a babble of voices with one, a well-modulated woman's voice, commanding and organising. Cassandra was aware of the change from sunlight to gloom as they entered the inn, of jolting as Nicholas carried her up a short flight of stairs and then there was a wonderfully soft, warm, safe feeling as she was lain on a bed.

Fingers unwrapped the swathing blanket; then there was silence. Nothing happened. After a moment, the woman's voice said, '*Monsieur?*'

Cassandra opened her eyes to find a tall, middle-aged woman looking down at her with raised eyebrows. Painfully, she turned her head and saw the expression of astonished horror on Nicholas's face as he, too, looked at her. Suddenly she was aware of just how little she was wearing. Slender bare feet protruded from the torn remnants of her stockings, her wet breeches were moulded to her hips and with her jacket and waistcoat gone the sodden, white linen shirt was as transparent as gauze across her breasts.

Without the constricting upper garments, every curve of her eighteen year old body was revealed. With a gasp, Cassandra grabbed the edges of the blanket round herself as the woman said, 'A word with you, *monsieur.*'

If she hadn't felt so ill and been so embarrassed, she could have found humour in the situation. Nicholas appeared to have been poleaxed, and the obviously highly respectable Widow Aubrac was completely in control of the situation.

Snatches of low-voiced discussion reached Cassandra's ears from the two who had withdrawn into the window embrasure.

'You expect me to believe you were unaware. . .'

'That she was a girl. . .not that she was a woman. . .'

'You prefer to travel with a *child* in disguise! *Monsieur*, this is a respectable house!'

'*Madame*. . . I assure you. . .' Nicholas was the picture of guilt, digging himself into a deeper hole with every word he uttered.

He obviously needed rescuing before *Madame* decided he was a total roué and threw him out. Painfully Cassandra levered herself up on one elbow and croaked. '*Madame*. . .'

Instantly the woman hurried to her side. 'Do not worry, *ma petite*. You are safe here. I have heard of these decadent English milords.' She shot Nicholas a cold look. 'Under my protection he will not touch you! I will write to your family and *Monsieur le Curé* will give you sanctuary under his roof until they come for you.'

'But it is not his fault—it is I who have been dishonest,' Cassandra protested. 'The Earl is the son of my godmother: I deceived him into thinking I was much younger than I am. Listen, I will tell you everything. . .'

'When you are warm, fed and rested, *ma petite*,' Slightly mollified, the woman turned to Nicholas. '*Monsieur*, you and I must talk later, but for now I must ask you to leave.' There was a knock at the door and servants staggered in with a hip bath and flagons of hot water. 'Your chamber is at the other end of the landing, you will wish to bathe and rest, *sans doubte.'*

Much later, warm, dry and lulled, Cassandra drifted off to sleep, aware only of the comforting crackle of logs in the grate and subdued noises from the outside world penetrating the closed shutters.

She woke to find the room full of sunlight, the shutters thrown open and the smell of chicken broth in her nostrils. *Madame* was setting down a tray, but when she saw Cassandra was awake, she bustled over to plump up the pillows and help her sit up.

Every muscle in Cassandra's body seemed to protest. Under the starched sheet her legs were stiff and sore, and when she picked up the spoon, her wrists were purpled with bruises.

'Nicholas?' she asked anxiously, suddenly fully awake, the memories of yesterday flooding her mind. '*Madame*, is he all right?'

Madame smiled slightly. 'Stiff and bruised as yourself, *m'selle*, but quite well. Somewhat chastened in spirit, I believe: I have remonstrated with him on his foolishness in indulging in such a charade.'

Looking at the aristocratic face, Cassandra could well believe it! What such a woman was doing running a country inn was a mystery, but in post-Revolutionary France, many people were forced to make shift as best they could.

Madame continued to talk as she straightened the bedclothes. 'I will never understand Englishmen! How could he have been so blind? You would not have deceived a Frenchman for one moment!'

'How long have I been asleep?' Cassandra swallowed the soup hungrily, it seemed days since she had eaten.

'You have slept the clock round. Now eat, and sleep again. Tomorrow, perhaps, you can get up.'

'But I need to talk to Nicholas.' All Cassandra could think of was the expression on his face as he realised just how she had deceived him. What would he do? Such impropriety would not be countenanced by polite society. Even the reputation of the Earl of Lydford would be damaged by such a scandal: no mother of a marriageable daughter would have him in the house again. Godmama would never forgive her if she prevented Nicholas from making a suitable marriage, as surely he soon must.

'Not in your room! It would be most improper for the Earl to visit you here. Besides, he, too, is resting. He came close to losing his own life in rescuing you.'

So it *had* been Nicholas who had dragged her from the water, and brought her back from the edge of death. Unconsciously she rubbed her wrist where his strong fingers had marked her. 'And the others? Our boatmen?'

'They are all safe, thank God.' *Madame* crossed herself piously. 'Even the one whose fall caused the accident will live, although he has a broken leg. Now rest again, that is enough talk for now.'

Cassandra was too weak to argue, even if *madame*'s autocratic manner had permitted it. 'Yes, *madame*,' she capitulated, her eyes closing even as she spoke.

* * * *

When Nicholas found her the next day, Cassandra was sitting quietly on a settle by the fire in the back parlour. In the high-necked grey gown *madame* had found for her and with her cropped hair, she looked like a novice nun. Her face was porcelain pale except for a livid bruise running from cheekbone to jawline on one side and she was flexing stiff fingers painfully in her lap.

'Cassie,' he said quietly.

Cassandra jumped, then bit her lip with pain at the sudden movement. Nicholas took one step towards her as if to comfort her then stopped, sitting abruptly in the wing chair on the other side of the fire.

'We have to talk.' He looked not at her but down at his clasped hands, and Cassandra wondered if he was too angry at her deception to face her.

'I know, Nicholas. . . I'm sorry. I was headstrong and foolish and I should never have allowed you to go on believing I was so young. But I knew you would not have brought me with you if you knew the truth.' For a moment the thought of Lord Offley's wet lips on hers, the prospect of marriage with such a man came flooding back and she shuddered. 'I would rather have died than remain!'

'You almost did,' he said sardonically.

'*Madame* told me it was you who saved me.' Still he did not look at her. 'Thank you for saving my life, risking your own for me. I am truly sorry.'

'*You* are sorry!' The words burst from him. 'I should never have taken you on that boat. You were frightened and I ignored it.' His anger was palpable. 'This has been a sorry escapade.' He got to his feet and thumped the mantelpiece with his clenched fist. 'I must have been mad that day in London!'

'But you weren't to know my true age,' Cassandra protested. 'It was I who let you go on believing I was fifteen.'

'Just how old are you, Cassandra?' he demanded, his voice hard. He was standing over her and she had to look up to meet his scrutiny.

'Eighteen,' she confessed quietly.

'Oh, Cassie!' He took her chin between long fingers, turning her face from side to side. 'Of all the stupid things to do!' There was a heavy silence, then he sighed and released her. 'What a damn fool I've been — I think I must have known all the time, I just didn't choose to see it. For heaven's sake, I nearly kissed you in Lyons!'

'You *did* kiss me in Paris.' Cassandra could have bitten her tongue as soon as she said it: the expression in Nicholas's suddenly hooded eyes warned her she was still on dangerous ground.

'Precisely! Cassandra, you are a woman, however little experience you may have of Society and the world. . .'

'Are you telling me I cannot trust you?' she whispered.

'Yes!. . . No!' He spun away, pacing the room in his inability to explain to her. 'That night in Paris I had been drinking, you had made me angry — and then to see you looking like that. . . I didn't stop to think.' He struggled to find the words to explain to this sheltered girl-woman just how provocative her behaviour had been. 'Our Society keeps unmarried girls and men apart for a reason: sometimes our natures overrule both sense and honour.'

Cassandra swallowed hard. The delicacy of Nicholas's carefully chosen words could not disguise the truth of what he was saying. If it had happened in Paris, it could happen again if they were thrown together in such intimacy. 'You are saying that you must send me back,' she stated bleakly. 'That you have no alternative.'

'I only wish I could send you back! Don't think I haven't considered it.' His smile was rueful. 'But I could not consign you to Offley's tender mercies! Nor can I send you directly to my mother: from here you would have to travel back to Lyons, then across the Alps into Switzerland and on to Vienna, and that is too perilous a journey even with a reliable escort.

'No, I have weighed all this since yesterday: you must continue to travel with me, but as my ward, under my protection. It is no further to Vienna through Italy than to retrace our steps.

'*Madame* will find you a wardrobe of discreet clothes such as you are wearing now and we must hope you can pass as a schoolgirl. I will engage a maid.' He broke off and looked at her. 'It will seem unconventional, but we are on the Continent: foreigners think all the English are mad, anyway. We must just avoid the company of our own countrymen.'

'But Nicholas, you will be sacrificing so much, missing so much of the Grand Tour if we have to avoid everywhere where English tourists will be.'

He shrugged. 'So be it. I doubt I'll have a decent night's sleep until I can deliver you safe to my mother, never mind an appetite for art galleries and antiquities!'

Cassandra knew she should feel guilty, perhaps she did. But overriding all other emotions was the thought that she would still be with Nicholas, for days, weeks to come. He was arrogant and dangerously disturbing, but he also laughed with her, shared with her and looked after her. For the first time in her life, she had a friend, a companion.

Her life before she'd run away had been desperately lonely. No doubt when she reached Vienna, Godmama would introduce her to girls of her own age who would become friends, but for the moment there was only Nicholas to fill that gap.

'Thank you, Nicholas,' she said fervently. 'I promise I'll behave with discretion—I made a good boy, but I'll make an even better schoolgirl!'

She fixed him with an imploring gaze, which he met with narrowed eyes and a slight, dubious, shake of the head. 'You'll be bored to tears back in skirts and with a chaperone. When the novelty wears thin. . .'

Whatever he was about to say was drowned by the rumble of carriage wheels on cobbles, followed seconds later by the raised voice of an Englishman. Nicholas jumped up and opened the door a crack. 'Hell and damnation! Upstairs quickly!'

'But Nicholas. . .'

'Don't argue.' He propelled her to the door, one hand painfully between her bruised shoulder blades. 'There's a party of about a dozen English. . .three carriages. Of all the cursed bad luck!'

In her room, Cassandra set the shutters open a crack so she could safely observe the new arrivals. There seemed to be two families with their servants. The older men appeared to be brothers, both florid and overdressed. They were accompanied by their wives — one stout and perspiring in the afternoon sun, the other thin and languid — and their sons.

Cassandra saw at a glance they were not of the *ton*. Rich merchants from their dress and manner, she guessed. The yard soon emptied, the noise transferring to the interior of the inn as they and their luggage were distributed among the available rooms.

Did this mean she would have to be confined to this chamber until these people — or she and Nicholas — moved on? Cassandra sighed heavily, already beginning to chafe at the restrictions of her new rôle. At least as a boy she could have slipped down the back stairs and into the stableyard and no-one would have spared her a second glance.

There was a light tap at the door and *madame* came in, accompanied by a pretty blonde woman in her early twenties, whom she introduced to Cassandra as Madame Vernet, the apothecary's wife. '*Monsieur* entrusted me to engage a companion for you, *m'selle*, and he has requested me to ask you to come down to dinner this evening with Madame Vernet.'

'But the other visitors. . .'

'They are not of the best society, *m'selle*.' The widow spoke with hauteur, as if her inn were used to better. '*Monsieur le Comte* thinks it would be useful for you to practise your new rôle among people who do not know him.'

'Oh, good!' A chance of escape, a change of company. 'What am I to wear?'

'*Monsieur* and I consider what you are wearing entirely suitable for a young lady not yet out.'

Cassandra smoothed down the light grey stuff of her skirt and sighed. Her new resolution to behave was being sorely tested sooner than she would have expected.

The rest of the party was assembled in the dining-room by the time Cassandra and her new chaperone entered. Colette Vernet had proved to be a friendly companion and an excellent dresser of hair. Despite her drab dress, Cassandra was pleased with the shining curls Colette had teased from her crop, and the Frenchwoman had brought her own rice powder to cover the bruise on Cassandra's cheek.

Daringly, Cassandra had crushed geranium petals to colour her lips and touched rose water behind her ears. All eyes turned to the two women as they entered, Nicholas's with relief at her modest demeanour, the touring party with frank curiosity that turned to indifference at the sight of two uninteresting females.

'My ward, Miss Jones. Ca. . . Catherine, Mr Bulstrode and Mr George Bulstrode and their families.'

Cassandra bobbed a neat curtsey, then took the seat next to the Earl, Colette at her side.

'You are most indulgent to bring your ward with you, my lord,' the elder Mrs Bulstrode observed archly. 'My two sweet daughters, Phoebe and Ariadne, pleaded with their dear Papa to permit them to accompany us, but Mr Bulstrode would not countenance it. Would you, Mr Bulstrode?'

'Certainly not,' her spouse replied robustly. 'I don't spend good guineas for them to attend Miss Simpkin's Academy in Bath so they can fritter their time on continental travel. No way to catch a good husband that, is it, my lord?'

Faced with a direct question, Nicholas was forced to participate in a conversation he clearly found distasteful. 'I am afraid I have no opinion on the matter, Mr Bulstrode. I am delivering my ward to the care of her great aunt in Nice: that is the sum total of my experience of the rearing of young girls.'

Cassandra could hardly contain her laughter. How Nicholas managed to convey such total boredom and a complete distaste for the subject without being openly offensive fascinated her. She could well believe all the stories she had heard of the arrogant Earl of Lydford.

The Bulstrodes appeared oblivious to the snub. They ignored Cassandra and her companion completely, except to request them to pass the buttered crayfish or the mustard, and addressed all their remarks to poor Nicholas.

Cassandra knew she had to avoid his eye or they would both set off laughing. But all desire to giggle left her when, to her utter astonishment, she heard her own name mentioned.

'Of course, Earl, you have been out of the country and will not be aware of the latest *on-dit* in Society. Poor Lord Offley has set off such a hue and cry after his young bride-to-be, who has quite vanished from her home. Why, he believes Miss Weston to be abducted, so sudden was her disappearance!' The younger Mrs Bulstrode was positively quivering in her inappropriately overtrimmed gown with the excitement of the tale.

'And he must be right,' her sister-in-law chimed

in, 'for what young girl would fly from such a distinguished connexion!'

Cassandra felt the colour rise up her throat and her heart began to thud painfully. Not for a moment had she expected anyone to make her flight public, let alone Lord Offley. But, of course, when she thought about it she could understand why. Her father might live cut off from Society, but he hoarded every penny and was known to be a warm man. Lord Offley, as profligate with his money as with his morals, would want Cassandra—and her dowry—back.

'Why, we have shocked dear Miss Jones,' Mrs Bulstrode senior said patronisingly, misunderstanding her flushed cheeks. 'I am sorry, my dear, but such sad stories should be told: they hold a moral for young girls.'

'In what way, since you hold her to have been abducted? If that were the case, it could not be her fault and the story holds no moral,' Cassandra remarked coldly. 'Or do you suggest she had connived in her own abduction? If that were so, I am sure it is not fit for my ears!'

Nicholas tapped her warningly on the ankle with the toe of his shoe, but Cassandra was enjoying the look of outrage on Mrs Bulstrode's florid features. The older woman was not to be so easily snubbed, however. Ignoring Cassandra, she turned to the Earl. 'I believe Miss Weston is a connexion of yours, is she not, my lord? This sad news must be a terrible shock for you.'

'One of my mother's numerous godchildren, I believe,' he said in tones of utter boredom. 'A scrubby child given to masquerades when I last saw her. The Dowager has always been more generous than wise in her patronage. Catherine, my child, if you have finished that Rhenish cream, I suggest you retire.' He turned to Mrs Bulstrode. 'She is not yet out, you know,' he remarked, by way of explanation for such an early dismissal.

Cassandra was glad to escape the overheated atmosphere and the ugly curiosity of the Bulstrodes. In her room she thanked Colette, who promised to attend her in the morning, but once the Frenchwoman had gone, she felt too agitated to undress and get into bed.

Instead she curled up in the window seat and rested her hot face against the cool green glass. In the moonlight, the dark Rhône slid silently past, its smooth surface giving no hint of the murderous currents beneath.

Those odious women! The thought of vulgar persons like that gossiping, bandying her name about! It had never occurred to her for one moment that news of her flight would reach more than her immediate and restricted circle. She had believed no-one would care, no-one would find her of any interest.

Now what was she going to do? What would Godmama say when she heard? The humiliation made her go hot and cold all over. The thought of waiting until the morning to talk to Nicholas was insupportable: she must see him now, find out if he would still take her with him in the face of this scandal.

When she reached his room, it was empty. Too agitated to sit, she perched uneasily on the end of the bed until she heard his feet treading lightly on the polished boards of the passage.

Almost as soon as he closed the door behind him, she had flung herself into his arms, sobbing against his chest. The candle he was holding guttered and snuffed with the draught she created, leaving them clinging together in the darkness.

'Cassandra. . .for goodness' sake,' he began, trying to free the arms that encircled him, but then the extent of her unhappiness and humiliation must have reached him and he said no more, but held her close until the sobs turned to hiccoughs.

His arms around her felt strong and sure, his body was a rock to which she clung. Gently he stroked her hair from her crown to the nape as if he was gentling a kitten and instinctively Cassandra snuggled closer.

'You shouldn't be here, you know,' he remonstrated gently.

'Those horrible people, Nicholas! Talking about me! Everyone knows. . .I'll die of shame. What am I going to do?'

'Pay them no heed — they'll find another scandal next week,' he said matter-of-factly.

Cassandra tipped her head back to look at him. In the moonlight his face was a white mask, but it seemed to her his breathing was not as regular as it had been.

'Cassie. . .you must go.'

'Not yet, we must talk about what to do, Nicholas,' Cassandra insisted, no less vehement for having to whisper.

'Not now, not here!' Nicholas freed himself from

her embrace and gave her a little shake. 'Cassie, this isn't proper and it isn't wise!'

'Oh, I know what you said, but I trust you, Nicholas. . .'

He looked down into the pale oval of her face, at her parted lips and her dark, shadowed eyes. 'Stop it, Cassie, I'm not made of stone! Be a good girl and go to your room.'

'Stop treating me like a child when you know I am not,' she said vehemently. 'You've seen I'm not a child. Why won't you discuss this with me? You just keep saying "Cassie, do this, Cassie, do that, don't worry, it'll be all right". But it won't be all right, will it?'

'If you don't get out now and go to your room it will never be all right,' he said between clenched teeth. 'What if someone finds you here? Do you *want* to be ruined?'

'But I *am* ruined in the eyes of Society, anyway. I've been travelling with you day and night for more than two weeks. What has changed? I need to talk to you, Nicholas. . .' She reached out her hands to him again, but he caught her wrists, holding her away from him.

'I tried to warn you in Paris you were playing with fire. There is a lot of difference between being ruined in name and in fact. You are not such a child; you understand what I am saying to you. Get out of this room *now*.'

He freed her wrists and turned from her, one hand clenched on the carved bedpost. In the sudden stillness of the room his breathing was ragged.

Cassandra could not pretend she did not understand him, not after his plain speaking earlier. He had obviously been attracted to her in Paris, and in Lyons, but had fought against it because be believed her so young. Now he had seen with his own eyes that she was a woman. Cassandra burned with the memory of his eyes on her body, but mixed with the embarrassment was a tingling pleasure.

And Nicholas was a passionate, experienced man, used to the company of women as experienced and willing as Lady Broome. Innocent young ladies were a bore—until such time as he would have to enter the Marriage Mart in search of a suitable wife.

With her trustfulness and in their enforced intimacy, she was putting an intolerable strain on him. And suddenly, staring at his wide shoulders, the crisp curl of dark hair at his nape, the strong hand gripping the bedpost, she realised she didn't care, she *wanted* him to feel like that about her.

Five minutes ago she had been in his arms, held close to him and she yearned to be there again. With a shiver, she remembered the heat of his mouth on hers in Paris, the strength of his arms as he held her on the river bank. 'Nicholas,' she began, then broke off, uncertain of what she meant to say.

'Damn it, Cassandra,' he ground out without turning. 'Will you get out of here!'

'But. . .' she stammered.

'Go!' He gestured abruptly with his hand and she turned and fled, banging the door behind her.

CHAPTER SEVEN

'THEN I can go back to being a boy?' Cassandra started to sit down on the low stone parapet of the bridge, remembered her skirts and checked the movement.

Nicholas gazed past her to the edge of the river where an old woman was collecting driftwood. 'I think it would be as well.' His tone was studiedly neutral, as it had been since the rather stilted breakfast they had shared that morning.

A little devil prompted her to ask, 'Why?' The question was rewarded by a sharp glance from Nicholas's green eyes.

'If people such as the Bulstrodes know of your disappearance, those in Society certainly will. The Bulstrodes are in no position to know whether I have a ward or not, but the *ton* most certainly do. The coincidence of my mother's missing god-daughter and a mysterious young woman travelling with me would be too marked to overlook.'

'Yes, Nicholas,' Cassandra averred demurely. 'That is a very good reason.'

And it was. But she knew the real reason as well as he did. Nicholas did not want the constant reminder of her femininity. Dressed as a boy and with the formality of the master-servant relationship restored, it would be easier to pretend she was simply young Cassie again.

In the cold light of day, she realised what a narrow

escape they had had last night from something they would have both bitterly regretted. She had only Nicholas's self-control to thank for that. . .

'Will we be moving on today?' she asked, gathering up her skirts to cross the cobbled bridge. 'I haven't any boy's clothes.'

'The apothecary's wife is buying some. I asked her this morning while I was making arrangements for the carriage.'

'And the rest of the luggage?' Cassandra rested her palms on the bridge parapet and watched the treacherous sucking water below that had so nearly taken her life.

'We can buy everything we need in Orange, according to Madame. Stop looking at the river, Cassie, dwelling on the accident will not help you recover from it.'

She shivered and decided he was right. Her restless sleep the night before had been full of swirling green water overlying the image of Nicholas's face and the remembered sensation of someone touching her skin with cold lips.

Raising her eyes from the surface to the water's edge, she watched a group of urchins chasing minnows in a muddy pool, shrieking with laughter. 'The river is not all bad,' she remarked with a smile, which froze on her lips at the sudden appearance of the Bulstrode family party strolling along the far bank.

The Mesdames Bulstrode were a startling vision, the elder in lilac, the younger in an argumentative shade of puce. Both were having trouble controlling overlarge poke bonnets in the strong morning breeze.

'Oh, yes, Cousin Nicholas,' Cassandra remarked in a high, clear tone. 'You are so right in observing that the state of the deserving poor in this country is much worse than that of our own. Good morning, Mrs Bulstrode.' She dropped a neat curtsey. 'The Earl and I were discoursing on the condition of the lower orders in these parts. The absence of a benevolent landowning class must be much to blame.'

'Well, they are all Papists,' the older woman announced sweepingly, before turning her attention to the Earl.

Nicholas, however, was too experienced in the ways of social climbers to be trapped by the Bulstrodes into a lengthy exchange.

'You are so right, Madam,' he agreed, straight faced. 'I wonder why that did not occur to us. Come Cas. . . Catherine, the wind is getting quite keen.' He raised his hat to the Bulstrodes and shepherded a demure Cassandra back towards the inn.

'You baggage!' he accused, as soon as they were out of earshot. '"Benevolent landowning class", indeed! Where did you learn to spout such nonsense?'

'The vicar's wife talks like that all the time. I did it rather well, I think,' she congratulated herself.

'You do like to sail close to the wind, don't you, Cassie?' he remarked drily. 'Now stay upstairs until the carriage is ready. I doubt my constitution will stand any more encounters between you and the Bulstrodes.'

How and when Cassandra would transform herself from demure young lady to valet exercised them both. It would not do to risk encountering the sharp eyes of the elder Mrs Bulstrode with Cassandra in boy's guise and Nicholas cravenly refused point-blank to risk the icy disapproval of Madame Aubrac by enlisting her aid. Nor could Cassandra change in an inn along the way or the postillions would gossip.

Eventually she hurried out to the carriage while the horses were being hitched up, drew the blinds and scrambled out of the dress and into her shirt and breeches. She was just tying her second garter when Nicholas joined her.

She was perfectly decently clad but, for some reason, she felt exposed in her shirt sleeves and stockinged feet. Hastily she pulled on the jerkin and fastened the buttons tight, jammed on her shoes and began to fiddle with her neckcloth. She knew she was mangling it, but Nicholas made no move to help her as he would have done two days before: he seemed as conscious as she of the changed condition between them.

But by the second day, as they neared Aix en Provence, it seemed the illusion of the clothes had worked, the truth about her age was forgotten and they were at ease with each other again.

Aix lived up to Cassandra's expectations of what a 'proper' foreign city should be. There were wide, clean avenues of limes, fountains on every corner and gracious squares where the inhabitants took the air in the evening.

To Cassandra's delight, it was warm enough to sit out after dusk. In the larger squares, enterprising restaurant owners had set tables out under the plane trees for couples to watch the promenaders while sipping wine and nibbling almond biscuits.

Cassandra had acquired a very decent suit of

black superfine, and with her best linen and polished shoes, looked respectable enough to sit with Nicholas pretending to be his *courier*.

'You are causing much interest amongst the young ladies,' she teased slyly. As the respectable family groups strolled past, several of the pretty daughters on their fathers' arms were sliding interested looks under demure lashes to where they were sitting.

Nicholas snorted. 'It's not me,' he teased back. 'I think the little redhead has taken a fancy to you. Take care, Cass, I don't want outraged fathers banging at our door.'

Far from being chastened, Cassandra burst into laughter, choking on her wine until Nicholas threatened to slap her on the back. 'It's good,' she finally managed to say. 'If I can deceive those girls, I can deceive anyone.' Greatly daring, she added, 'I do believe you're jealous of my success, Nicholas.'

'Impudent whelp!' Nicholas aimed a cuff at her ear. 'I would have you know that respectable bourgeoises hold no fascination for me.'

No, she thought, taken unaware by a sudden stab of jealousy. It wasn't inexperienced, unsophisticated chaperoned girls he wanted, it was the older, knowing, society women who attracted Nicholas. Preferably those safely married to complaisant husbands.

Cassandra gave herself a little shake and picked up the *Gentleman's Guide*. 'It says here that Aix will please us more than any city we have seen in France.'

'If you're going to start quoting the guidebook, it's time you were in bed. Come on, brat, you've broken enough hearts for one evening.'

* * *

From Aix, they turned due East and took the winding road through St Maximin and Brignoles. High ground rose sharply on either side covered with a fragrant scrub of lavender and wild thyme, baking under the hot sun.

Even glimpses of snow on the distant Alps could not make the journey seem any cooler. Nicholas tossed aside his jacket and loosened his cravat and Cassandra followed suit, too hot to worry about her shirt sleeves and exposed throat.

The road was rough and the low scrub of the *maquis* crowded close. The postillions were nervous. In every inn along the way, people were telling vivid tales of banditry, and now they were convinced every clump of trees contained brigands waiting to attack the carriage.

As the shadows lengthened, Nicholas cleaned and checked the pistols in the carriage holsters. When he reached for the balls to reload, Cassandra could contain herself no longer. 'Please show me how to shoot them, I've always wanted to try.' She leaned forward, eyes shining and reached for one of the long-barrelled weapons.

'Don't touch!' Nicholas looked quite shocked at her bloodthirsty interest. 'They aren't toys, Cass.'

'Yes, but what if we're attacked?' They, too, had heard the tales of brigands at every inn along this coastal route to Nice.

'The postillions have horse pistols,' he began, then broke off, looking thoughtful. 'Perhaps there is something in what you say. Look, it loads like this. Leave the hammer down and don't point it at anyone. When you need to fire, you cock it like this.'

Cassandra watched as his strong thumb lifted the hammer, then eased it back down slowly.

'Here.' He handed her the unloaded gun. 'Try with this one.'

The hammer was stiff and she had to use both hands to cock it, the metal cold and unfriendly against her hot hands. Suddenly she didn't want anything to do with guns, but he took her hand in his, aiming it and the weapon out of the window.

'Like this. Hold it steady and squeeze the trigger. Aim for the body, it's the biggest target, you are more likely to hit something than if you aim for the head.'

Cassandra swallowed hard and handed the gun back. 'Thank you.' There was nothing exciting in the prospect of killing or maiming a man, however villainous.

Frejus, however, was reached without incident. They put up for the night in a passable inn where the patron boasted of the parties of English tourists who had passed that way the week before. 'They all took the sea passage, of course, milord. To avoid the brigands, you understand.' He rolled his eyes to emphasise the dangers. 'Desperate men, milord! They would slit your throat for the clothes on your back. Much safer to take my brother-in-law's boat.'

Nicholas turned from the landlord's cheerful relish of the dangers ahead to see Cassandra turn as pale as a ghost.

'Nicholas. . .no. . .please, not a boat! You didn't say anything about another boat!'

'All right, Cass,' he spoke calmly. 'We'll say no more of it today: tomorrow we can look at the sea.

Perhaps you'll feel better when you see how calm it is.'

Next day the sea was indeed calm, but Cass was not reassured. Panic tightened her chest and her feet seemed rooted to the shingle beach. In vain, the landlord's brother-in-law demonstrated the fine lines of his boat, the strong arms of the boatmen and the wisdom of the captain. Cass shook her head mulishly and refused to move.

'The lad was almost drowned on our way down the Rhône,' Nicholas explained to the landlord, who was obviously of the opinion that a firm master would simply toss the young valet on board and be done with it.

'*Les anglais*,' he muttered, shaking his head in disbelief at such indulgence.

'Thank you, Nicholas,' Cassandra whispered fervently, some of the colour restored to her face. 'I know I shouldn't be such a coward.'

Nicholas cast a swift glance round and finding them alone gave her a swift, hard hug. 'No, you're not a coward. You very nearly lost your life: I should never have suggested it.'

Cassandra shivered, despite the hot sun on her back. The casual embrace was meant to reassure, she knew that, but she could still feel the pressure of his fingers on her skin beneath the fine lawn shirt. He was already striding ahead, shouting at the postillions to harness the horses. The gesture had obviously been as fleeting as the moment to him, she thought, with a tinge of regret.

The road left the coast to cut inland through the thick forest of pine and chestnut hugging the slopes of Mont Vinaigre. The rutted dusty track climbed steeply in hairpin bends up the flank of the mountain to a height of almost a thousand feet.

Jolted by the deep ruts, Cassandra watched Nicholas as he sat with one hand resting on the holster set in the coach door, his eyes alert, despite the heat that seemed to bake through the very fabric of the coach. Eventually the heat and the motion lulled her into an uneasy doze from which she woke stiff-necked and dry lipped as the coach descended into the little fishing village of Cannes.

'Are we there?' she asked, not too certain where 'there' was.

'Almost.' Nicholas relaxed against the cushions with a long sigh. Cassandra realised just how alert he had been for the last twenty miles, despite his reassuring words to her earlier.

Cannes was no more impressive than Frejus had been and the inn considerably worse. They were relieved to be leaving the next morning after a breakfast of coarse bread and evil coffee and now with the threatening mountain road and its danger of brigands behind them, they were both in almost holiday mood.

The route from Cannes to Nice lay along the coast: a winding, often alarming road hanging on the very cliff edge. The sea sparkled blue below them, sometimes hidden by clumps of pines, and white farmhouses set in the hillside made the land seem peopled, even though they saw scarcely anyone except a goatherd and his dog.

After the insignificant village of Antibes, the road dropped almost to sea level offering a continuous view over the dazzling Mediterranean with fishing boats bobbing at anchor. Cassandra stuck her head out of the carriage window and breathed in the smell of hot pine resin, the crisp tang of the sea and the scent of herbs in the dusty air.

Nicholas seized the hem of her waistcoat and hauled her back into the carriage. 'Get back in, brat—or you'll be out of the window at the next bump in the road!'

'Why are you laughing at me?' Cassandra demanded, seeing the grin on his face.

'You look like a retriever pup who has just had her first scent of game!' But as he looked down into her indignant face, flushed with heat and excitement, her hair awry, her eyes sparkling, he thought he had never had the urge to kiss one of his gun dogs.

The carriage suddenly slowed and one of the postillions shouted out. Nicholas put his head out of the window. 'What is it? Why are we stopping?'

From the other window Cassandra had already spied the problem: a broken-down farm cart was slewed across the road, its meagre contents spilling out and the ancient driver tugging at the reins of an equally ancient mule.

'Get down one of you, and help him or we'll never get to Nice,' Nicholas ordered. The man did as he was bid, walking awkwardly in his heavy boots. He vanished round the cart: seconds later there was a sudden cry, then silence.

'What the Devil!' Nicholas jumped down, leaving the door swinging. 'Stay there, Cassie, while I see what is happening.'

As he strode towards the cart, the driver took to his heels. Then there was a thump swiftly followed by a cry: from her vantage point Cassandra watched in horror as the second postillion slumped to the ground, a knife-hilt protruding between his shoulder blades.

For a moment she was frozen, then she scrambled across the carriage to the open door. 'Nicholas! Behind you!' she shouted, seeing two ruffians emerge from behind the cart, each with a cudgel and a curving knife in his hands.

Everything happened so fast it was blurred. Nicholas stooped, picked up a rock and threw it with unerring accuracy to catch the nearest brigand in the centre of the forehead. The man fell as if poleaxed. The second man cursed and began to back away, holding the murderous knife in front of him.

Nicholas had already snatched up the fallen man's knife and was advancing when a shadow seemed to slip from behind the horses, arm raised.

'Behind you!' Cassandra shrieked again, but too late. The man had brought the cudgel down in a crashing blow on Nicholas's shoulder, sending him sprawling to the ground.

Cassandra saw red. Unknowingly her fingers curled round one of the pistols, slipping it from its holster. The smooth wood of the butt felt right in her hand and this time the hammer pulled back smoothly under her thumb.

Without conscious thought, she brought the muzzle up, aimed at the broad, leather-jerkined back and fired. The recoil shot her backwards painfully onto her tailbone. Eyes streaming, shoulder numb, she scrambled down from the coach, brandishing the other pistol.

'Get away from him! Get away or I'll kill you!'

she yelled in English. The message was clear enough: the brigand grabbed his injured colleague and stumbled off into the pines. Of the man Nicholas had hit there was no sign.

Cassandra ran, stumbling in her haste and fell on her knees beside Nicholas. He was stirring, his eyes black in a deadly white face. 'Nicholas!'

'Stop pointing that pistol at me,' he managed to say, then broke off, retching painfully.

'Sit up.' Cassandra half dragged him into the shade of the cart and propped him against the wheel. 'I'll fetch some water.'

After several deep draughts, he reopened his eyes and looked at her, a ghost of a smile on his lips. 'Bloodthirsty brat! Where are all the bodies?'

'One of the postillions is all right, he only had a tap on the head. He's looking after the other one in the carriage. The brigands have gone.'

'I'm not surprised!'

'I only shot one of them,' Cassandra protested. 'I think the others were taken by surprise; they didn't know there was anyone else in the carriage.'

Nicholas shifted his position and grimaced. 'I think they've broken my collarbone.'

Cassandra probed gingerly, wincing as he did. 'I don't think you have — but it is bound to be very badly bruised. Can you get up? We need to get all of you to a doctor — and besides, what will we do if they come back?'

Unsteadily, leaning on her shoulder, Nicholas made his way back to the coach. The stabbed postillion was slumped silently in one corner, the other stood holding his head and moaning.

'There's money in it for you if you can drive us

on to Nice,' she said firmly to the man with the headache. 'You have done well, the Earl will not fail to reward you.'

It was almost dusk by the time they entered Nice at a decorous trot. Cassandra was too preoccupied with her patients to heed the famous groves of oranges and lemons or admire the white *bastides*, their doors and windows smothered in brilliant blooms.

To her relief, Nice was every bit as civilized and fashionable as the other coastal towns were not. The hotelier summoned a doctor with dispatch and made them comfortable in his best suite, while the postillion was carried off to the servants quarters to have his wound dressed by the barber surgeon.

'*Monsieur le docteur* will be here soon,' the hotelier announced. 'It would be best if you get your master undressed and into bed while you wait. I will send up wine and hot water.'

'Undress. . .er, I. . .'

'You are his valet, are you not?' The man shrugged his shoulders at the stupidity of the English. 'You have not had a blow to the head? You understand what I am saying?'

'Perfectly,' Cassandra replied haughtily. 'I will look after *Monsieur le Comte*. You may leave.'

Nicholas was slumped back against the pillows, his face faintly green in the subdued light. Cassandra bit her lip, undecided how best to get him undressed. She told herself that she was being unnecessarily modest, and that in an emergency such as this, propriety could not count. Even Godmama would tell her not to be such a little ninny.

She pulled off his shoes and stockings then his neckcloth. He did not stir. Emboldened, she unbuttoned his shirt, pulled it loose from the waistband of his breeches and tried to ease it off his shoulders. After a few minutes struggling to no avail, she sat on the edge of the bed and pulled him forward to rest against her breast while she slid the shirt free.

She should have let him back down onto the pillows, but instead, Cassandra found herself holding him, his naked back warm and smooth under her fingers, his heart beating rhythmically against her chest. She had never realised that a man's skin could be this smooth, that the play of strong muscles would be so alluring to the fingertips.

Her hesitant, gentle touch seemed to rouse him and he stirred, murmuring incoherently. His lips moved against her throat and Cassandra stiffened with shock at the intimacy and pleasure of the sensation. How long they would have stayed like that had not the doctor's knock at the door intervened, she did not know.

Doctor le Blanc greeted Cassandra in excellent English, clucked with disapproval to find Nicholas still half-dressed and had him out of his breeches, into a nightshirt and between the sheets in a trice.

She was relieved to see how competent and efficient the doctor seemed. He kept up a constant flow of inconsequential but reassuring chatter while he probed and checked Nicholas from top to toe.

'Very good, my lord, very good,' he said as Nicholas stirred and opened his eyes. 'No breaks, I am happy to say, although that is a most serious contusion on your shoulder. It will be painful for some time as it is so near the bone, but nothing a fit young man like yourself cannot endure!

'. . .and you have found a most excellent hotel which is fortunate when you consider the number of your countrymen resident already in our lovely town.'

'Does that account for your excellent English, *monsieur*?' Nicholas asked between clenched teeth as the doctor pulled his nightshirt back over his shoulder.

'But *certainement*, milord. Many of my patients are of the English nobility, here for the excellence of the climate and the efficacy of our seabathing. I would recommend a course of immersions for your wound.'

Cassandra had retreated to the window when the doctor arrived, glad of the opportunity to regain her equilibrium. She rubbed her fingertips together, still feeling Nicholas's body so warm and strong and yet, for once, so vulnerable.

It had seemed such a good idea to reassume her former rôle, but however much she might play the boy, she could no longer deceive herself that her feelings for Nicholas were anything but those of a woman for a man.

'Cass. . .that is your name, is it not?' The doctor was at her elbow and had obviously been talking to her for some time. 'I have sent a message to the apothecary to prepare a salve. It must be applied three times a day and rubbed in well. The day after tomorrow, milord must go down to *la plage* and immerse himself in the sea for ten minutes: it does not matter if he cannot swim.'

'He swims very well,' Cassandra replied absently.

'So much the better. *Au'voir*, milord, send for me if you have the slightest discomfort.' He bowed himself out of the chamber as Nicholas shifted uncomfortably against the piled bolsters.

'Slightest discomfort! French understatement, no doubt.' He looked across at Cassandra's pinched face and held out a hand to her. 'Cassie! Come over here. You saved my life, you know. . .'

Cassandra walked to him as though he pulled a string and took his warm, strong hand in hers. His fingers closed over hers and stroked the knuckles.

'And how are you? It must have been a terrible shock.'

His sympathy was enough to precipitate tears. Two large drops gathered and rolled down her cheeks and she hung her head to hide them.

'I thought you were going to be killed. . .and the knife in the postillion's back and the blood. . .and those terrible men. . .' She took a deep breath and asked, 'Do you think I killed him?'

Nicholas didn't answer. Instead he pulled her onto the bed beside him, gathered her against his good shoulder and held her until the tears dried. Gradually in the safety of his arms, Cassandra's tense body relaxed, her eyes felt heavy. Without conscious thought, she snuggled closer and let herself drift. Under her cheek, Nicholas's breathing slowed and they both slept.

They were roused by a soft knock on the door. For a long moment, Cassandra could not remember where she was. She blinked and looked up to find her eyelashes almost grazing Nicholas's unshaven chin. 'Cassie! What on earth..?' he began.

The knock was repeated and she scrambled off

the bed, scarlet with confusion, avoiding Nicholas's eyes as she pulled down her jerkin.

'*Entrez*!' he called when she was a safe distance from the bed, but his voice carried less than its usual authority and Cassandra guessed he was as shaken as she at the position they had woken up in.

The door opened to reveal a little party assembled outside: the apothecary's assistant with a package sealed with wax, a chambermaid with a tray full of food, a waiter equipped with cutlery and a cloth, and the *patron* to supervise all.

Cassandra was relieved at the diversion: a glance at the clock on the mantel showed her that she had slept in Nicholas's arms for over an hour and she had no notion of what she should say to him.

By the time she had laid a tray on Nicholas's knees, poured him a glass of wine and settled herself with chicken casserole, she had decided that the only thing to do was to play Cass the valet to the hilt. She must drive from his consciousness all awareness of Cassandra, the woman who had slept beside him in his embrace. She was honest enough to recognise that if he took her in his arms again, she would do nothing to stop whatever might follow—and she wanted him to hold her so much. . .

'You look much better,' she said briskly, whipping away the tray and bringing him warm water and cloth. 'I think you ought to go back to sleep again. I'll leave you in peace and go and find out about the seabathing.'

'Cassie?' He seemed bemused by the transformation from vulnerable femininity to brisk efficiency. 'Is anything wrong?'

'Wrong? Of course not.' She shook out the starched tray cloth with a snap, not meeting his eyes. All she wanted to do was throw herself back into his arms and tell him. . . What? That it was the only place she felt content?

To her intense relief, Nicholas was up and about when she tapped on his door the next morning.

'What about the salve?' she asked, gathering up discarded clothing to avoid looking at him.

'It's all right, I put it on myself. Smells disgusting, so it must be doing some good.'

Cassandra could feel herself blushing with relief. Her sleep had been troubled by half dreams, half fantasies of rubbing the salve into Nicholas's naked shoulder. She had woken angry with herself for such immodest thoughts. The thought of what Nicholas might assume if he realised how her thoughts dwelt on him was mortifying. Why, he might imagine her to have a *tendre* for him!

All it was, she told herself firmly, was the natural attraction of finding herself in the constant company of one of London's most eligible men, a man who had offered her sanctuary and a means of escape when her world had been turned upside down. Why, as soon as she reached Vienna, this attraction, the dreams she had of him, would fade as other companions filled her life.

'Should you be up?' she enquired, folding a shirt.

'Of course. I can't lie in bed on a beautiful day like this. It would take more than a blow from a ruffian's cudgel to keep me on my back. Now, here's some money: go and do some shopping, buy what you like — some lace or some sweetmeats. I'll see you here for dinner, I'm going to try the good doctor's seabathing.'

'Shouldn't I come?' Cassandra asked thoughtlessly.

Nicholas caught her eye and pointed to the window. 'Lean out and to your left and you can just see the men's bathing beach. I assume you didn't go and look last night!'

'No.' Cassandra did as she was bid, then gasped with shock at the glimpse of bare flesh. 'Nicholas! They have no clothes on!'

'Then I suggest you stay well away from the shoreline, Cassie! In fact, take care where you wander if you go out.' The door banged shut, leaving Cassandra gaping after him.

Despite the money burning a hole in her pocket, Cassandra didn't feel like mingling with the crowds. She headed away from the centre, climbing through the narrow streets past the close-packed stone houses to the ramparts crowning the town. Below her lay a vista of the sea to one side and, in the distance, white capped mountains. In between the land was full of fruit trees, already heavy with oranges, lemons and pomegranates; the hot air hummed with the song of cicadas.

Even the simplest house among the groves was neat and white painted, hung about with bougainvillea, roses and climbing vines. Cassandra wandered down into an olive grove touching the ancient twisting trunks in wonderment; they seemed a thousand years old.

She found a shady patch under an olive and sat watching the spear shaped leaves trace patterns as they filtered the sunlight. Below her a goatherd was leaning on his staff and flirting with a dark-eyed girl who had brought him a dinner basket.

Cassandra leaned back against the gnarled trunk and closed her eyes. This was all she had ever wanted: to get away from home, to travel, to experience foreign ways and see strange sights. This place was idyllic, almost paradise, yet, like Eden, it had its serpent.

Every time she closed her eyes, she could feel the touch of Nicholas's body under her palms, feel his lips on hers, hear the warm strength of his voice caressing her. It was no use pretending to herself any longer: she was falling in love with him.

And he would never love her, however much it seemed on occasion he was physically attracted to her. The Earl of Lydford had no time for gauche girls fresh out of the schoolroom.

She could imagine his embarrassment, how kind he would be if he discovered her *tendre*. She could live without his love—somehow—but she couldn't bear his pity.

CHAPTER EIGHT

'CASSANDRA! Wait a moment!'

She hesitated on the threshold of the bedchamber, her arms full of Nicholas's freshly pressed shirts, then reluctantly came back into the room.

'Yes?'

'I need to talk to you, sit down.' Nicholas gestured to the chair opposite him in front of the cold fireplace. 'I've scarcely seen you the last two days, you haven't even eaten your meals with me.'

Cassandra sat down awkwardly, still hugging the shirts to her chest. 'The doctor said you had to be quiet,' she said defensively. 'And you did say I could explore the town.'

'I have no complaint if you wish to go about enjoying yourself.' He hesitated, obviously at a loss to know how to deal with her in this uncommunicative mood. 'I was worried about you.'

Still she wouldn't look at him, risk meeting his troubled eyes. Instead she sat scuffing the parquet with the toe of her shoe.

'I know what it is that's troubling you,' he began, then broke off in surprise at the tide of scarlet confusion that swept up to the roots of her hair.

Cassandra felt sick with humiliation. How could he have guessed how she felt for him? Oh, the mortification of it! He was going to be kind about it, she could tell. Tolerant of this puppy love. . .he wouldn't take her seriously, or worse, he would pity her. . .

'I can see I was right,' he began. 'It pains me to embarrass you, but I think we should talk of it.'

'How did you guess?' Cassandra whispered, raising haunted eyes to meet his concerned look.

'It was natural you should be upset to find you had fallen asleep in my bed the other evening. After all, you are a gently brought up young girl: but we shouldn't reproach ourselves for what was entirely innocent.' He leant forward and patted her hand gently. 'We had both suffered a terrible shock, it was natural we should fall asleep like that. Try not to feel so conscious of it, Cassie, nothing happened, after all.'

Cassandra could only gape at him, she was so taken aback at his words. And she had very nearly blurted out her love for him!

Nicholas misinterpreted her shocked expression. 'Don't look at me like that, Cassie!' He stood up and ranged around the room while he searched for the right words for what he had to say. 'I admit there have been moments when my. . .instincts have led me to regard you in a way I now regret. . .'

'Like that evening in Paris?' Cassandra's voice was sharp with reaction.

'Yes, like Paris.' Nicholas turned to face her. 'But I promise that won't happen again, Cassandra.' He managed a laugh, although it sounded hollow in the high-ceilinged room. 'Do you realise how good you are for me? Why, I declare, by the time we arrive in Vienna, my mama will not recognise the dissolute rake she left behind, so responsible and sober will I have become.'

* * *

He was as good as his word. Two weeks later as their carriage neared Venice, Cassandra reflected that she could hardly have had a more sober, correct, *boring* companion if her Godmama had appointed a strict chaperone for her.

Nicholas had dutifully pointed out the beauties of the Plain of Lombardy, encouraged her to read improving passages from the guidebooks he acquired along the way and ensured she went to bed early after a good dinner.

Even the excitements of passing from one independent kingdom or duchy to another were kept from her, for Nicholas insisted she stay in the carriage while he ruthlessly bribed officials and negotiated passports and health certificates at the endless customs posts.

By the time they reached Padua, Cassandra had decided she had been quite mistaken: far from being in love with the man, she actively disliked him.

With bad grace she clumped on board the *burchio* waiting to take them down the Brenta Canal from Padua to Venice and glowered out at the unlovely town crowding the banks.

'Stop sulking, Cassie,' Nicholas said sharply, then seemed to relent. In a softer tone, he added, 'I'm sorry, I should have realised: are you frightened to go on a boat again?'

'No.' She scowled down into the greenish depths of the still water. It was true, she wasn't afraid, she was quite simply bored. 'I'm bored: I'm tired of dirty inns and bumpy roads and greasy food — and no diversions *at all*.'

That was only part of it. Nicholas had withdrawn into the half avuncular, half patronising manner of their first meeting in London. If he had ever found her tempting or alluring, it was quite plain he no longer did. Sulking was not going to improve matters, but she was too hot, tired, dusty and cross to care.

'If you don't take that mulish look off your face, I'll tell the officials in Venice that you haven't got a bill of health and they'll shut you up in the Lazarrette for forty days with all the pestilential seamen!'

Cassandra glowered at him: he was only half-joking. 'Well, it would have to be more entertaining than the last fourteen days!'

Nicholas's eyes narrowed, and not against the slanting evening sun. 'You are asking to be put across my knee and have your britches paddled, my lad,' he began between clenched teeth.

'I would like to see you chance it!' Cassandra knew she was going too far, but she couldn't stop herself. She had tried being good and obedient and meek, and he treated her like a troublesome scrub of a boy. The knowledge that she must look like one only rubbed salt in her wounded vanity. Her hair was full of dust no brushing would remove, the fleas last night had been worse than usual and she had had no clean linen for three days.

'When we get to the *palazzo*. . .' Nicholas began, real displeasure in his voice.

'Oh, be quiet!' Cassandra was on the verge of tears and didn't care who knew it. Abroad was dangerous and squalid, travel was boring and uncomfortable and Nicholas was a beast. Or perhaps he was just a man and they were all like that.

She sniffed loudly and cast him a darkling look, half expecting him to carry out his threat and put her across his knee. She was saved from whatever retaliation Nicholas was contemplating by the arrival of another party of travellers with a pile of baggage.

Wordlessly he handed her a large pocket handkerchief and then ignored her: they embarked for the fairytale city of Venice in a mood of sullen antagonism.

The *burchio* was a long, flat-bottomed craft with an awning of canvas over metal hoops; the passengers were a mixed bag who would have entertained Cassandra under different circumstances. Opposite her a soberly dressed lawyer, with his equally sober young family, divided their disapproving glances equally between the two loud-voiced gallants perched precariously in the stern and a gaudily dressed and painted woman who winked at all the menfolk unwise enough to catch her eye. A party of peasants complete with malodorous goat added to the general discomfort.

By mid-afternoon on the second day, Nicholas, glancing sideways at Cassandra's set face, began to worry that she was not sulking but sickening. 'Cass,' he began in a low voice, then saw her face light up for the first time in many days.

'Oh, look!' She pointed out under the half-moon of the awning to where the banks of the canal opened out into a vast lagoon. Across the shimmering water the towers and palaces of Venice hung like a mirage. Cloud shadows chasing across the water and mud made the whole scene unreal and dreamlike. 'Nicholas, it's beautiful,' she whispered, hardly able to speak.

'It is rather fine,' he remarked casually, then

grinned at her fierce expression, 'Oh, yes, you're right, it *is* wonderful — a dream city.'

Their passage across the lagoons of Chioggia and Malamocco gave them different vistas every few minutes as the boatmen wove between mud banks and islets. At last they entered the Canale della Giudecca, a waterway as wide as the Thames at London and as crowded, with craft of all sizes, from sea-going galleys with banks of oars, to the narrow black gondolas Cassandra had read so much about.

Reading of Venice in the seclusion of her father's study bore no resemblance to the reality of the scene before her amazed eyes. The noise of barge-men shouting, the bustle of constant activity between the shore and the boats, the vivid colours under the brilliant sun and the exotic shapes and colours of the buildings were so overwhelming, Cassandra forgot her miseries and discomforts.

'Ouch! Cass! Let go of my arm.' She hadn't even realised she had hold of him. Hastily she let go and smoothed down the creased cloth of his sleeve with a penitent hand. 'Never mind that.' He was pointing ahead. 'There's St Mark's and the Campanile.'

Cassandra was trying to find the correct page in the guidebook without taking her eyes off the gorgeously exotic facade of the Doge's Palace, its delicate pink and white walls seeming to float on the water, its walls crowned with Arabic ornaments and spikes.

No sooner had the barge drawn up alongside the crowded pavement than Cassandra had scrambled ashore and was hopping from one foot to the other with impatience, while Nicholas retrieved their luggage. 'Come on,' she urged, 'we go up here to get to the Piazza. . .'

Nicholas had to seize her by the collar to restrain her. 'Not now, Cass! Wait here and guard the luggage while I hire a gondola to take us to the *palazzo*.'

'A *palace*! We're staying in a palace?' All thoughts of exploration fled.

'If you hadn't been sulking for the last sennight, I would have told you. It's been hired by my friend Beckwith, but he's been summoned to Rome by his uncle at the Embassy, so we'll have the place to ourselves.'

Cassandra felt immense relief at the thought of such privacy and comfort. In a private lodging she would have only the servants to deceive, no sharp-eyed noblemen to avoid, no sharp-tongued harridans to gull.

Travelling in the gondola after the heavy barge was like riding a horse after being in a carriage. The gondolier, dextrously propelling the swift craft with strokes of his oar, dodged between the shoals of boats ferrying people of all classes about their business.

They made their way up the Grand Canal, under the Rialto Bridge, then turned sharply into a little side canal no more than twelve feet wide and flanked by twisting alleys and landing stages.

Their gondolier finally drew into the side of a minute square with marble steps leading down to the water. The paving was decorated with coloured inlays and in the centre a little fountain bubbled.

Close to, Cassandra saw how the fine frontages were stained with water marks and the stucco was peeling to expose the stonework. Greenish water lapped at the walls and Cassandra's nose wrinkled at the smell. Nicholas noticed her expression and laughed. 'The tide will not flush these little waterways as it does the main canals. Is the palace not as grand as you expected?'

'It's wonderful,' Cassandra protested. 'So old and mysterious.' She would have said more but for the appearance at the door of a black-coated major domo flanked by footmen. With a gesture, he dispatched them to unload the rowing boat loaded with luggage which had followed the gondola and advanced on Nicholas.

'My lord!' He bowed low. 'Welcome to the Palazzo Lucca. Signore Beckwith is devastated that he cannot be here to greet you, but all is prepared. Pray enter!'

Nicholas rolled his eyes at Cassandra and followed the self-important little figure as it swept up the steps to the main door. Cassandra would have followed, too, but she paused, her eye caught by a flash of colour at a window in the facade to her right.

A woman, dressed in a robe of emerald green taffeta, was leaning on the sill watching their arrival, idly brushing out the mass of coppery-gold curls which cascaded over one bare shoulder. Cassandra knew she was staring, but she had never seen such a gorgeous creature before. As she watched, a man's bare arm appeared, caressing the naked shoulder and the woman turned and disappeared into the shadowy room.

'I thought you said there was no one else staying

here,' she hissed to Nicholas when she caught him up in the monumental entrance hall.

'There isn't.' He turned in surprise as she tugged at his sleeve.

'But I thought I saw someone in the window over there.' She pointed to the wing of the *palazzo*.

'That's another house,' he explained. 'Every building is crowded in against its neighbour, land is so scarce.' He turned away and mounted the staircase in the wake of the major domo.

Cassandra raised her eyebrows behind his back and mused to herself that she was certainly learning a great deal about the world. She could hazard a guess at the woman's profession, but somehow the broad daylight made her state of undress seem even more scandalous.

They were shown into a suite of rooms overlooking the canal at the front and the courtyard at the side. Nicholas's bedchamber faced directly across from the courtesan's balcony and Cassandra hurriedly closed the carved wooden shutters. 'The sunlight's bad for the draperies,' she explained, as Nicholas blinked in the sudden gloom.

'The perfect housewife,' he remarked drily, but made no move to re-open them. 'Baths and hot water for myself and for my valet,' he commanded the major domo, but the man was already ushering footmen in with hip baths and brass water jugs.

Cassandra retreated to her own room, which adjoined Nicholas's with a shared balcony between them. As she closed the shutters, she peeped across at the opposite window, but it, too, was shuttered.

The magnificence of her chamber stunned her with its cool, high ceiling adorned with cherubs and gods disporting on swirling clouds. The walls were lined with painted and gilded panelling interspersed with vast, cloudy mirrors. The bed was piled high with silk-covered pillows and hung with billowing draperies.

Cassandra caught a glimpse of herself in the glass and shuddered. Her hair was dark with dust and perspiration; her skin was dirty, too, but under the grime she suspected that she was not only tanned, but freckled also. She tore off the restricting jerkin with a sigh of relief and threw off the rest of the clothing. The wide boards were cool under the soles of her feet and she wandered naked across the room to peer more closely at her reflection.

Her shoulders and breasts were milk white in contrast to the golden tan of her face and hands. The poor food and the strains of the journey had honed her already slender body and the unaccustomed freedom of striding around in breeches had sculpted her leg muscles, chasing away all traces of girlish plumpness.

Suddenly self-conscious, Cassandra crossed to the door onto the landing and turned the key. The major domo would not be inclined to knock before entering the room of a mere valet. Doubtfully, she contemplated the tall double doors connecting her chamber with Nicholas's. There was no key in this escutcheon.

Need she worry? Nicholas had always been scrupulous in respecting her privacy, even when they were sharing a room. But yet, she felt uneasy. Perhaps it was the opulent femininity of the room, the air of decadence hanging over the whole city. She carried the painted and gilded chair from the dressing table and wedged it as best she could under the door handles.

The bath was deep and hot and when she had washed all over once, she unlocked the door, retreated behind a screen and rang for yet more water. Luxuriating in the scented warmth, she let herself drift, running through memories of the journey in her mind. It was remarkable how quickly being clean lifted her spirits and improved her temper. Why, she felt quite in charity with Nicholas again.

Unbidden, the memory came back of lying against his long body, safe in the shelter of his arms, and more disturbing, the recollection of that kiss in Paris, the response it had kindled in her. . .

Idly, she squeezed out the sponge and saw how wrinkled her fingertips had become. Time to get out before she resembled a prune! A pile of large linen towels were heaped on a chest and Cassandra draped one around herself under her armpits, tucking it in at the front. She found a smaller one and began to rub her wet hair, so much easier to dry now in its boyish crop.

Glancing up, she gazed at the ceiling once more, the painted scene suddenly making sense. Why, it was no innocent pastoral scene as she had thought: instead, gods and satyrs chased — and caught — naked nymphs through wooded glades And when they caught them. . . Her mouth dropped open at the explicitness of what was depicted there. Did men and women *truly* do that? And, if they did, was it as pleasurable as it was depicted here?

Fascinated, Cassandra walked slowly backwards,

her head tipped right back as she followed the unfolding scene.

'Cassandra?' Nicholas's voice called, but she was scarcely aware of it. The next second there was a crash, a curse and Nicholas was lying on top of her, inexplicably entangled in a chair.

'What the devil!' he gasped. 'Why was that chair there? Are you hurt?'

Cassandra pushed the wet towel from her mouth and the hair from her eyes. He had knocked the wind out of her as they had fallen together and for a moment she couldn't speak.

'Cassandra?' His green eyes, full of concern, were very close and her damp limbs were entwined with his.

'I'm all right,' she managed to say. 'You knocked the breath out of me. Why didn't you knock?'

'I did—but there was no reply. I was worried about you, thinking you might have fallen asleep in the bath and drowned yourself!'

It seemed to Cassandra that indeed he was concerned for her: he was pale, his breath uncertain and he held her to him strongly. He was stroking her bare shoulder lightly and his gaze was on her mouth. . .

'Nicholas. . .' she began hesitantly.

'Yes?' His voice was husky, his face so close his breath fanned her cheek.

'I wanted to ask you something, but I think you will be shocked.'

He brushed the wet hair away from her temples and smiled down at her. 'You can ask me anything, Cassandra.'

'Well. . .this ceiling.' She freed an arm and

pointed upwards. 'I. . . I mean. . .does that sort of thing really go on between men and women? I thought I knew. . .you know. . .what happens. But nothing like *that*!' She pointed to a particularly rapacious and inventive satyr.

Nicholas seemed stunned, then he broke into helpless laughter, rolling over and releasing her as he did so. He sat up, hands on knees and regarded her as she gathered up the folds of towelling.

'Cassie, my mother would thoroughly approve of your influence on me!' He ignored her puzzled frown and got to his feet, ruefully rubbing a bruised knee. 'Hurry up and get dressed, dinner will be ready. And,' he paused in the doorway, 'what the blazes was that chair doing there?'

'I. . .er. . . I couldn't find the key.'

'For future reference, Cassie, that trick only works when the door opens towards you. Although, if you wish to cripple your would-be ravisher, this method is quite effective.'

'But Nicholas — what about the ceiling?'

'Ask my mother. It is a godmother's duty to explain such matters to a young girl. I am certainly unequal to the task!'

The servants had left clean linen set out on the chair and Cassie dressed swiftly. Nicholas's sudden eruption into her room had driven everything from her head, even the impropriety of finding herself scarcely clad in his arms. Now everything she had felt while she sat under the olive tree in Nice and thought of Nicholas came back to her. She felt again the touch of his caressing fingers on her bare skin and a shiver ran through her, bringing with it, inexplicably, a vision of the woman in the green robe. Nicholas might anger and irritate her, make fun of her, but she was still in love with him and she still yearned for his touch.

And it was so improper to feel like this, she scolded herself, as she tied her neckcloth. A well-bred young lady should admire and respect a man she believed she loved, but the warmth of affection was all that should animate her. Surely this desire to be in his arms, to taste his skin again with her lips, to feel his strong body against hers was shameful and sinful?

She was feeling somewhat shaken when she knocked on the door of his chamber, but outwardly she was composed as Nicholas opened the door to her.

The marble-floored dining salon was even more ornate than the bedchambers. The long table had been laid with two places at one end and candles cast pale shadows on the polished wood. The shutters were still half-closed against the early evening light and the air was warm and heavy.

'Nicholas,' she whispered, as servants began to carry in dishes. 'Is it the Venetian custom for master and valet to dine together like this? And why has the major domo given me such a magnificent bedchamber?'

He waited until the servants had withdrawn to their station against the wall before replying, and even then seemed strangely reluctant to look her in the eye.

'I . . . um, suspect that Antonio, the major domo, has penetrated your disguise.'

'Oh.' Cassandra was surprised at the man's perception, but even more puzzled by Nicholas's diffidence. He was fiddling with the long stem of his wine glass, uncharacteristically ill at ease. 'Then he knows I'm a. . .girl? Doesn't he think that's odd?'

'I believe he has jumped to the obvious conclusion. Have some turbot.'

'The obvious conclusion?' Her brow furrowed in puzzlement, then the serving forks fell with a clang onto the silver serving platter. 'You mean he believes we're. . .that I'm your. . . But that's absurd! You must tell him, Nicholas—at once—that I'm no such thing!'

'And how do I explain you to him if you are not my mistress?' he asked drily, finally looking her in the eye. 'An Englishman with a mistress in Venice is so commonplace as to be beyond remark. . .'

'Dressed as a boy?' Cassandra interjected in amazement.

'Dressed as *anything*.' Nicholas sipped his wine thoughtfully. 'But a runaway, especially a well-bred female runaway, will be a cause for gossip and rumour. Remember where we are: this is Venice, the home of intrigue. There are many English residents and tourists in the city.'

'But what about my reputation?' she wailed, then realised how ridiculous she was being. She had abandoned that the moment she had donned breeches and escaped from her home. Too late now to quibble over the precise cause of her disgrace.

The same reasoning had obviously occurred to Nicholas. He said nothing, but gave her a hard stare and continued to eat his fish fastidiously.

Finally, after the servants had served a platter of quail, he remarked, 'And I'm not certain what the penalty for abduction is in Venice: breaking on the wheel, probably.'

Put like that, masquerading as his mistress seemed the lesser of two evils. They finished the meal in virtual silence, both lost in their own thoughts. When at last Nicholas pushed back his chair and stood up, Cassandra demanded, 'What are we going to do now? It's a lovely evening, can we go to St Mark's Square?'

'You are going to bed and I am going out,' he announced firmly.

'Where to?'

'Really, Cassandra, you are beginning to sound like a nagging wife. You need a good night's sleep.' He sounded out of patience with her. 'I need a game of cards, some good company and perhaps some dancing.'

'Dancing? Ha!' she ejaculated scornfully. 'Painted women, more like!'

'What a good idea,' he said smoothly. 'Why didn't I think of that? Some grown up company for a change.'

He was gone before she could think of a suitable retort. Back in her room, she kicked angrily at the flounced drapes around the bed, then threw herself down among the cushions. She complained bitterly out loud about being left behind, suppressing the small voice inside that told her she was being very unfair and that after two weeks of playing the duenna, he deserved some entertainment.

Her eyes focused on the painted ceiling again. Did gods and goddesses really do that sort of thing? Did anybody do that sort of thing? Was that what the courtesan across the square spent her time doing? Did Nicholas like. . .? Her hectic thoughts were interrupted by a soft tap at the door.

'Come in!' She sat up hurriedly.

'Good evening, *ma donna*. Do you have any commands for the household?' The major domo seemed quite unperturbed to be addressing a young lady in valet's clothing as if she were mistress of the household.

'Yes.' Cassandra sat up straight, suddenly full of enthusiasm. 'I want some new clothes—some nice clothes.'

'Men's attire or women's?' Antonio enquired calmly.

'Men's, I suppose,' she said gloomily. 'But some fine fabrics, please, Antonio. Silk and linen. . .'

'It will be as you wish, by noon tomorrow. Does *ma donna* require wine and biscuits now?'

'No, thank you. I don't want anything to eat, I want to go out.'

'But, of course, I will bring you a cloak, and perhaps a mask would be wise.'

So, it seemed that guarding her formed no part of Antonio's duties! Cassandra threw open both shutters and windows and walked out onto the balcony. Below her the previously quiet canal was now busy with gondolas, each bearing a cargo of richly attired men and women out for the night's entertainment.

'Shall I order you a gondola?' Antonio had reappeared with a cloak of dull black silk, a half-mask dangling by its strings from his fingers.

'No, I will walk—I have a map in this guide-book.'

As she swung the cloak around her shoulders, Antonio pointed from the window. 'Follow this *calle* here and eventually it will take you to St Mark's Square.' He looked at the map she had opened out. 'You will be quite safe if you avoid these *sestieri* — in those areas, the low types inhabit. Stay with the crowds and carry only a few coins secreted in your clothing.'

Cassandra put on the *domino* and mask, which covered the upper part of her face. Behind it she felt anonymous and irresponsible: no longer Miss Cassandra Weston of Ware, but a citizen of Venice going out to enjoy the evening like any other.

The narrow *calle* flanking the canal twisted and turned, sometimes widening into the forecourts of *palazzi*, sometimes into little squares where several paths met. Several times she had to flatten herself against the brickwork or stand in a doorway to let a group pass noisily on their way to the Opera or to one of the many public balls whose music floated across the water.

Finally, more by good luck than by careful attention to her map, Cassandra reached St Mark's. The entire square was a confusion of people and a babble of languages. Cassandra spied an elderly gentleman rising from a table outside a coffee house and darted quickly to seize the seat.

'*Uno caffè*,' she ordered, pleased with her few words of Italian gleaned from her father's books.

Languages she could only guess at filled her ears: as she sipped her coffee, she began to differentiate one from the other.

A group of naval officers, swarthy and dark-haired were Greek — she recognised a few words close to the classical form. Two tall men, deep in a business discussion must be Jews by their long ringlets and fur-trimmed hats, and to her delight a group of turbanned and berobed Turks strolled across looking arrogantly about them.

There was a multitude of fortune-tellers, minstrels and conjurors — even a man with a dancing bear — all soliciting for money in loud voices and with extravagant gestures. Cassandra pushed the pocket containing her money more securely into her inner garments: pickpockets were the same the world over from Ware market to Venice, and as she watched she saw an embroidered handkerchief vanish into a voluminous sleeve without the owner being any the wiser.

As the night became darker, the flares and lamps lighting the piazza shone more brilliantly. Cassandra ordered more coffee, then nearly dropped the cup in shock as a courtesan swept into sight, a small black page at her heels. There was no mistaking her trade: her hair fell loose, dyed an improbable array of colours, plumes topping a silk turban. Heavy earrings brushed her shoulders, but the most shocking thing was her gown, cut so low in the bodice that her breasts were totally exposed, the nipples painted gold.

Respectable people passed her with scarcely a glance, then Cassandra saw others like her, drawn like moths from the darkness into the illumination of the piazza.

With a start, she found someone bending over her, whispering in her ear. Her Italian could not cope with the rapid words, but the tone of invitation was unmistakable in any language. His garlic-laden breath was hot on her face and lacking words she pushed him roughly away. He fell against another table and wandered off laughing, quite unperturbed by her rejection. In alarm, Cassandra doubted her disguise: even behind the concealing mask had he realised she was a woman?

At that moment a youth strolled past with an older man, the latter openly fondling his shoulder. With a deep sense of shock, she realised that being a boy was no protection here. The next rake who wandered in her direction was met with a scowl so ferocious, he veered away at once, and Cassandra relaxed slightly.

The crowd fell back and a group of men wearing strange silken togas strolled across the square. Her reading of the guidebook told her that these were some of the senators who governed *La Serenissima* under the Doge.

The clock in the tower struck twelve and Cassandra knew she should retrace her steps and be safely home before Nicholas returned. But her feet were aching now and the darkened lanes beyond the Square were subtly threatening. She would hire a gondola and glide home in style.

She was hesitating on the water-steps, unsure of how to hail one of the many gondoliers when a man and a woman passed her so close the silk of the woman's gown swished against her cloak. Cassandra stepped back, a word of apology on her lips, then froze as she realised the man was Nicholas.

He handed his companion down into the narrow craft and waited until she was settled on the heaped cushions before joining her. Cassandra had ample time to take in the woman's appearance. She was undoubtedly a courtesan but young and beautiful, her fresh skin subtly tinted, her hair loose on her shoulders, confined only by a twist of silk scarf. Her gown was as outrageous as the others and Cassandra realised she must be wearing tight stays to thrust forward her small, naked breasts. Her nipples had been rouged a deep ruby and a single red stone quivered on a gold chain between them.

As soon as Nicholas joined her she insinuated herself into his arms, long ruby-red fingernails scoring lightly down his thigh. Cassandra watched, mesmerised, until he bent to nuzzle the courtesan's white throat, then turned with a small, choking sob and stumbled away into the shadows.

She was hardly conscious of the journey back, but some instinct must have guided her footsteps for, at last, she found herself standing under the awning of a wine seller's booth at the head of the *calle* leading to their *palazzo*.

'*Signore*?' The man was proffering a horn beaker brimming with red wine. Unheeding, Cassie took it and drained it in three gulps, unprotesting as he filled it again. This time she sipped it slowly, her mind full of dark thoughts of how she would like to deposit that courtesan in the deepest, dirtiest canal in Venice—then pitch Nicholas in after her!

So much for his fine talk of reform and responsible behaviour! Why, he had just abandoned her so eager had he been to go out—she groped for a word and came up with the ugliest she could remember—*whoring*! Images of the painted ceiling flashed through her mind, but it was Nicholas's face on the satyr's body, the painted breasts of the courtesan on the nymphs.

She tossed the wine seller a few coins and stumbled miserably towards home. The door was open and a watchman blinked sleepily at her from his chair in the hallway as she dragged herself up the stairs. She pushed open the door into Nicholas's chamber, driven by an obscure need to touch something belonging to him.

On the bed lay his brocade dressing gown and she picked it up, smelling the ambergris he used. 'Oh, Nicholas,' she whispered miserably. What did she expect? He was a man of the world, used to indulging himself. He had not asked to chaperone a sulky, inexperienced girl across Europe. . .

'*Where the hell have you been*!' Nicholas roared at her, standing framed in the connecting doorway to her room.

Cassandra was so startled she jumped, dropping the robe to clutch the bedpost in shock. Her heart thudded in her throat. 'I. . . I thought you were out.'

'That is all too obvious!' He strode into the room and took her roughly by the shoulders. 'Where have you been sneaking off to? I managed to get Antonio to admit he'd allowed you to go out—but that's all I'd expect from a Venetian rogue of a servant!'

'Let go, you're hurting me!' Cassandra tried to free her arm from his iron grasp, but he only pulled her closer, a look of revulsion crossing his face as he smelled the wine heavy on her breath.

'You're drunk!' he snarled. 'Who have you been drinking with?'

'No one,' she protested, twisting in his grasp.

'Don't lie to me,' his eyes glittered: Cassandra had never seen him so angry. 'And what else have you been doing tonight?'

The implication was clear, even through the fog

of wine that was muddling her thoughts. 'You think I've been. . .that I would. . . How dare you!'

'What am I to think, with you wandering the streets like a. . .'

'Like a courtesan?' she finished for him. 'I know what a courtesan looks like.' Her chin came up and she looked him straight in the eye. 'She has long, unbound hair twisted with a vermilion silk scarf; she paints her face, but lightly if she is young. Her breasts are bare and her gown is sequinned and she paints her nails to match other parts of her body which should remain concealed. She laughs a lot and when she does, the ruby round her neck. . .'

Nicholas jerked her against his chest, glaring down into her defiant face. 'You little witch! You followed me!'

'I did not — but if you flaunt your whore across St Mark's Square you should not wonder if you are seen!' She wrenched herself free and ran acrosss to the balcony, desperate for air. She felt sick with the heat and wine and the sordid argument.

He followed her swiftly and before she knew what he intended, he had upended her across his knee and brought his hand down hard across the seat of her breeches. With the strength of pure outrage, Cassandra twisted free, bringing up her hand to fetch him a vicious crack across the cheekbone.

The force of the blow snapped his head back and brought tears to her eyes. Nicholas stood frozen, one hand to his face, then turned on his heel and slammed the window shut with a clap that bounced off the walls of the little square.

Cassandra clutched the balcony rail as a wave of sickness swept her from head to foot. When she recovered herself, she raised her head slowly and found herself meeting the quizzical gaze of the woman in the room opposite. She was lit by a branch of candles at one side and Cassandra saw a fleeting smile touch her lips. The woman raised her hand in a small salute, then slowly turned and vanished into the room.

CHAPTER NINE

A THIN dawn light penetrated the little courtyard, touching warm fingers on the damp stonework behind Cassandra's head. She blinked and shook her head, wincing at the pain behind her eyes. So this was what an excess of wine felt like. . .

Cassandra struggled to her feet, grimacing at the stiffness in her cold limbs. She must have dozed off eventually, after a miserable hour or two. Instantly the memory of the terrible quarrel with Nicholas hit her: the shocking words she had used to him, the humiliation of being put over his knee like a recalcitrant schoolboy—and worst of all, to have raised her hand to him. How could she, how *could* she, have struck Nicholas!

No gently brought up young lady would use violence under any circumstances, save to protect her virtue or her life. And however hypocritical he was being, she sensed Nicholas's anger was prompted by his wish to protect her.

Cassandra heard the creak of oars and leant out over the rail to watch a vegetable boat emerge from the miasma of mist rising from the canal. The city was beginning to wake and go about its business: a servant from the *palazzo* ran down the steps and hailed the vendor. After much haggling and jesting, conducted in whispers, the servant returned, his wicker basket laden with saladings and fruit.

Silence fell again, broken only by the slap of the

boat's wake against the greenish stonework of the landing steps. Cassandra turned unhappily towards her chamber window, then paused as a man's voice, low and sensual, broke the peace in the courtyard.

Standing back in the concealing shadows of the architrave, Cassandra watched as a cloaked figure stopped on his way from the house opposite to the steps. He was looking up to the window where the Titian-haired woman in the green wrapper leaned out, calling softly down to him.

As the church clocks began striking five, the gentleman swept an elaborate bow, gesturing to a sleek black gondola which had drawn up in readiness. Intrigued by the pantomime of parting, Cassandra forgot her woes, watching the lovers. The woman beckoned, and as the man approached again, tossed down a round object. The gallant caught it one-handed, laughing up at his lady as he broke open the fruit.

A pomegranate. Cassandra had never tasted one, but she recognised the faceted red flesh and smooth exterior of the fruit. Somehow, it added to the fairytale mood of the scene with the mist rising off the canal and the sleeping city slowly rousing all around them.

The magic held Cassandra until the carved stern of the gondola slipped from sight, then with a sigh she turned to slip into her room. As she moved, she found herself caught in the steady gaze of the courtesan. The woman smiled as she had before, then beckoned with one long-nailed finger.

'Me?' Cassandra mouthed foolishly, looking round, but there was no one else in sight. The woman nodded and gestured again. Cassandra hesitated, intrigued by the summons, yet unwilling to run the gauntlet of the servants, who would all be about their business by now.

Suddenly emboldened, she swung a leg over the balustrade, gripped the heavily carved stonework, and in a moment had reached the safety of the courtyard, with only a scraped knuckle and a burst seam to show for her foolhardiness.

The door opened silently as she approached and closed just as quickly when she entered. A maid-servant holding a candle ushered her upstairs in silence, then abandoned her at a chamber door with a bobbed curtsey.

Cassandra scratched tentatively on the carved panels and a soft voice called, 'Come in, little one.' It was English, exotic and musically accented, but English none the less.

The chamber was heavy with brocade hangings, dominated by a huge canopied bed and lit by many candles, each multiplied over and over in the silvery mirrors which hung on every wall. The air was redolent of attar of roses and a hint of cinnabar, and Cassandra's feet sank into the deep pile of a Turkey carpet as she hesitated inside the door.

'Come in, little sister,' the woman said gently, sinking gracefully onto a sofa with a gesture for Cassandra to come and sit by her.

Startled, Cassandra blurted out, 'You know I'm not a boy?' Mesmerised, she sat as she was bid, next to the courtesan, unashamedly staring.

'But, of course. You may call me Lucia. And you are?'

'Cassandra.'

'Cassandra.' Lucia rolled the name round her

tongue as if tasting it and nodded in approval. 'You will take your *colazione* with me.' It was an assumption, not a request and Cassandra abandoned all thought of her English Society manners. This was no afternoon tea party at the Vicarage.

The maid was already laying the breakfast table with hot rolls, fruit and chocolate. The mixture of warm fragrances was so appetising that Cassandra could hardly contain her hunger.

To her surprise, her hostess showed as hearty an appetite as she, and for several minutes neither spoke. At last, Cassandra sat back with a contented sigh, warm, full and clear headed.

Lucia shifted slightly to regard her guest. 'So! Now you feel like a human being again. It is always a mistake not to eat, my child. How old are you?'

'Just eighteen,' Cassandra confessed. Being lectured on the importance of eating properly was not what she had envisaged when she had entered this house.

'Ah.' Cassandra shifted uneasily under the courtesan's appraising gaze. 'Just eighteen, just arrived in Venice and you have had a *disputa*, a, what do you call it. . .?'

'Quarrel?'

'*Si*. A quarrel, with your lover.'

'He is not my lover!' Cassandra protested hotly. 'He is the son of my godmother and I am travelling under his protection.'

'Dressed as his valet? And it is part of the masquerade that he beats you? You English!' She cast her eyes heavenwards.

'He doesn't beat me! Well, that was the only time and I had been very provoking. . .' Her voice trailed away as the resentments of last night resurfaced. 'But he deserved what I said about his whore.' Then she realised in whose company she found herself and went scarlet with embarrassment.

'There is no need to avoid the word in my company, although courtesan is more accurate, both for myself and for the lady who the Earl of Lydford was escorting.'

'You know who he is?' Cassandra looked at Lucia with new respect, noting for the first time the shrewd intelligence in her eyes.

'It is my business to know.' She shrugged, a lazily sensuous movement, even in the presence of another woman. 'My sisters and I are well-informed. We are professionals, after all.'

'Your sisters?' Cassandra was confused.

'Venice is a city of women. Men rule it — and we rule the men. Men work against each other for their own power. Our strength lies in our combined power: even the wives of the men who come to us are our sisters. We trust each other. It is accepted.'

The idea of women selling themselves, yet still retaining their independence and their dignity, astonished Cassandra, yet, looking at Lucia, the only comparison she could draw was with her god-mother, an independent great lady.

'But why did you ask me here?' she blurted out.

'Because you need my help.' Lucia snuggled back into the cushions and tucked her long, bare feet up. 'You say he is not your lover, this Earl of Lydford. . .'

'Nicholas.'

'*Niccolo*.' Lucia tried out the name. 'But you do

love him?' Her plucked eyebrows rose
interrogatively.

'Yes,' Cassandra whispered. Having said it out
loud, she knew it was true. This was no hero-
worship, no *tendre* of a young woman for an experienced man. It was certainly not gratitude. She
wanted him in every possible way, and forever. 'But
it's impossible.'

'Perhaps. Do you want his heart or his body?'

'Both,' Cassandra confessed. 'I want him to love
me and marry me.'

'Ah,' Lucia looked thoughtful. 'This is more
difficult. He wants you, that is self-evident.'

'It is?' Cassandra's eyebrows shot up. 'There have
been occasions. . .' She blushed. 'We have been
thrown together by circumstance and he is a man of
the world. . .'

'So he starts to make love to you and then he
feels guilty and stops. Oh, the English and their
sense of guilt!' Lucia frowned at her. 'Silly little
virgin, do you think he would be so angry with you
if he did not want you?'

'Perhaps not. But I am a great nuisance to him, I
have ruined his Tour, perhaps even his reputation,
if we are found out.'

'You keep making excuses for him, yet you are
angry and hurt,' Lucia remarked shrewdly. 'Why?'

Cassandra got to her feet and began to fidget
around the room. The question was disturbing,
forcing her to confront her real feelings. 'I'm jealous,' she said eventually. 'I want him to see *me*, not
an irritating child he's been saddled with or a
distracting body he must try and ignore. If he thinks
of me at all, it's either as the little girl I was when

he last met me, or as a package he must deliver intact to his mother, because his duty demands it.'

'So you want him to recognise you are a woman. A woman who can say "yes" or "no" to him. . .'

'I suppose so.' Cassandra bit her lip, forcing herself to be honest. 'But I want him! I know it's wrong, but I want him to love me. . .to make love to me. He has always had everything he wants. . .'

'And now there is something you desire?' Lucia laughed. 'And you need to learn how to use a woman's power to make him see you and only you.'

'But how?' Cassandra sank down on the sofa, suddenly aghast at what she was saying.

'You go home and go to bed, little one. Sleep. Eat your dinner in your room. Let your Niccolo believe you are not well, and when he goes out to the Turkish Ambassador's ball this evening, come back here to me.'

'How do you know where he is going this evening?' Cassandra asked, although nothing about this amazing woman would surprise her now.

'All Society goes to the Ambassador's masque. And so do the courtesans. And for one evening you will be one of us, for your Niccolo only. And then you may love him or not, as you decide. Now go — and take care no one sees you leave.'

Remaining in her room was simpler than Cassandra had feared. The encounter with Lucia seemed some sort of mad dream. How could she even contemplate anything so outrageous as to seduce Nicholas? She sent a message by Antonio that she was feeling unwell and would take her meals alone and received by return a curt note from Nicholas.

It is not to be wondered at that you feel unwell after your behaviour last night, he wrote. For myself I have no wish to set eyes on you until you have had time to reflect on your conduct and make amends. The servants have been informed that you will remain in your room until they receive my orders to the contrary.

It was signed curtly, Lydford.

Cassandra read this missive through twice, unable to believe her eyes. So, he wanted her to confess her faults, while he offered no word of contrition for his conduct in putting her over his knee like a child! All doubts about Lucia's wanton plan vanished: she would show him she was a woman!

Cassandra screwed up the paper and hurled it at the wall. It missed, sailed out of the open casement and into the canal where it sank gently beneath the greenish waters.

It was nine in the evening when she watched Nicholas emerge from the front door and make his way down the steps to his waiting boat. He was obviously dining out before the ball. Despite her anger with him, Cassandra felt her heartbeat quicken at the sight of him, magnificent in full evening attire. A heavy opera cloak lined with scarlet silk was thrown back over an evening suit of corbeau blue cloth. His neckcloth was immaculate in its complex folds, a single fob glinted against the dull sheen of soft silver threads in his waistcoat.

The major domo hovered, in his hand Nicholas's mask dangled by its strings. Against the Venetian servants, Nicholas's rangy height was even more apparent.

More than anything else, Cassandra wanted to be

with him, on his arm. To be helped into the boat by him with the solicitude he had shown his companion of the night before. . . But after tonight, perhaps. . .

With the Earl's departure, the public rooms of the *palazzo* rapidly emptied of servants, making it easy for Cassandra to slip out and across the courtyard. The door opened before she even knocked and once again she was conducted silently into Lucia's presence.

The courtesan was already dressed in evening finery, although without paint. A large bathtub, lined with white linen stood in one corner, a manservant filling it with flagons of warm water. Lucia sent him away and paused to consider a collection of glass phials.

'Sandalwood, I think,' she mused. 'Heady, but not clinging. You will be able to wash it off later, and that may be important, for you may yet change your mind, little sister! Now, take off your clothes, and into the bath with you.'

An hour later Cassandra was being laced into a corset which produced a figure which she had no idea she possessed. She looked down, startled, at a surprising amount of cleavage, but oiled, warm and faintly lightheaded from a glass of sweet wine, she felt no inclination to protest.

The maid helped her into a gown the colour of crushed raspberries and began to fasten it. 'But what about my hair?' The boyish crop, even though it was beginning to grow into soft curls, was ludicrously at odds with the soft folds and low cut bodice of the silk gown with its gauze overdress.

'But a wig, of course!' Lucia sat Cassandra to the

dressing table, pulled back her hair with a ribbon and arranged a blonde mass of ringlets on her head. 'There!'

Cassandra gazed into the glass and a creature who was not Cassandra gazed back. Only her dark, direct eyes, shadowed by uncertainty, were familiar.

'Now, to paint your face. We will do it together.'

Cassie sat obedient as a child as Lucia went to work with her brushes and myriad little pots. She brushed kohl around her eyes until they were huge and dark, then thickened the lashes with a black powder. She brushed Cassandra's skin with rice powder, clucking over the fading sun-freckles. And then she painted her mouth with a red gloss the exact colour of the gown.

The sensuous touch of the brush following the curve of her lip made Cassandra pout. 'Perfect,' Lucia murmured. 'Now, remember, do not bite your lips and be careful when you drink.'

Lucia, satisfied at last, led her to a full-length glass. 'There!'

Cassandra gasped. A total stranger stood there, sophisticated, beautiful, intriguing. Yet despite the paint and the tumbling blonde curls, there was no hint of coarseness or wantoness. The neckline teased, but did not reveal, the lines of the gown flattered rather than flaunted.

'Now: slippers, a fan, a mask and you are ready. Not even your father would recognise you!'

Cassandra smiled ironically. What her father would say if he could see his only child now beggared description. 'Lucia, this is beautiful,' she stroked the gown, 'but I'm still not certain I can go through with this.'

Lucia steadied the kohl brush as she shaded her own eyes. 'We are going to the Turkish Ambassador's ball and you will dazzle your Niccolo. What comes after is in your hands.'

'I can't do it, Lucia!' When he found out, his anger would be unimaginable! Cassandra looked round wildly for the maid to unlace her gown.

'Silly child!' Lucia swept over and pressed her into a chair. 'I do not recognise you and I created you myself. You do not have to decide anything. . . yet. Follow your instincts. Here, drink this slowly and try on your mask.'

Cassandra slipped the heady wine then tied the strings of her mask. It covered her eyebrows, cheek-bones and subtly altered the shape of her nose. Lucia was right; she could not recognise herself. And besides, she thought philosophically, there would be such a throng that perhaps Nicholas would never see her.

'But my voice? What if he should speak to me?'

'Oh, he will speak to you, that is certain.' Lucia smiled her slow, mysterious smile. 'You speak French? Good, then lower your voice, use a French accent and say only a little, with many French words. That will intrigue even more.'

Cassandra shrugged, still sceptical that Nicholas would even notice her among the throng of beautiful women but the heavy scents of the room, Lucia's confidence, the sweet potency of the wine, all came together, and suddenly she was careless of what the night might bring.

'Wait,' said Lucia suddenly, as the maid settled their cloaks around their shoulders. 'One jewel is all you need.' She clicked her fingers and the maid brought a casket, waiting while her mistress stirred the contents with one long finger. 'Ah, yes, the very thing. This is a little gift for you, my child.'

She held up a flexible gold necklace, fashioned in the shape of a serpent. In its delicate jaws it held a rose quartz egg on a gold chain. Lucia fastened it around Cassandra's neck where it hung, the jewel trembling on the swell of her breasts.

'Thank you,' Cassandra breathed, touching the ornament as she followed her companion from the room.

The journey was short, but their gondola had to wait, jostling for position with the dozens of others at the watergate to the Ambassador's imposing *palazzo*. Despite Lucia's assurances, Cassandra was amazed to see groups of courtesans arriving, rubbing shoulders quite openly with nobility of all nationalities. English voices carried on the night air, mingling with the growl of Russian, German gutterals and mellifluous Mediterranean accents.

The entrance court was as bright as noon with turbanned servants lining the walls, each with a flambeau to light the guests threading slowly up the marble stairs to where the Ambassador greeted the company.

Lucia ignored the main throng and insinuated herself through a side door, up a flight of stairs and emerged, Cassandra in her wake, virtually at the Ambassador's elbow.

He recognised her at once, bowing low over her hand with an intimate murmur of greeting. Cassandra realised all at once why Lucia had been so confident of her plan: the Turk was obviously a favoured client. The Ambassador's dark eyes gleamed appreciatively as he bowed to Cassandra and she found herself smiling back at the hawkish, moustachioed face.

He snapped his fingers and an elegant young man, dressed like the Ambassador in national dress, hurried to his side. Cassandra heard Nicholas's title murmured and the aide nodded and gestured politely for the ladies to precede him into the crowded salon.

It took some minutes to locate the Earl. He was standing listening to a middle-aged man whose evening dress was bedecked with orders and medal ribbons. Cassandra recognised Nicholas's rising boredom and stifled a giggle before sudden panic gripped her.

'I must be *mad*,' she whispered, pulling back against Lucia's light grip on her elbow.

'Do not worry, little one,' Lucia whispered in return. 'Go and fascinate your Niccolo: he will never know it is you — unless you choose to tell him! I will not be far away.'

The aide waited politely until the senior diplomat noticed him and broke off an exposition of the Russian situation.

'His Excellency, my master, has commanded me to introduce these ladies to your eminences. . .' The aide allowed his words to tail off discreetly as he melted backwards into the crowd.

The diplomat's obvious irritation at the interruption vanished abruptly as his gaze fell on Lucia. She looked magnificent in her favourite emerald green, her white bosom scarcely contained in a jewelled net bodice, her Titian hair tumbled in artful disarray.

'Hurrumph!' He stared for a moment through his quizzing glass, then it fell from his fingers as he surged forward to bend over Lucia's proffered hand. '*Madame*! Your most obedient!' He had no eyes for anyone, let alone Cassandra in her more modest attire and the Russian situation had obviously been instantly forgotten.

'Sir Humphrey,' Lucia purred. 'I have met you at last! I have heard so much about you: tell me, is it true that only your subtle intervention saved the talks at. . .' She had already borne him off towards a curtained alcove and Cassandra never did discover Sir Humphrey's great contribution to European statesmanship.

She was looking after them with bemused admiration for Lucia's tactics, when Nicholas's voice in her ear remarked, 'Very prettily done — it is always a pleasure to see an expert at work.'

Cassandra started, realising with horror that she was all alone with Nicholas. He was looking at her with blatant admiration in his eyes, a warm smile playing round his lips. For the first time, she was experiencing all his charm, uncomplicated by their difficult, ambiguous relationship.

This was the man whom prudent London mamas warned their susceptible daughters against: not because he was a seducer of innocents, but because he would steal their hearts without for a moment taking them seriously. Many lures had been cast before the eligible Earl of Lydford, but none had hooked him.

Cassandra took a long, unsteady breath and the rose quartz jewel quivered between her breasts, drawing Nicholas's eyes to the soft swell.

'Monsieur?' Cassandra hastily remembered the rôle she was playing and held out her hand to him. Nicholas took it and turned it so that his warm lips met the inside of her wrist in a lingering caress. Her heart leapt so she thought he must feel it in her pulse, but he drew her hand through his arm and began to stroll towards the terrace.

She forced herself to relax and move sinuously against him as he bowed and nodded to various acquaintances as they progressed through the crowd. A black page paused before them with a tray of wine glasses and Nicholas took two, offering one to Cassandra.

She took a cautious sip and realised it was champagne. The bubbles tickled her nose, but the taste was unthreatening and she drank more deeply.

Nicholas was intent on reaching the less crowded terrace and skilfully evaded all attempts to detain him with conversation. Outside it was much quieter, although couples and small groups strolled and chatted along the wide, balustraded space overhanging the Grand Canal. He found her a bench, its cold marble smothered in heaped cushions, and leaned against the wall at her side.

Cassandra could hear the slap of tiny waves as gondolas disturbed the water below, then quite forgot her surroundings as Nicholas spoke to her.

'Will you tell me your name, *ma belle*?' he asked. 'I am Nicholas. . .'

'Earl of Lydford,' she finished for him, rolling her r's.

'You know? I am flattered.' He dropped onto the bench beside her, stretching out his long legs, quite at ease.

'I make it my business to know,' she said, remembering Lucia's words. 'You may call me Antoinette.'

There was a small silence as they sipped their wine, their eyes meeting above the rim of the glasses. A vague uneasiness stirred somewhere in Nicholas's mind, an evocation rather than a memory. A frown creased his brow and his companion noticed it at once.

'Something is wrong, Nicholas?' Her voice was husky, low; the dark gaze behind the mask questioning.

He tried to express what he was feeling. 'I thought you reminded me of someone. . .but no, it is a passing fancy. I cannot even recall who it might be.'

'I, Antoinette, have never met you, Nicholas.' Cassandra let her hand rest lightly on his sleeve. 'I would have remembered *you*.' Panic gripped her: there must be something about the way she moved, the way she held herself, that could not be disguised, and she was still not ready to commit herself to this masquerade.

Very well, then, she would use Lucia's arts to divert his thoughts. He had known her in many rôles in their weeks together: tomboy, nurse, demure young lady — but never seductress. This was frightening, but excitement was racing in her veins.

She let her hand drift down his arm until her fingertips brushed his knuckles, then flexed her fingers, grazing the smooth flesh with her nails. She felt his instant reaction, and suddenly she was aware of her own power over him. This was what Lucia had meant when she spoke of the power her sisters wielded over men.

His free hand came over hers, trapping it. Again,

he turned it, but this time, instead of carrying it to his lips, he rubbed one fingertip over the sensitive palm, the swell at the base of her thumb. A wave of tingling heat passed over Cassandra's body, absurdly out of porportion to the lightness of his touch.

She met his eyes, unaware that her painted lips were parted invitingly, that the snake on her breast rose and fell with her tremulous breathing. Nicholas was intrigued by this courtesan who responded like an innocent girl. It had to be artifice, she was obviously a professional, but the fantasy of inexperience was powerfully erotic.

'You are refreshingly different, *ma belle*,' he murmured against her hair. Cassandra felt herself swaying instinctively against him, driven by her love, her need, for him. His warm lips grazed tantalisingly down the curve of her jaw to the soft hollow of her throat.

She had to touch him. She was beyond thinking how a courtesan should behave, beyond teasing and flirting. Cassandra put up her hand, caressing the nape of his neck and instantly her memory supplied the recollection of his bare back under her palms in Nice.

Spreading her fingers in his hair, her thumb rubbing the strong tendon of his neck, Cassandra was hardly aware of the balustrade behind her shoulders, the yielding cushions beneath her.

Nicholas could feel the pulse jumping beneath his lips, the warm, supple body yielding in his arms and knew he had to stop this now, whilst he still could.

Footsteps rang on the marble and with a mixture

of relief and regret, Nicholas sat up, running one hand through his hair and tugging at his cravat.

Cassandra, her heart in her throat, came back to reality with a start. The terrace was now virtually empty, but Lucia was approaching them with Sir Humphrey in her wake. All that had happened, Cassandra told herself, was that he had taken her in his arms, yet she felt stripped naked before everyone.

Behind the mask, Lucia's eyes were quizzical. 'We came to tell you that supper is being served and dancing will follow. Will you not join us? It would give us great pleasure, would it not, Sir Humphrey?'

The diplomat was totally under her spell. 'Of course. . .of course. Damned good supper, by the look of it.'

Nicholas responded readily, taking Cassandra by her hand to escort her once more into the salon.

'One moment,' Lucia put out her hand. 'Look, my dear, your lace is torn. Gentlemen, allow us a moment while I pin it up. Please, go ahead, we will meet you inside.'

As soon as they were alone, she pushed Cassandra back on the seat and stood before her. 'What are you about, little one! You must tease, tantalise, flirt with him. Inflame him, yes — but not yield to him! At least,' she added thoughtfully, 'not yet.'

'I couldn't help it,' Cassandra wailed. 'I love him, I do want him. . . How could I realise it would be like this? What am I to do, Lucia? I have no experience. . .'

'You have two choices: flee now while you can; or take him back to my *palazzo* and there give yourself to him.' She shrugged her shoulders. 'You want him to know you as a woman. But I wonder if you understand truly what that means. . . I cannot dictate to you whether you follow your heart or your head, you must decide. Come now, they will be becoming impatient.'

Nicholas had heaped a plate of dainties from the buffet for her and Cassandra ate with an appetite, telling herself it would mop up the wine, clear her head.

To her own amazement, she kept up her part in the lighthearted badinage which passed between their party, remembering to keep her voice low and accented. Yet, all the while, she was aware of Nicholas at her side, the touch of his sleeve against her bare arm, the caress of his fingers as he handed her peeled sections of fruit.

His regard was warm on her; she sensed his impatience to touch her was reined in only by the demands of good manners. Even as she chatted and flirted, her mind whirled on a treadwheel of indecision. What should she do?

The safest thing would be to disappear now. But meeting his eyes as he smiled down at her, she knew she wanted more than anything to be in his arms, for him to kiss her again as he had in Paris, for her to show him her love.

She wanted to be his wife, to be with him always. By giving herself to him tonight, he might come to love her as she loved him. But it was a terrible risk. He might reject her and an illicit love affair would be a betrayal of everything she felt for him, of her upbringing and sense of what was right.

'You are very thoughtful, *ma belle*,' he said lightly, tipping up her chin.

The touch sent the blood burning through her veins and she smiled at him, moving closer, wanting to be held. 'Let us dance, Nicholas. Listen — the waltz.'

She had never performed this daring, intimate dance with a man as her partner. The Vicar's four daughters, with whom she was friendly, had wheedled their dancing master into teaching them the waltz and Cassandra had learned it from them.

But dancing and giggling with Verity Lamb while sister Charity played the spinnet was quite a different matter than standing close to Nicholas, his hand resting lightly at her waist, the other clasping hers. She gathered up her skirt gracefully in her free hand and tried to concentrate on the steps of the dance, not the touch of his palm against hers.

At home to have danced more than twice with the same man would have been shockingly forward, but in Venice, such conventions held no sway. Dance after dance passed, and Nicholas took no other partner, had eyes for no-one else.

As the clock struck three, he pulled her closer than the dance demanded and whispered huskily, 'I can bear it no longer, I must be alone with you. Come to my *palazzo*.'

'No.' Cassandra was startled into bluntness, then remembered Lucia's whispered instructions earlier in the evening. 'I never go to a gentleman's house. . .'

The look of disappointment on his face gave her a feeling of power, of strength, she had never before experienced. This assured, experienced man was in her thrall, hanging on her decision. She wanted him — and he was hers.

'You would leave me?' His eyes were dark and glittering, although he kept his voice light.

'No, my lord. I did not say that. Come, instead, to my *palazzo*. Come home with me.'

CHAPTER TEN

THE blaze of torchlight on the Grand Canal seemed almost to ignite the water, so bright were the reflections on its dark surface. To Cassandra's relief, she had to give no orders to the boatman: Lucia's gondolier followed his mistress's instructions to return speedily to her *palazzo*, but by a route his passengers would not recognise. He steered south, not north, turning off to avoid the main waterways.

Cassandra was lost within seconds, but their route was of small importance beside the effect of being alone with Nicholas in the intimacy of the gondola. Now, in the velvety darkness, with the discreet silhouette of the gondolier above them, she felt panic, and a sudden doubt. Despite her overwhelming love for this man, was she doing the right thing? Would he understand that she was driven to break all the codes by which she had been raised only because she loved him?

Through the thin silk of her gown, Nicholas's thigh was warm and hard against hers. He put his arm around her shoulders, drawing her close against his chest, his lips moving in her hair.

Cassandra stiffened, then made herself relax as one hand slipped under the lace at her shoulder and he began to caress her skin. Any maidenly shrinking would betray her instantly—but how was she to restrain his mounting passion until they reached the *palazzo*?

'Nicholas,' she whispered. 'Do you intend to stay long in Venice?'

'Umm?' He was disinclined for conversation, his response merely a mumble as he nibbled delicately at her ear.

'How long do you stay in Venice?' she persisted, unable to prevent her treacherous body moving more closely into his embrace.

Reluctantly he freed his mouth. 'That depends on what there is to stay for.' He bent his head and trailed kisses across the swell of her breasts, his lips fretting at the confining lace.

Cassandra swallowed hard, filled with a strange mixture of panic and desire. 'Oh, there is much to stay for Nicholas,' she managed to gasp out.

'As I am discovering,' he responded huskily. An unwelcome thought seemed to strike him, and he straightened up, still holding her close. 'I am not entirely my own master in this matter,' he said with heavy irony, his eyes on the dark water.

In the light from a lighted courtyard, Cassandra saw his face harden with remembered anger. 'Why not, my lord?'

'I am encumbered,' he said shortly. 'Encumbered by a troublesome child for whom I have responsibility. I must take her to my mother in Vienna. If I do not strangle her first,' he added bitterly.

Some devil prompted Cassandra to probe further. 'You jest, of course, Nicholas! You have your little daughter with you? Do you not like *les enfants*?'

'She is no relative of mine, thank the Lord! And she is not truly a child, although she is as unruly and ungovernable as one.'

There was real feeling in his voice and Cassandra

realised she was still unforgiven, both for her words and for the blow. 'Surely, if you are giving her your protection, she should be meek and grateful in return? Why,' she fought to keep the anger from her own voice, 'I am sure you must have been like an indulgent elder brother to her, *mon cher*.'

It was too dark to read his face, but Nicholas shifted uncomfortably on the cushions beside her and Cassandra felt a small stab of triumph. So, she had pricked his conscience had she?

But not so much, it seemed, to make him forget his grievances! 'The wretched chit had the impertinence to lecture me—*me*—on my behaviour and morals. When I consider that I saved her from the most dissolute, the most diseased rake in London. . .' Nicholas had forgotten the woman beside him in his bitterness.

Cassandra was frightened by his vehemence, then remembered Lucia's suggestion that his anger was fuelled by his desire for her. It seemed difficult to believe, looking at his set profile and stiff back. His hands no longer caressed her, but rested tensely on his thighs.

To her relief, the gondola bumped up against a landing stage and the gondolier jumped ashore to secure it. Cassandra realised they had reached the back of Lucia's *palazzo* and set herself to distract Nicholas in case he should recognise their surroundings.

'You are very quiet, my lord,' she purred, as he handed her out of the gently rocking boat. She kept her fingers linked with his as she drew him towards the door already standing ajar. 'Forget your troublesome ward—you are with me *ce soir*. . .' She let the phrase trail off provocatively, and it had the desired effect.

Nicholas gave himself an almost imperceptible shake and smiled down at her as they passed into the darkened hallway. 'No man could forget he was with you, *ma belle*,' he murmured.

His ardour led him to catch her in his arms as they mounted the stairs, spanning her slender waist with his hands and turning her towards him as he stood on the step below.

This position brought them mouth to mouth. He kissed the corner of her lips, then ran the tip of his tongue around their curve, the strength of his hands pulling her tight against his hard body.

'Nicholas,' she protested gently, against his lips. 'Upstairs. . .we will be more comfortable upstairs in my chamber.'

'Then let us make haste, or I swear I will have you here where we stand!'

Cassandra felt the scalding blush sweep from her toes to the roots of her hair. She had never dreamt that the depth of a man's passion and urgent desire could lead to lovemaking on the stairs! She was just reflecting that it was fortunate that the darkness masked her dismay, when he stopped and swept her up in his arms.

'This door?' He hardly waited for her nod of acquiescence before shouldering it open.

Cassandra expected him to set her on her feet as soon as he had kicked the door closed behind them. Instead he tightened his embrace, crushing her breasts against the soft linen of his shirt front as he bent his head to claim her lips.

This was what she had been waiting for, yearning

for, since she had realised her love for him. She tightened her arms around his neck, unconscious that she was inciting, compelling with her fingertips.

His mouth was hot, sweet and demanding, invading hers with an intimacy that shocked yet thrilled. Cassandra felt certain that if she did not draw breath in the next few seconds she would surely faint, yet rather than withdraw, he deepened the pressure with erotic expertise, teasing her tongue tip with his own. Her senses spinning, she forgot all her doubts, all her fears, in the tide of her love and longing.

She was aware of him moving towards the bed, although he never freed her lips. He stooped, laying her gently amongst the yielding cushions, and sat beside her.

Cassandra lay fighting to control her tumultuous breathing, watching him through the slits in her mask. A small branch of candles afforded enough light to gild the sheen of perspiration on his taut face, and his eyes glittered greener with desire.

Nicholas watched her for a long moment, deliberately it seemed to her, prolonging the tension in the room. When at last he did move, it was to reach out with one long finger and free the jewel that trembled beneath the lace, caught in the cleft of her breasts.

The merest brush of his fingertip left her quivering with desire; he took the rose quartz between thumb and forefinger rubbing its cool smoothness gently, insistently, his eyes never leaving her face. While he fondled the jewel, his little finger stroked the satin sheen of fine skin, gently at first, then with increasing pressure.

A tiny gasp of shock and surrender escaped

Cassandra's parted lips: if he kissed her now, she would be lost, would give herself to him utterly without heed to anything. . . But it would be worth it, worth anything, if there was a chance he could come to love her, too.

'Damn these masks,' he growled, fumbling in her hair for the strings. 'Intriguing they may be, but they're damnably inconvenient. . .'

In a moment they would be face to face, not Nicholas and Antoinette, but Nicholas and Cassandra. Suddenly she knew she, Cassandra, could never do the things that 'Antoinette' would do. To make love to him in disguise would be pointless, empty, wanton. To make love to him as herself, she realised, was impossible.

It would betray her own honour and, in doing so, tarnish everything she felt for Nicholas. The realisation doused her passion more effectively than a douche of cold water. With a sinuous twist, she slipped from beneath his hand and off the bed.

'When I return, Nicholas,' she whispered huskily, 'then you may take everything. . .starting with the mask. But I must fetch wine and fruit for later and make certain we are not disturbed.'

'I'll wait then, *ma belle* — but impatiently.' He swung his long legs up onto the bed and leaned back against the cushions. The smile he sent her was melting with desire as she escaped, pulling the heavy door closed behind her.

She leaned her shoulders against the panels, achingly aware of Nicholas on the other side, fighting to control the urge to run back into his arms, whatever her conscience told her.

Lucia's sharp hiss brought her to her senses. 'Why

have you left him?' She was standing at the foot of
the stairs as Cassandra ran down. 'What is wrong?
Why are you not in your Niccolo's arms?' Her sharp
eyes missed nothing in the flushed face turned to
hers.

'I cannot do it, it would be wrong! Oh, but Lucia,
I love him so.' Her voice broke on a sob.

'Make haste then!' Lucia drew her into the
chamber where her maid was waiting. The two of
them began unlacing the gown, loosing the wig and
freeing Cassandra's own hair.

'Wear this,' Lucia bundled her into a plain wrapper and began scrubbing at her face with a thick
cream. 'Here, take the rest of the pot and this linen
to apply it, check carefully in a good light that there
is no paint left around your eyes and hairline. Now
go!'

Propelled into the chilly dawn light of the courtyard, Cassandra stopped, looking round wildly.
How was she to get into her own *palazzo*? Then she
saw the door standing ajar: Lucia's influence no
doubt. She ran up the steps, then paused, one hand
on the heavy iron ring, and looked back. Behind
the lighted window, Nicholas's shadow crossed and
recrossed the room: he was becoming impatient.

Fear lent wings to her feet as she sped towards
her chamber. Candles burned on the dressing table
in front of the mirror and she stooped to scrutinise
her face as she scrubbed the linen over the last
remnants of kohl under her lashes. Dragging of the
wrapper, she bundled it into the clothes press and
kicked the slippers out of sight.

The water in the pitcher on the washstand was
cold but Cassandra splashed it over her neck and

breast to wash away the lingering scent of sandalwood, replacing it with a splash of her usual innocuous rosewater.

The jewel! It still hung around her neck. Her fingers were fumbling with the unfamiliar clasp when the front door crashed shut with the force of a thunderclap echoing around the marble halls.

Cassandra whisked into bed, dragging the covers up to her chin, then lay back on the pillows steadying her breathing. Nicholas wouldn't come to her room — why should he? It was only her guilty conscience that prompted the fear.

As she closed her eyes, she heard him enter his chamber, shutting the door with slightly less vehemence this time, no doubt to avoid waking her. She could chart his progress around the room by his footsteps and the sound of drawers being opened and closed, his shoes being kicked across the floor with a muttered imprecation: then there was silence.

Cassandra had just started to relax when the connecting door eased open. She caught her breath, then forced herself to breathe deeply and slowly. Between slitted lids, she watched Nicholas in his brocade robe standing on the threshold regarding her. She turned slightly on the pillows to watch him more easily and muttered as though restless in her sleep.

How long he stood there she had no idea, although it seemed long minutes rather than seconds, but he made no move to come further into the room or to speak to her.

In the end, it was her own guilty conscience that made her feign waking. 'Nicholas?' She injected as much sleepy puzzlement as she could into her voice. 'What's wrong? What time is it?'

He hesitated, one hand on the edge of the door. 'Nothing, nothing's the matter. Don't worry. I'm sorry I woke you.' But he did not go back through the open door. Instead he moved slowly to sit on the end of her bed, his eyes steady on her face.

After a moment, he said, 'You look tired, Cassie.'

'I am. I haven't slept much.' She looked at him, seeing how the excitements and disappointments of the night had left him drained. 'Are you all right? You look ill.'

'I will survive.' He smiled wryly. 'Like you, I have had no sleep.'

He fell silent again, and once more it was Cassandra who spoke. 'Why are you here, Nicholas?'

'I felt the need to see you, but I didn't intend to disturb you. Cassie, I'm sorry. . . I felt, I feel. . . I should never have shouted at you, never have struck you. I had neglected you, no wonder you felt rebellious. . .'

'Nicholas, there is no need for this.' If he felt guilty, Cassandra felt a thousand times worse. His anger had turned to remorse, but she could feel no satisfaction at his apology. She put out a tentative hand and he took it gently.

'Coming to Venice was a mistake, I should never have brought you here. It was selfish of me.' He was patting her hand in a way totally removed from the caresses of an hour ago. 'Sleep now, we will make more plans tomorrow.'

When he had gone, she let out her breath in a huge sigh of relief. She did not deserve to have escaped the night's wild masquerade without discovery, she knew that. But she knew also that her heart would never escape the pain of unrequited love. Her fingers touched the jewelled snake and she sat up and unclasped it. The clasp unlatched easily now there was no need for haste.

The gold pooled into a supple coil in her palm and she stirred the jewel with her finger, evoking the touch of Nicholas's finger on her skin. No, she had not escaped unscathed: she was no longer the innocent girl who had set out on this mad masquerade six weeks before. Love hurt.

It was two heavy-eyed and silent people who sat down to break their fast at ten o'clock that morning. The servants, used to the effects of Venetian entertainments on visiting foreign guests, moved with unobtrusive silence around the table, then melted away discreetly.

Nicholas regarded Cassandra over the rim of his cup. She looked drawn and tired and he cursed himself for having woken her in the early hours. But the overwhelming need to look at her had drawn him to her door.

After letting himself be so thoroughly duped by the artful mock innocence of the young courtesan, he had had to reassure himself what true innocence really was. Cassandra must be about the same age as Antoinette, he supposed, although it was hard to believe as she sat there in prim black suiting, her face scrubbed and her hair tied back in a queue. What a contrast with that silken creature last night. And what a contrast with the scene he interrupted when he had gone looking for Antoinette! The ageing diplomat, flushed and dishevelled, ridiculous in his passion. . . Nicholas shuddered fastidiously.

Cassandra glanced up from the roll she was crumbling and caught his thoughtful regard.

'Don't look at me like that, Cassie! I'm not angry with you—I told you I was sorry I was so harsh with you.' Colour flooded her cheeks, and seeing it he spoke again, more gently. 'I was only angry because I was frightened for you. You don't know how dangerous this place can be; you are too innocent to even guess at the viciousness beneath the surface glamour.'

'No, of course, I'm not afraid of you, Nicholas,' Cassandra said briskly, pushing back her chair and getting up. 'You said we were leaving, shall I go and direct that our bags are packed?' He was becoming too kind for comfort!

'I have already told Antonio to prepare for our departure.' He, too, stood. 'Now I am going out to arrange for our travel papers. Do you wish to come with me? It will be a long and tedious business, I fear.'

'No, thank you. I would rather pack my own things myself.' If Nicholas was to be gone all morning, it would give her the chance to slip across to Lucia's house and return the wrapper and slippers. And satisfy her curiosity as to what had transformed Nicholas from lover to penitent.

When he had gone, Cassandra went back to her chamber, folded the slippers and jar of salve into a neat parcel inside the wrapper and tucked the whole under her arm. She was just descending the stairs when she heard Nicholas talking to the major domo in the hall below.

'Tell me, who is the occupant of the *palazzo* opposite?'

'La Puttana.'

'The whore?' Nicholas translated.

'A very great and powerful lady,' Antonio said drily. 'And a dangerous one. She is said to have the. . .ear, shall we say, of our most powerful senators. Few dare to cross her, for she has influence with many of the diplomats and ambassadors, and acts herself as their agent.'

'I see,' Nicholas said slowly. 'Perhaps I have an enemy I am unaware of. . .' He caught himself thinking aloud and added more briskly, 'I am not certain when I shall return, Antonio, but make sure all is ready for an early departure tomorrow.'

'As you command, milord.' Antonio bowed the Earl through the doors and vanished into the salon, leaving the way clear for Cassandra to flit down the stairs.

Once more the door into Lucia's *palazzo* opened as if by magic. Cassandra wondered if the little maidservant was in truth a mute as she gestured her towards the stairs.

The courtesan was in bed, sitting up sipping a cup of chocolate. She looked tired, and for the first time since Cassandra had met her, she realised that Lucia was not in the first flush of youth.

Her skin, now bare of maquillage, was smooth but there were fine lines at the corners of her eyes. Her hair had been captured into a long plait over one shoulder and the severity of the style emphasised the intelligence and experience in her face.

Cassandra could well believe that she was in the presence of a powerful and influential woman and wondered again at Lucia's background and parentage.

'Well, little one? How is your Niccolo this morning?'

Cassandra grimaced. 'Subdued. Very out of character: I'm not used to him like this. Why, he apologised for being so angry with me.'

Lucia smiled, and it was not a pleasant expression. 'And that does not make you happy that he is no longer cross?'

'No, it doesn't! I am sorry to seem ungrateful, Lucia, but I should never have done it, never agreed to such a deception.'

'It will do you no harm to realise early what hypocrites men are,' Lucia remarked coldly. 'And your Niccolo is no exception.'

'But what happened last night when I had left?' Cassandra perched on the end of the bed. 'I expected him to be angry, but he seemed chastened.'

'A man like that is not used to rejection.' She laughed shortly. 'And he came across Sir Humphrey and myself: trust me when I tell you that Sir Humphrey was nothing if not ridiculous! Your Niccolo has the intelligence to see that what is exciting and romantic when you are young and dashing and firm-fleshed, is ludicrous and sordid when one is flabby and ageing.'

Cassandra was taken aback by the vehemence and contempt in Lucia's voice. She experienced a flash of pity for Sir Humphrey—and to her surprise—for Lucia, too.

So, that explained Nicholas's revulsion. Suddenly

she wanted to be in the fresh air, away from the cloying scents and veiled intrigue.

'I came to return these.' She laid her bundle on the bottom of the bed. 'And to say *adieu*, we leave early tomorrow.'

'Goodbye, little sister.' The courtesan's hard face softened. 'Do not despair: if you want him enough, you will get your Niccolo. Keep on loving him and one day he will realise he loves you, too.'

Cassandra shook her head sadly. 'No, I do not think he will ever love me. Perhaps you are right and he wants me, but that is not enough. Goodbye, Lucia—and thank you for trying to help.' She crossed and hugged the older woman, surprised at the sentiment in her eyes.

'Write and tell me what befalls!' Lucia called after her as Cassandra descended the stairs.

Cassandra spent the rest of the day alone in her chamber, trying to convince herself she had made the right decision.

Nicholas returned late in the afternoon, a fat portfolio of visas and passes to show for his pains. His encounters with bureaucracy had not, as Cassandra expected, fatigued and irritated him. Instead he seemed stimulated, once more the self-assured Earl of Lydford.

'It amazes me that we do not require permits to breathe in this city,' he exclaimed, tossing down the papers for her to peruse.

'How very impressive!' Cassandra ran a finger over one embossed and self-important document in Italian. 'What is this?'

'A certificate stating that neither of us has the pox,' Nicholas supplied wryly. 'That cost me more than any others — I had to bribe the doctor not to examine you.'

'Examine me?' Cassie cringed inwardly at the thought of such an indelicate procedure — to say nothing of the scandal. 'Thank goodness everyone in this city has their price! And this?' She held up a scroll.

'Our permission to leave the Venetian Empire. It is rather easier to get in than to get out. At least, once having secured your person they demand a high price for your freedom.'

Antonio brought in wine and salted almonds. 'The packing is complete, my lord. Do you dine at home?'

'Yes, we do,' Nicholas rejoined, with feeling. 'And an early night!'

'Now this looks like a *proper* passport!' Cassandra exclaimed, examining a leather-bound document the size of a small book.

'Indeed, it is. That is our entry into the Austrian Empire: once we enter Trieste, it will be the only document we need until we reach Vienna. And that,' he added with feeling, 'cannot come soon enough for me.'

Cassandra bit her lip. 'I *am* sorry, Nicholas. I know I have ruined your Tour. You haven't seen Rome or Florence or any of the great buildings and treasures you must have planned on visiting.'

'Never mind, brat: it wasn't your fault.' Nicholas smiled at her as he poured himself some wine. 'I cannot deny I shall be more relieved than I have ever been in my life when I hand you safe over to my mother's care, but mad as it sounds, I have enjoyed this journey.'

'You have? Why, you've been embarrassed in front of your friends, near drowned in the Rhône, attacked by bandits, bitten by every flea in North Italy and last night. . .' Hastily Cassandra shut her mouth, almost betrayed into indiscretion.

'Last night?' Nicholas's eyebrows shot up. 'What about last night?'

'Well, you obviously didn't have a very nice time,' she said feebly.

'No, I didn't have a very nice time,' he agreed with a grimace. 'But that was my own stupidity.' There was a pause before he continued. 'I have enjoyed your company, brat.' He raised his glass to toast her. 'And you have been a good influence on me. No doubt my mother will say it was time I assumed responsibility for something other than my own pleasures.'

'I am sure Godmama will say it is high time you were married,' Cassandra riposted tartly.

'No doubt.' He poured her a small glass of wine and pushed it across the table. 'Within hours of my arrival, she will have a bevy of eligible young women ready for my approval. The only consolation is that she has better taste than my Aunt Augusta.'

Emboldened by the wine Cassandra asked, 'Do you not want to get married?'

'I know I must marry. There's the title and the estates to consider. But I want more than an alliance, more than a social arrangement.' He twisted the stem of the glass between finger and thumb. Cassandra held her breath and sat still: it was almost as though he were thinking aloud to himself. 'To me, marriage should be more than that. I want a wife with character and a lively mind, not some little mouse who acquiesces because I am her husband.'

'Surely there are young ladies in the Marriage Mart who would fit the bill?'

'I have yet to encounter one!' He pitched his voice into a mocking falsetto. 'Yes, my lord, anything you say, my lord. Of course, the moon is made of green cheese, Lord Lydford, if you say so.'

Cassandra laughed at him. 'Surely they are not all such silly ninnies.'

'Of course they are not — until their mamas school them in the ways of husband catching. No, what I really need is a wife like you.'

She went very still. There was a ringing in her ears as her pulse raced and she realised her fingers were cramped on the arms of her chair. 'Me?' she croaked.

'Not *you*, of course, but there must be one of them with a sense of fun! Someone with your resourcefulness and spirit. But I expect yours will disappear when you climb into petticoats again, more's the pity.'

Clocks struck seven throughout the house and Nicholas drained his wine. 'We must dress for dinner: I will tell you then my plans for the journey.'

Cassandra glared at his retreating back, fighting down the urge to throw something at him. Not *her*, of course! Miss Cassandra Weston was *quite* unsuitable!

Why, she had a sense of fun, and resourcefulness and spirit, so he said. There were even moments when he found her attractive, however hard he tried to forget it. But was he so obtuse that he could not put these ingredients together and recognise that she would be the ideal partner for him? Or was it that Miss Cassandra Weston was not good enough for the arrogant Earl of Lydford and therefore beyond consideration?

'Oh. . .!' She kicked the tableleg, wishing it were Nicholas's well-muscled calf. Just let him wait until they reached Vienna—she'd show him she was the same person in petticoats or in breeches!

CHAPTER ELEVEN

'I CANNOT believe it is but two months since I left
Ware,' Cassandra marvelled out loud as their carriage threaded its way along a highway lined with
heavily imposing palaces and town houses, the
Imperial splendour a world away from the sedate
buildings and maltings of her home town.

'It seems like six,' Nicholas replied repressively.
He regarded her sombrely from the opposite corner
of the carriage, 'You are going to have to behave
yourself here, brat: this isn't Venice!'

'What do you mean?' Cassandra asked, her eyes
on a magnificent team of horses pulling a carriage,
its door emblazoned with a coat of arms, every
panel glinting in the sunlight.

'For one thing, the city is full of diplomats and
their wives from every corner of Europe. If you
make a scandal, there will be nowhere to retreat to
and no corner where your business will not be
known. As I said, this is not Venice: here, Society
is regulated and regimented. If it is discovered that
you had spent just one night in my company, no
allowance will be made for the predicament you
found yourself in. One slip of the tongue and you
will be ruined.'

Cassandra contemplated him thoughtfully from
under her lashes, her excitement quite gone. If she
was ruined, what would the scandal do to her
Godmama and Nicholas? His words chilled her: for

202

the first time in many weeks, she was afraid. Both she and Nicholas had concentrated on attaining the goal of reaching Vienna and his mother, without thought of how their unexpected appearance could be presented to Society.

And for the first time doubts bubbled up in Cassandra about Godmama's attitude to her flight from Lord Offley and her home. What if Godmama agreed with Papa? If she thought Cassandra wilful and disobedient in not going through with the marriage? And what if she blamed Cassandra for compromising Nicholas and blighting his chances of a good alliance? The thought of him marrying anyone else but herself was agony, but she knew it must happen.

It was a very subdued and nervous Miss Weston who finally climbed down from the carriage in the courtyard of the English Ambassador's residence, a voluminous cloak concealing her valet's clothes, the collar turned up around her face.

Seven weeks in Nicholas's company had made her sensitive to every nuance of his voice and, through her own distress, she recognised the tension underlying his apparent composure as he dispatched the major domo to announce his arrival to the Dowager Countess.

'Stand over there,' Nicholas hissed to Cassandra, gesturing to a more shadowy corner of the sunlit room while he paced restlessly over the Turkey carpet.

Minutes later the servant reappeared and bade them follow him to Lady Lydford's suite.

'Are the Ambassador and my uncle, Sir Marcus Camberley, at home?' Nicholas enquired, engaging the man's attention as Cassandra followed quietly in their wake. 'It is several weeks since I read a newspaper, but I imagine they are very much occupied with the Treaty.'

'There are still many negotiations in progress, my lord. Although the Congress has long ended, there is much business to attend to. However, we expect both His Excellency and Sir Marcus to return for dinner.'

The major domo flung open the double doors into the Countess's salon and announced, 'The Earl of Lydford, milady.'

As the doors closed behind them and Nicholas strode forward, Cassandra shrank back against the gilded panels, wishing she could melt into them and vanish.

The Dowager Countess was seated on a bergere armchair, a white Persian cat on her lap and a most becoming lace cap on her dark curls. From the drift of paper at her feet and the gilded chocolate cup at her side, it was evident her Ladyship had been engaged in perusing her morning's correspondence when the news of her son's unexpected arrival had been brought to her.

'Nicholas! Darling!' She extended both hands in greeting, the heavy lace on her morning gown falling back to reveal smooth white arms. The movement sent the cat jumping to the floor, its plumy tail waving in irritation.

'Mama!' Nicholas stooped to kiss her on both cheeks, then stepped back to regard her. 'You look even more ravishing than the last time I saw you, how do you manage it?'

'I do, don't I,' she riposted with a twinkle in her

dark eyes, so like her son's. 'I was stifling in London with those boring matrons with their boring little daughters. No conversation, no intrigue. . .and the fashions!' She shrugged delicately, 'What could I do? Your uncle needed me—at least, so I told him.'

She regarded her tall son shrewdly, and Cassandra saw the sharp intelligence behind the coquettish pose. 'Sit down, Nicholas, and tell me why I have the unexpected pleasure of your company. I am, of course, delighted to see you, but why are you not in Florence admiring the frescoes, as my reckoning tells me you should be?'

There was a silence while Nicholas took his time settling in a chair. He crossed one long, booted leg over the other and brushed an invisible speck of dust from the knee of his breeches.

'It's a long story, Mama. . .'

Cassandra held her breath, catching her lower lip between her teeth with the tension of the moment. Unnoticed, the white cat stalked over to where she stood and showed its displeasure at being neglected by sinking its claws into her stockinged ankle.

Cassandra let out a shriek of pain and clutched her leg. Lady Lydford's sharp gaze moved rapidly from her son's face to the slight figure by the door, apparently noticing it for the first time.

'You! Boy! Come here and stop provoking my cat.' The summons was sharp. Lady Lydford had obviously sensed her son's reticence and was becoming suspicious.

Cassandra obeyed, limping over until she stood directly in front of her godmother. She waited, eyes cast down, fingers twisting in the cord of her cloak.

'Take off that cloak,' Lady Lydford ordered

quietly. Swallowing hard, Cassandra let it drop and stood revealed in breeches, waistcoat and shirtsleeves.

'Lydford,' the Dowager began frostily, after one comprehensive look at the shivering figure, 'what leads you to believe that bringing your *fille de joie* into the Ambassador's Residence — into my rooms — is acceptable behaviour?' Her small figure seemed to grow by degrees as indignation filled her. 'In what way did I fail in your upbringing that you believed I would be complaisant? Or did you merely assume my eyesight was failing?'

'Mama, this is not a *fille de joie*,' he said firmly.

'Godmama,' Cassandra interjected, falling on her knees beside the outraged Lady Lydford, her cheeks burning with mortification. 'He hasn't. . .I mean. . .I'm not. . .' Her voice faltered, she was so overcome with nerves and emotion.

'Cassandra?' Lady Lydford uttered in a voice of rising incredulity. 'Can it really be you? Here? Dressed like this?' There was real anger in her eyes as she turned to confront her son. 'Lydford, what is the meaning of this. . .outrage!'

'Godmama, don't blame Nicholas. It is not his fault.' Cassandra pleaded.

'Hold your tongue, Cassandra,' Nicholas commanded brusquely. 'Mother, this is not how it looks. Can we all sit down and I will explain everything: it is a long story.'

There was a long, considering pause, before his mother replied evenly, 'Very well.' Thankfully, Cassandra sank into a bergere armchair next to Nicholas. Beside her, she heard him draw a deep breath, but his voice was steady when he began the tale of their adventure.

'Seven weeks ago Cassandra came to the London house seeking you. It was a foolish thing to do, but when I tell you that her father was coercing her to marry Lord Offley, you will see what desperate straits she was in.'

'Offley!' The Dowager shuddered. 'He must be mad: that man is no suitable bridegroom for a gently reared young girl.'

'Exactly. Cassandra was desperate and lacking all female friends, she had no one to turn to but yourself.'

'I disguised myself as a boy and took the stage to London. It never once occurred to me you might not be at home,' Cassandra burst out, lifting her hot face to her godmother's cool scrutiny.

'My poor child.' Lady Lydford reached out and gently touched the soft cheek. 'What a terrible position to find yourself in.' Her tender tone became barbed. 'And, of course, my intelligent and resourceful son could find no better way to settle the crisis than to drag you across Europe dressed like that?'

'It seemed like a good idea at the time,' Nicholas said firmly. 'At first I was going to leave her with the housekeeper: then Aunt Augusta turned up and my valet broke his leg.'

'Oh, stop rambling Lydford! What has my sister to do with your valet breaking his leg?' She broke off and regarded him through narrowed eyes. 'Did you say *seven weeks* ago? Am I to understand that for all that time you have had this child in your company, unchaperoned and dressed like this?'

'It seems like seven years, I have to confess, Mama!' He flashed a teasing smile at Cassandra as she glared indignantly at him. 'But when we got to Paris. . .'

'Paris! Why were you in Paris?'

'I thought you were still there. I was going to leave Cassandra with you and continue my Grand Tour. . .'

'As if nothing had happened, I suppose,' his mother finished drily. 'There are moments when you remind me so much of your dear father. *If* you had troubled to read my last two letters to you, you would have been aware of your Uncle Marcus's posting to Vienna, and my intention to accompany him. But in any case, it does not take over a month to travel from Paris to Vienna.' Her dark brows rose interrogatively.

'We went via Lyons, Nice and Venice,' Nicholas admitted.

'And then there was the accident on the Rhône and the footpads on the coast road,' Cassandra added helpfully.

A delicate shudder passed through the Dowager's frame. 'I think we will save the detail for later. Nicholas—go away. I am quite out of patience with you. And remember: you have no valet and you have not seen my god-daughter for ten years. I don't want to see you until dinner. Cassandra, stay with me.'

After the door had closed behind Nicholas, Cassandra turned imploringly to Lady Lydford, 'Please don't blame Nicholas, Godmama, he had little choice.'

'Nonsense,' the Dowager responded robustly. 'I

can think of at least two perfectly sensible courses of action.' Then she smiled. 'So like his dear father, so impetuous.' She drew Cassandra down to sit beside her. 'I suppose he took off without a thought to the practicalities of the situation. You have been travelling as his valet, I apprehend: that would necessitate a degree of intimacy I assume?'

Cassandra blushed fiery red remembering the kiss in Paris, sleeping in his arms in Nice, the heat of his passion in Venice. 'We had to share a bedchamber on occasion — but Nicholas was always, I mean, he never. . .there was always a screen around my bed.'

'And nobody penetrated your disguise?' Lady Lydford's eyebrows rose in surprise. 'For myself, I knew as soon as I saw you that you were no boy.'

'Peacock, your butler knows. And after I fell in the Rhône, and nearly drowned, the keeper of the inn — a French gentlewoman — she knew my secret. And in Venice, the major domo of the *palazzo* where we stayed: he knew, but he assumed we were. . .' She couldn't complete the sentence under that critical gaze.

'Quite. But, of course, no such thought entered either of your heads.'

'Of course not!' Cassandra protested, trusting her averted gaze would be mistaken for modest shock, not a guilty conscience.

'And you would have me believe that my short-tempered, self-centred, pleasure-seeking son remained equable and considerate throughout this escapade? You have had a thoroughly pleasant time in his company?'

'He was frequently very angry with me. I talk too much, you see, and I wanted to see the sights, and I answer back too much for a valet. But I did enjoy it — apart from the fleas, and nearly being drowned, and when I thought Nicholas was dead and I had to shoot the footpad.'

The Dowager rolled her eyes upwards. 'You have your dear mama's spirit, I see. Tell me no more now, that is all behind you. As for your being here, I think I can see how we may contrive to account for your sudden appearance. But, for now, we must get you out of those clothes before anyone in the household sees you. And you need a bath.'

The Dowager rang for her dresser, explained the situation to that formidable female in a few well chosen words and sent Cassandra off in her charge to bathe and rest. As she glanced back at the door, she saw her Godmama deep in thought, her firm little chin sunk in one palm, the merest frown shadowing her brow.

That evening Cassandra sat in the window seat in her room in the wing of the Embassy occupied by Sir Marcus Camberley and his sister. The street below was bustling with the fashionable life of the city. Society was making its way to dinner parties and soirées before the curtain went up in the theatres and opera houses for which Vienna was famed.

If only she had her boy's clothes again, she could have slipped out and joined the throng in the City of Music. But her godmother had ordered them removed and, Cassandra strongly suspected, burned.

It was strange how, now she had achieved the long-desired sanctuary and her tale was told, she was not as elated as she had expected. True, the worry that her godmother was going to send her packing back to her father had proved unfounded. She should be thankful, but surprisingly she was not: the freedom and independence she had enjoyed for the past two months were now at an end. Once more she would have to conform to the strictures of Society which ruled and regulated the existence of every well-bred unmarried girl.

And her closeness to Nicholas, to the man she loved, would be the first sacrifice she'd have to make. He would become as remote as any other gentleman to her: this was the price she must pay for her reputation. Already she was realising what a high price that was. Over those past few weeks they had been closer than many a married couple in so many ways.

There was a tightness that was almost pain around her heart at the thought that she would never share that closeness again, see his quick grin as they shared a secret jest, feel his warm skin beneath her fingertips, burn to the pressure of his lips on hers. Now he was in Vienna, he would soon forget her. Godmama would see to it that he was introduced to all the right people: his sense of duty would do the rest.

The scene outside blurred as unshed tears gathered at the back of her eyes and she was rubbing them angrily when the door opened and her god-mama swept in, followed by a petite, sombrely dressed woman of middle years.

'Araminta, my goddaughter, Cassandra Weston. Cassandra, Miss Araminta Fox, my cousin.'

Cassandra got up hastily and bobbed a curtsey, stumbling slightly over her unaccustomed skirts.

Miss Fox held out a well-tended hand and nodded gravely, 'Miss Weston, I am very pleased to make your acquaintance.'

Cassandra glanced at her godmother, uncertain how much this lady knew of her predicament.

'Araminta is the only person in whom I have confided,' Lady Lydford remarked, gesturing to them to seat themselves. 'She has been lately acting as companion and housekeeper to her brother, the Bishop of Arundel, but following his recent marriage, she finds herself free to travel and I invited her to join me. It is our great good fortune that she arrived, unexpectedly early, two days ago.'

Miss Fox took up the tale. 'And as I was feeling rather indisposed after the journey, I have not been out into Society. For all anyone knows, you and I arrived together yesterday, having travelled in each others' company from England.'

'After all,' Lady Lydford finished triumphantly, 'who could be a more respectable chaperone than the sister of a bishop, and my own cousin?'

'But how could you have known of my predicament?' Cassandra felt slightly breathless. This upright spinster seemed to be entering into a scandalous intrigue with all the evident enjoyment of an actress!

'Why, I am sure you would have been in correspondence with me, Cassandra,' Lady Lydford said carefully. 'We would have been exchanging letters for some time, and as soon as I heard of Lord Offley's disgusting pretentions, I enlisted the aid of my trusted cousin.'

'Of course, even in the Bishop's Palace, we had heard whisperings of Lord Offley's reputation. Rest assured that had I heard of your predicament, I would have done all in my power to assist you, so no-one would doubt the truth of this story for a moment.'

Cassandra's brain whirled at the facility these two respectable ladies were showing for intrigue. 'But would no one have met us on our journey?' she enquired dazedly.

'Certainly not,' Miss Fox rejoined stoutly. 'My brother always insists I travel in a private carriage and stay in only the most select inns, avoiding English tourists.'

Cassandra could not doubt it. 'How will all this be explained, though? Surely it is not a tale we can recount openly?'

'Indeed not,' her godmother agreed. 'Leave that to me and to gossip. Tomorrow morning, the dress-maker and hairdresser will call. In the afternoon, I will hold a small tea party for a few select friends.'

'Only those of the utmost discretion, my dear Sophia!' said Miss Fox, with a wicked twinkle.

'But, of course,' her cousin assured her with mock gravity, 'I am counting upon it.'

Cassandra closed her eyes and leaned her slightly aching head back on the cushions. How could she have doubted her godmama for an instant?

'Sophia, my dear, this is a most select and mysteri-ous gathering you have invited me to!' Through the hinge-crack in the painted Chinese screen, Cassandra could see the Ambassador's wife settling herself by the fireside. 'I am quite agog—you have precisely the air of mischief you had about you when you were engaged in one of your pranks at Miss Lucas's Academy.'

'My dear Dorothea, that was quite thirty years ago — and just as I did then, I rely upon you now for your support and good sense, just as I do with Araminta.'

'But tell me the secret. . .' She broke off as the major domo flung open the double doors into the salon and announced,

'Lady Hartley.'

The Naval Attache's wife, resplendent in purple, swept into the room, greeting her hostess warmly. Cassandra felt confused, as she was followed rapidly by a group of four ladies of similar age and bearing, all equally agog to hear the reason for this intriguing summons.

Cassandra took advantage of the noise of greetings and the rustle of silk gowns to seat herself more comfortably in her hiding place. Godmama had suggested she observe the beginning of the tea party to ensure their stories matched. It would also be far less intimidating to meet these influential ladies, all pillars of the English community in Vienna, after observing them for a while without being observed herself.

Once the introductions to Miss Fox had been made and the tea tray brought in, Lady Lydford cut across the individual murmurs of conversation. 'Ladies, I have to confess I have asked you here with an ulterior motive.'

'We suspected as much.' The oldest lady present, Mrs Spencer, wagged her folded fan in a knowing way. 'Your note contained such a hint of mystery I immediately cancelled an engagement at a picnic.'

'You may have been surprised that my cousin, Miss Fox, has not been out in Society since her arrival last week.'

'We assumed you were indisposed by the journey, my dear Miss Fox,' the Ambassador's wife remarked. 'Personally, I am always prostrated by the shortest journey: you are quite a heroine to set forth on such an arduous journey alone.'

'Ah, but I was not alone,' said Araminta primly, looking down at her hands folded in her lap.

There was a moment's silence, but Cassandra could almost feel the suppressed excitement in the high-ceilinged salon. Now, they were thinking, now we come to the scandal.

'Some of you may be acquainted with Lord Offley, or at least know of his reputation,' Lady Lydford dropped the words quietly into the silence. The result was as if she had said 'Fox!' to a flock of hens.

'*Lord Offley!*' exclaimed Lady Hartley in awful tones. 'That libertine rake! What connexion has he with you, Miss Fox?'

'Absolutely none, I am glad to say,' Miss Fox responded roundly, her back becoming, if possible, even more stiff. 'At the Bishop's Palace, however, we are not unaware of the opprobrium which attaches to that individual: I hesitate to call him a gentleman.'

'And knowing of that reputation, my sweet cousin did not hesitate to come to my aid when I apprised her of the crisis.' Lady Lydford paused, and gestured towards Mrs Spencer's cup. 'A little more tea? Or perhaps a macaroon?'

Cassandra marvelled at the skilful orchestration of the group: the ladies were hanging on every word, tea cups quite forgotten as they anticipated an awful revelation.

'No, no, thank you, Lady Lydford, I have quite sufficient.' Mrs Spencer could bear it not longer, 'What crisis?'

The Dowager put her own cup down on the piecrust table beside her with deliberate care, and leaned forward in a confiding manner. Like marionettes on strings, the assembled ladies leaned forward, too.

'I have a goddaughter,' she began, low-voiced. 'She is just eighteen, and has spent her entire life on her father's estate in Hertfordshire, quite secluded. The poor child is motherless; her father, I must tell you, is a scholar of most eccentric habits.'

Knowing looks passed between the ladies at this point, and behind her screen, Cassandra smiled at this masterful understatement.

'Contemplating matrimony on his own behalf, her father has contracted her in marriage to Lord Offley.' Ignoring the sharp intake of breath around the tea table, Lady Lydford pressed on. 'This sweet child, who is not yet out, and who knows nothing of the ways of the world, is, as you may have guessed, a considerable heiress.'

Heads nodded. 'Nothing short of a fortune would tempt *that man* to forsake his bachelorhood for a respectable marriage,' Lady Hartley opined. 'Why, I heard the other day that he had formed a connexion with *both* daughters of a wealthy cit and was found. . .' At this point her voice dropped to a whisper, and strain as she might, Cassandra could hear nothing but the gasps and exclamations of horror which swept the little group.

'Exactly so,' remarked Miss Fox, leaning back once more in her chair. 'You may readily understand, dear ladies, why, when I received a letter from Sophie telling me of her goddaughter's predicament and entreating my aid, I lent myself to a scheme that under other circumstances, I would not have countenanced.'

The ladies could hardly contain their excitement at these horrid revelations. Lady Lydford inflamed them further by saying in a voice of quivering intensity, 'I know, dear friends, that I may rely on you all for the utmost discretion and support.'

There was a chorus of murmured assent around the little circle, and she continued. 'I arranged for Cassandra to slip away — with her maid, of course — and meet my cousin in London. From there, they set forth on their journey to Vienna for my goddaughter to seek sanctuary at my side.'

'And not a mile too far from the influence of such a man!' added the Ambassador's wife. Seeing the most influential lady present had endorsed the plan, the others lost no time in adding their voices in support.

'But are you certain she was not seen on her journey? What if he has hastened after her?' enquired Mrs Spencer, anxiously.

'I am quite certain,' said Miss Fox, straight-faced, 'that she was not seen in my company on the journey.'

Cassandra smiled wryly at the skill of the two

ladies in manipulating the conversation. Miss Fox's
obvious utter respectability and Lady Lydford's
scandalous revelations combined to make a most
titillating tea party.

'Now Cassandra is off his hands, her father will
not concern himself further with her. I intend to
bring her out myself, and, of course, present her at
Court when we return to London — once mourning
for Princess Charlotte is over.'

'A large fortune, you said?' ventured one of the
ladies, as if it were a mere detail.

Lady Lydford tilted the heavy teapot on its stand
and replenished a cup. 'Oh, more than respectable,'
she rejoined, equally casually.

Watching through the gap in the screen,
Cassandra admired her godmother's skilled manipu-
lation of her audience, then found her admiration
replaced by a small frisson of apprehension. If Lady
Lydford was as intelligent as she appeared, it was
going to be very difficult to keep secrets from her.
How could she hide the way she felt for Nicholas
from his mother?

She was jerked out of her brown study by Miss
Fox enquiring if she should fetch Miss Weston from
her room.

'If you would be so kind, Araminta.' Lady Lydford
turned to her guests. 'I am sure our friends will be
sensible of a young girl's feelings and not allude, in
any way, to the distressing circumstances. . .'

Cassandra picked up her skirts and tiptoed out of
the door behind the screen. She found Miss Fox
waiting for her at the head of the grand staircase
which swept up in a double curve from the ballroom.

'Could you hear all that passed?' Miss Fox

enquired, pausing to tease out one of Cassandra's newly dressed curls high on her forehead. 'You look quite charming, my dear,' she added, nodding with aprobation at the high-waisted, high-necked sprigged muslin gown. 'Just arrange your shawl a little lower on your arms. There, that should have given the old pussies time to smooth down their fur before your appearance.'

Seeing Cassandra's look of astonishment at her frankness, she added drily, 'If you had spent as many hours in the company of clerical wives as I have, my dear, you, too, would be an expert on gossiping middle-aged ladies!'

Cassandra's heart was thumping uncomfortably by the time she was ushered into the salon by Miss Fox, and she felt her colour rise under the scrutiny of the assembled ladies.

Her embarrassment and the effort of remembering not to stride in her unaccustomed skirts kept her almost tongue-tied as the presentations were made, and she sank down gratefully at her godmother's side and accepted a cup of tea.

'. . .from Ware in Hertfordshire, ma'am,' she was replying to the Naval Attache's wife, while trying not to listen to Mrs Spencer whispering to her neighbour.

'Such a pretty child, and quite nice style.'

She caught her godmother's eye and received a small nod of approval, which gave her the courage to respond quietly and calmly to the unexceptionable questions the ladies were asking her.

She was just asking her godmother's permission to join a party driving into the country the next day, when the major domo announced, 'The Earl of Lydford, my lady.'

Cassandra knew the blood had been driven from her cheeks by Nicholas's unexpected arrival, but fortunately the ladies were far more interested in the eligible Earl of Lydford than in her reaction to him.

He stood just inside the room, self-assured and extremely handsome in a coat of deep blue broadcloth, his long legs encased in a pair of white trousers which Cassandra knew were new. His waistcoat was pale yellow silk with a broad grey stripe that she had helped him choose in Lyons, and at his throat, the snowy folds of his cravat were impeccable.

He strolled across to bend over his mother's hand, calmly ignoring the frigid glint in her eye. 'Mama, if I had any inkling you were entertaining so many charming ladies, I would have hurried home sooner.' He began to bow to the ladies in turn. 'Mrs Spencer, it must be at least two years since I had the pleasure; Lady Hartley, I trust I find you in good health. Miss Fox, I was sorry to miss you at breakfast. I must admit to rising late after yesterday's journey.'

Cassandra watched him making his rounds of the room, leaving the ladies flushed and fluttering in his wake. His technique, she realised, was to make each and every one of them believe that were it not for the inconvenient existence of their husbands, he would be slain by their charms.

'Mountebank!' she hissed at him as, finally, he stopped before her, eyes twinkling and bent low over her hand.

'At last, Miss Weston! Or may I call you Cassandra, for we are as good as cousins? Last time we met, I was in a ditch rescuing your puppy, was I not?'

'Up a tree, and it was my kitten,' Cassandra replied tightly.

'Of course, it was. May I sit here?' Not receiving a reply, he sat down anyway, accepting a cup of tea from his mother while assiduously avoiding her eye. 'Even at the tender age of fifteen, I was your devoted slave.' Nicholas gave her a sudden grin which made her heart lurch.

'So far from being my slave,' she rejoined with spirit, 'you did nothing but pull my pigtails and twit me about my freckles!'

The ladies laughed approvingly at these childish reminiscences, but Lady Lydford cut in hastily. 'Enough of this, Nicholas, you must not tease Cassandra! You forget, she is no longer a child of eight.'

'There is no danger of that, Mama,' he said smoothly, turning his attention to Miss Fox as the colour rose hectically in Cassandra's cheek.

The infuriating man! Cassandra set down her cup with a sharp click, and schooled her face so as not to scowl. What game was he playing? He had obviously not been expected at this afternoon's tea party, that much was obvious from Lady Lydford's mien, however well she covered up her irritation.

But if she thought Nicholas had done with his sparring, she was mistaken. 'Another macaroon, Cassandra?' He offered her the plate with a warm smile.

'Thank you, no,' Cassandra replied coolly, trying

to think of a safe, neutral topic of conversation. Finding none, she lapsed into silence.

'Forgive me,' he said in a slightly lowered voice. 'My teasing has discommoded you.'

'Not at all, my lord.' She was pleased at the indifference in her tone. 'I am sure you were only humouring me, for you think of me as a child — one who was an inconvenient brat in the past, perhaps?'

'My dear Cassandra, now you are threatening to discommode *me*!' She had certainly succeeding in disturbing some of his air of assurance; there was a glint in his eye that was not all amusement, and one finger tapped the arm of the sofa.

'Oh, no, my lord!' Cassandra protested sweetly. 'Why, I declare nothing could discommode you — not raging torrents, nor foreign footpads.'

'Touché, Cassandra,' he whispered. 'Changing from breeches into skirts has done nothing to improve your temperament.'

Their secret squabble was interrupted by the Ambassador's wife rising to her feet, apparently a signal to the lesser ladies to take their leave, also.

In the flurry of goodbyes, Cassandra received several promises of future invitations. Lady Hartley said that her daughters would be charmed to take her about with them. 'I expect you, Lydford, will have many calls on your time,' she remarked archly as he bowed her out.

As soon as the door closed behind the last guest he collapsed gracefully into a chair, legs stretched out on the carpet. 'Mother, I congratulate you. A more worthy collection of influential gabblemongers you would be hard put to meet anywhere. And if I recollect, only Lady Hartley has daughters to dispose of.'

'You are out of touch, Nicholas. The elder is betrothed to Sommerson, and the younger is the reigning beauty in Vienna. She has no need to fear competition.' Lady Lydford dismissed the Marriage Mart and turned to her son in renewed irritation. 'What were you about, Lydford? You nearly ruined my entire strategy, arriving like that. Why, you might have put Cassandra completely out of countenance with your foolery.'

Nicholas snorted inelegantly. 'Ha! Nothing puts Cassandra out of countenance, as I have found to my cost these last seven weeks. Why, if someone particularly disturbs her, she takes a pistol to them.'

Stung, Cassandra protested. 'Nicholas, that isn't fair! I thought he had killed you!' Her throat tightened with hurt. 'I didn't *want* to shoot anybody.'

'Lydford!' his mother began, but Nicholas had already jumped to his feet and taken one of Cassandra's hands in his.

'I'm sorry Cassie, that was unworthy of me. You were wonderful.'

Time seemed to stand still as she let her hand rest in his, and their eyes locked and held. Then Lady Lydford cleared her throat, and the moment was gone, but not before the Dowager had seen Cassandra's face, and the suspicion which had been growing all day, crystallised in her mind.

CHAPTER TWELVE

'CASSANDRA!' Miss Fox hissed in reproof.

Hastily Cassandra roused herself from her day-dream and resignedly waited for the criticism that was surely to follow. She glanced down to check that her skirts were modestly arranged and that her satin slippers were still on the picnic rug and not on the springy woodland turf.

But no doubt Miss Fox was about to point out — as she had been doing all week — that Cassandra had once more committed some error of deportment or etiquette.

'The chicken leg,' Miss Fox continued, low-voiced. 'Do not gnaw it!'

She was not aware she had been: but weeks of pretending to be a boy, staying in wayside inns where daintiness would have betrayed her, had made settling back to being a demure young lady extremely difficult. Her sheltered homelife was no help, either. Cassandra soon discovered she had absolutely no talent for social small talk. Papa believed one should only open one's mouth when one had something worth saying, and gossip about gowns, affaires of the heart and the weather were outside her experience.

Sighing, she dropped the well-nibbled bones back on her plate, and dutifully turned her attention to the conversation of the other two young ladies sharing the rug with her and Miss Fox.

Lady Hartley had been as good as her word, and had arranged this picnic outing to the woods to introduce Cassandra to her daughters' circle of female friends. The elder daughter, Charlotte, secure in her new status as affianced bride, was holding court to a little gaggle of confidantes, all agog to hear of her bride clothes and wedding plans.

Lucy, the younger and more beautiful, caught Cassandra's eye and giggled. The two girls next to Cassandra had filled the past twenty minutes with an impassioned discussion on the relative merits of smocked or ruched edgings for a new gown, and Cassandra smiled ruefully back at Lucy.

'Will you not walk a while, Miss Weston?' Lucy called, already getting gracefully to her feet.

With hardly a glance at Miss Fox for permission, Cassandra scrambled to her feet, managing not to catch her toe in her hem as she was wont to do, and joined her new friend.

'May I call you Cassandra?' Miss Hartley asked. She slipped her hand through Cassandra's arm, as they gained the gravel path encircling the ornamental lake, which made this such a popular picnic spot.

'I wish you would,' Cassandra confessed frankly. 'I find all this formality rather daunting.'

'And you must call me Lucy.' They strolled on in companionable silence for a few minutes, then, when they paused to admire some ornamental waterfowl, Lucy continued, 'I believe Miss Fox said you have not been much in Society? That you have lived quietly in the country with your father? I do envy you. We scarce see anything of dear Papa these days, he is always so engrossed in diplomatic affairs.'

Cassandra smiled wryly. 'It certainly affords the opportunity to study the character of one's parent,' she said ambiguously.

'Indeed, it must.' Lucy took the comment at face value. 'I understand he is quite a noted Classical scholar? And you yourself, I think, are quite an accomplished student.'

Oh, dear. Cassandra groaned inwardly. That would be another black mark from Miss Fox, who had impressed on her vigorously the absolute necessity of avoiding the label of 'blue stocking'.

'It would quite ruin your chances if the gentlemen thought you *scholarly*,' she had said forcefully. 'Your little. . .' Miss Fox paused with a shudder, '. . .jest last night about the relative characters of Napoleon and Julius Caesar, while no doubt very clever, is precisely the thing to avoid.'

'Oh, no,' Cassandra denied hastily. 'I'm no scholar, although I can read some Greek and Latin. It does make it more interesting when one visits antique sites.'

'You have travelled then?'

'No. . .not yet, but I hope to, if Godmama is so kind.' Every conversation was fraught with traps! Cassandra was finding guarding her tongue every second very tiresome, even with someone as pleasant as Lucy.

'I do think your Godmama splendid,' Lucy said enthusiastically. 'I am so looking forward to her party tomorrow evening.' She paused, and added, not quite casually enough, 'Is the Earl intending to be there?'

'I presume so, I scarcely see him,' Cassandra admitted truthfully. It was almost as if he were avoiding her: but that was silly. After all, he had his own life to lead, why should he concern himself with a debutante his mother happened to be launching into Society? Everything was different now—she was hardly the Cassie with whom he had shared those weeks on the road. By the time Godmama and Miss Fox had finished with her, she'd be just another insipid young lady!

'Oh,' Lucy appeared disappointed. 'I was looking forward to renewing my acquaintance with him— we all were,' she added rather quickly.

'He has been out a great deal meeting his friends since he arrived. And I belive he has been seeing his tailor.' And, no doubt, attending the Opera and ballet and less reputable entertainments! Cassandra stifled the thought of opera dancers and actresses, and added, 'And, of course, Godmama has been taking me about so much to visit and to the *modiste*. I hardly see Ni. . .the Earl.'

'He is a very fine man, is he not,' said Lucy, quite failing to sound uninterested. 'So handsome, so well-dressed.'

'And so eligible,' Cassandra finished, rather drily. Thinking about Nicholas and actresses was doing nothing to improve her frayed nerves.

'Indeed, yes!' Miss Hartley's blue eyes were sparkling. Cassandra looked at the piquant little face and the artlessly arranged ash blonde curls and wondered just how well Nicholas knew her. What was it like to be fragile and dainty and so beautiful it took men's breath away? To be fair, she had to admit that Lucy seemed quite unaffected by her own loveliness, quite unconscious of the effect she produced.

Combined with her friendly charm and lively wit, Cassandra could quite understand why Lucy was the reigning beauty. And if Nicholas was a good catch, then so, too, was the well-connected, well-dowered Miss Hartley. Perhaps Godmama and Lady Hartley were even now planning to bring them together.

It was a painful thought, but not quite as difficult to face as the thought of Nicholas allied with one of the silly peahens they had left behind in the glade just now.

'Nicholas!' Lady Lydford fixed her only son with a cold eye as he strolled into the dining-room the next evening. 'Where do you think you are going in those clothes?'

Startled, the Earl glanced down at his irreproachably tailored trousers and evening coat and replied simply, 'Out — why?'

There was a slight pause while he took his seat and the soup was served. Across the polished expanse of walnut, Cassandra caught her godmother's eye and raised her own brows in response.

'You cannot have forgotten that tonight is the party I am giving for Cassandra. Why are you not wearing knee breeches?'

Nicholas put down his spoon. 'Oh, lord, I had forgotten. I'm engaged to play cards with Morton this evening.'

'Send a note: you can go on later.' His mother was crisp. 'I want you here to greet our guests. It is very important that you are here to lend Cassandra your support at her first soirée.'

'I'm sorry, Cass,' he began. 'Of course, I'll be there. . .'

'Don't call her Cass!' his mother wailed despairingly. 'How will I ever get her launched successfully if you don't watch your tongue?'

Cassandra and Nicholas ate lamb cutlets in attentive silence, while Lady Lydford rehearsed the guest list. It appeared to her goddaughter that the guests had been chosen with two purposes in mind: to launch her, certainly, but also to introduce Nicholas to as many eligible young women as possible. And, of course, he already knew Miss Lucy Hartley. . .

At the end of the meal, Nicholas vanished to change into satin knee breeches and evening coat. Cassandra, too, went up to her room for her abigail to tidy her hair and adjust her dress.

Godmama had decreed that a cream voile dress was entirely suitable for a first party dress. Looking in the long pier glass Cassandra had to agree it made the most of her rather unconventional looks.

With her chestnut hair and brows, debutante white would have looked insipid while the modestly scooped neck and high waist made the most of her height and slight figure.

In the hands of a skilful hairdresser, Cassandra's boyish curls had been transformed into a modish crop set off by a simple tiara and Godmama had presented her with a pair of simple pearl drop earrings.

'My dear, you look simply charming,' Godmama said from the doorway. In her hands she was carrying a pair of kid evening gloves. 'Here you are, Cassandra, let me help you with the buttons.'

Cassandra smoothed on her first pair of grown up evening gloves with a shiver of almost sensual pleasure at the smoothness of the fine leather. Then the pleasure turned to apprehension at the daunting thought of being the centre of attention at her first real party.

'Don't worry, Cassandra.' Godmama tipped up her chin very gently and looked into the intelligent, troubled dark eyes. 'I'll be there, and so will Nicholas.' She made no comment at the sudden flush that tinged Cassandra's cheeks and added, 'I know this week has been a difficult one for you, but you are quite ready to go into Society now. Forget your worries and enjoy tonight.'

An hour later, Cassandra realised, to her own amazement, that she was having fun. She had bobbed curtseys to all the formidable chaperones and heard many of them complimenting her to her godmother. Their charges were all girls she had already met, and suddenly small talk and chatter came easily.

It was exciting to meet so many pleasant young men, and flattering to observe their open admiration, as they competed to fill her dance card. Lady Lydford had engaged a string quartet to play country dances and had invited enough young people to make up twenty couples, but as she had said to Cassandra, 'No waltzes, we will save those for your ball.'

Godmama had opened up the Large Salon for the dancing, and arranged for card tables in the library for the older guests. As the dowagers soon became engrossed in their whist, the younger party were able to enjoy themselves without the close supervision of their elders.

Even so, Cassandra knew she must not dance more than two dances with any one gentleman, and was laughingly resisting the blandishments of Christopher Hartley to join him in just one more set, when Nicholas strode over.

'My dance, I think, Miss Weston.' The smile he bestowed on Mr Hartley was perfectly pleasant, but the young man hastily relinquished all claims and retreated.

'Nicholas!' she protested as they took their places in the set. 'This isn't your dance and you were very short with Mr Hartley.'

'Well, you shouldn't flirt,' he said with no sign of teasing.

'I wasn't.' Cassandra said, as they joined hands and parted again.

'You'd danced with him twice already.'

'There's nothing wrong with that, and I wasn't going to dance with him again. I was telling him so when you interrupted.' It was very difficult having a satisfactory quarrel in the middle of a country dance. 'And in any case, why are you counting? You're not my chaperone!'

The music was ending with a scrape of violins and Cassandra dropped a cursory curtsey, raising her eyes, sparkling with indignation, to meet his.

There was an expression on his face she could not recognise. Despite all the moods she had seen in Nicholas over the past weeks, she had never experienced this one. 'Are you cross with me?' she hazarded, her indignation overtaken by puzzlement.

He seemed about to reply when Lord Stewart appeared by her side, claiming the next dance as his. 'Sorry, Lydford,' he said heartlessly, 'the lady's mine!'

Lord Stewart, against whose frivolous high spirits

she had been warned by Miss Fox, proved to be a thoroughly entertaining partner. He was witty and amusing and his flirtatious sallies, while quite unthreatening, were flattering in the extreme. Cassandra found herself laughing up at him, completely captivated by his easy charm.

Lady Lydford emerged from the card room to find her son, arms folded, glowering at the sight of her laughing goddaughter.

'Ah, Nicholas! There you are. Doesn't Cassandra look charming this evening? And young Stewart is obviously captivated. You know,' she said, lowering her voice and leaning towards him confidingly, 'I have great hopes of that particular connexion. He might be only the second son, but his grand-uncle left him his entire fortune and Sir Marcus speaks very highly of him for the Foreign Office.'

Nicholas snorted inelegantly. 'Popinjay!'

'Nonsense, dear, he is merely high spirited. I think they look charmingly together. Oh, see now,' she added, apparently unheeding of the effect this conversation was having on her son, 'he's making Cassandra blush!'

Nicholas did not reply immediately, but followed the couple's progess with his eyes. 'I would have a care, Mama,' he said eventually, turning to face her. 'I would not place too many hopes on securing Stewart: he has a reputation as an accomplished flirt.'

'Like you, Nicholas, dear?'

'Just like me, Mama! And it is just as futile for you to strew my path with all these hopeful young ladies. Now I must join Morton's party.' He bowed gratefully over his mother's hand and left, unaware that Cassandra's eyes followed him from the room.

They were not the only eyes that followed the tall, lithe figure. Cassandra saw Lucy Hartley's concentration falter momentarily before she danced on. Well, that was one consolation. Nicholas might, for some reason she didn't understand, be out of charity with her, but he had paid her more attention than he had any of the other young ladies present.

She recognised a small flame of hope and ruthlessly suppressed it. Nicholas was not for her, she had to resign herself to that. But, enjoy the company of other men as she might, it was Nicholas she loved and wanted — and always would.

'May I escort you to supper?' Lord Stewart was at her side.

'Yes, please.' Cassandra rewarded him with a smile and allowed herself to be led away. A breaking heart was no excuse for bad manners, she told herself firmly.

The next morning, Cassandra came across the jewelled snake necklace coiled at the bottom of a drawer. She stared at it, suddenly cold, remembering Venice, remembering how close she had come to betraying both herself and her love for Nicholas.

It was too dangerous to keep; both for itself and for the memories it evoked. And if she found a respectable jeweller and sold it, she would have a little money of her own for emergencies. Cassandra slipped the jewel into her reticule and went downstairs thoughtfully.

She had the breakfast room to herself. Godmama, as usual, was partaking of chocolate and sweet rolls in her room and Miss Fox, according to the butler, had gone out for a walk.

'And Lord Lydford?' Cassandra enquired casually, toying with a little thin ham.

'He was up early this morning, Miss. He went out about eight o'clock, intending to ride.'

The butler bowed himself out. Left alone, Cassandra regarded the breakfast table. The ham was excellent. She helped herself to another slice and buttered some bread. She sipped her coffee and contemplated Nicholas's puzzling behaviour. What had put him so out of sorts? He had acted like an elder brother, and a particularly proprietorial one at that.

She was still musing when the door opened and the object of her thoughts strode in, banging it shut behind him. He was looking pale and fatigued and thoroughly out of temper at finding the breakfast room occupied.

'Coffee, Nicholas?' Cassandra enquired sweetly.

'Thank you,' he replied curtly, jerking the chair opposite her away from the table and slouching in it, long booted legs thrust out.

'Have you had a nice ride?' Now she had him alone, perhaps she could provoke him into revealing what was wrong.

'Not particularly,' Nicholas was obviously disinclined for conversation. He took the proffered cup and unfolded a newspaper with an irritable snap.

'I didn't realise you read German,' Cassandra remarked, peering across at the heavy Gothic script.

'I don't. I was merely trying to indicate — tactfully, I thought — that I would prefer to eat my breakfast in peace and quiet.'

'Well, have some ham, then,' she suggested help-fully. 'You know you're always irritable in the morning until you've had something to eat.'

There was a deadly silence while Nicholas low-ered the paper and regarded her with hard green eyes. 'I suggest you watch your tongue, Cassandra. My mood early in the morning should be quite outside your experience — do not forget our acquaintance is supposed to be of a week's duration. Mama can scheme to her heart's content, but it will all come to nothing if you cannot curb your prattle.'

Cassandra counted up to ten in Greek beneath her breath, very slowly. 'It is excellent ham,' she said out loud.

'Damn the ham!' he exploded, jumping up from the chair, which fell back on the polished boards with a clatter.

'Nicholas!' Cassandra assumed an expression of outrage. 'You should not use such language in front of me — it is most improper.' She knew she was goading him, but here he could not threaten to send her packing back to her father, or put her over his knee as he had in Venice.

'Why, I must congratulate Mama on the transform-ation she has wrought,' he said slowly, his face hardening as he eyed the slim figure in the demure sprigged muslin gown. 'No-one would recognise Cass the valet now — or a certain young lady in a Paris bedroom.'

Cassandra gasped, the flush rising hectically to her face. How could he remind her of that! She was half on her feet when he rounded the table and sat on the edge, so close she was forced to sit down again. He seemed to tower over her.

'That wasn't fair,' she said in a voice that shook, and not only with indigation.

'If you want me to forget those weeks we spent together, Cassandra, you must stop invoking the memories,' he said, in a reasonable voice that still retained the hard edge of anger. 'Now you want to be treated like a young lady. You want insipid compliments and well-turned phrases. You want nice safe flirtations and gestures from your pack of young admirers. Like this.'

He picked up her hand in his. Her fingers felt suddenly cold against the enveloping warmth of his, still slightly roughened from the reins. He bent his head and brushed the briefest of touches across her knuckles, then surrendered her hand with a flourish.

'Well, Miss Weston? Will that suffice? It will have to, won't it? One step out of line, one indication of your impetuous nature, and the carefully woven illusion is shattered.'

'Oh, no, my lord,' Cassandra countered furiously. 'Lord Stewart, to take but one example, is considerably more ardent in his attentions. And, I may say, he is considerably more gallant than you; he says my natural high spirits are charming!'

'Stewart will never make you a declaration,' he said contemptuously. 'It is known he is hanging out for a wife with good connexions.'

'I know that; I am not as gullible as you seem to think. Don't forget, Nicholas, I have just spent seven weeks in the company of just such another gentleman! But Lord Stewart is witty and he is fun to be with — two qualities you are singularly lacking this morning!'

She stood up, galvanised by irritation and found

herself standing so close to him her face was almost touching his neckcloth. The familiar scent of him, his warmth, filled her nostrils and seemed to take all power of movement from her.

The room was very still, the only sounds were of Nicholas's breathing, and the steady tick of the clock echoing her own heartbeat. Cassandra stood, fighting the urge to wrap her arms around him, bury her face in his chest and never let him go.

Nicholas did not move, and slowly she raised her head to look at him. He was regarding her steadily with hooded eyes, the trace of a smile touching his lips. 'It is very unfair, Cassandra,' he said softly, 'but well-bred young ladies can't expect to have fun.'

He kissed her then, before she had a chance to move her face away. The kiss echoed his voice, cool and sardonic, devoid of emotion or passion, but none the less thorough for that.

Cassandra jerked away angrily, face aflame. 'How dare you! I did nothing to warrant such behaviour from you! And you have the effrontery to warn me against Lord Stewart. . .why you. . .' She stuttered to a halt, lost for words.

Nicholas stood up quite calmly. 'But that is my point, Cassandra. Lord Stewart is *exactly* like me: and if you behave as recklessly with him, you may expect the same response—but considerably less discretion.'

Cassandra swung away from him, trying to hide the tears that welled in her eyes. Goading him had worked only too well: he was saying things she didn't want to hear, things that hurt because she loved him. 'Oh, damn it, Cassie, I didn't mean to make you cry!' There was an exasperated tenderness in his voice that made her heart thump. 'Come here.' Nicholas pulled her into the comfort of his arms, in an embrace so different from what had just passed between them, he could have been a different man.

'I'm not crying,' she protested unconvincingly.

'Then you obviously have something in your eye,' he said, humouring her. 'Have you a handkerchief?'

He was already reaching for her reticule as she stammered, 'No!'

He pulled the protruding corner of white linen. With horrible inevitability, the snake necklace uncoiled itself and lay gleaming in a shaft of sunlight.

Her sharp intake of breath was the only sound in the room as Nicholas stooped and picked up the jewel, letting it run between his fingers.

'How did you. . .' he began slowly, then as he looked at her betraying face, realisation dawned. 'It was you! You connived with that wh. . .' He bit back the word, his fingers white on the metal coils. 'Why, Cassandra? To get back at me because I had been angry with you? It must have seemed very amusing to humiliate me.'

'I didn't mean to. . .' she began.

'To let it go so far?' he queried dangerously. 'I am sure you didn't! I hadn't thought you would be so spiteful.' He looked at her through narrowed eyes, recollection blazing. 'Nor would I have suspected you capable of such seductive wiles.'

Cassandra felt the fiery blush rising as she recalled just how willingly her body had answered his. His face changed, hardened. 'What a fool I've been, worrying about your chastity all those weeks, when you knew full well how to rouse a man. Where did you practice, Miss Weston?' he sneered. 'With your father's ploughboys? Or the stableboy who was so willing to lend you his clothes?' If he had struck her, the shock could not have been greater. She expected—deserved—his anger. His contempt burned like acid. But how could she tell him that her responses had been instinctive, driven by her love for him? He would think it a lie, a subterfuge to extricate herself.

'Still no excuses? No convenient story to account for it? No, I suppose even your fertile imagination baulks at explaining this away.' The necklace swung from his fingers, mocking her.

'Nicholas. . .I. . .'

'No more, Cassandra,' he said icily.

The necklace moved in the sunlight, stabbing her eyes. 'Here.' He held it out. 'Take your whore's device. You can always sell it. Or you may have need of it again.' He smiled humourlessly at her. 'Why, I almost find it in me to feel sorry for Lord Stewart.'

Cassandra snatched it from his hand and ran from the room. At the foot of the stairs she paused. Her heart thudded and she felt sick with the force of Nicholas's attack. Yet she could not cry.

Fortunately, no one was about. She needed fresh air, to get away from these enclosed, silent rooms, the corrosion of Nicholas's contempt. On an impulse, she tugged the bell-pull in her room and summoned her maid.

Five minutes later, in bonnet and pelisse, Maria dutifully at her heels, Cassandra was strolling heedlessly down one of the wide promenades, in company with a throng of fashionably dressed people. She soon found herself in the Prat, which Godmama had mentioned to her as being an unexceptionable place to walk.

As she walked, she brooded on Nicholas's reaction. She could not blame him for his anger, nor for the conclusions he had drawn from her behaviour. At that moment, if the pavements of the Prat had opened and swallowed her, she would have been grateful for it. But she had to think about it: she would have to face him again, behave as if nothing had happened, knowing that every time he looked at her, he would recall her body quivering against his.

With her maid silent beside her, Cassandra walked on, deep in thought. After a while, Maria, who had been wondering what could have upset her mistress so, noticed that the set, frozen look relaxed and a touch of colour came back into Cassandra's cheeks.

Lucia's words at that first meeting in Venice had returned to her; Lucia saying that, if Nicholas had been indifferent, he wouldn't become so angry with her. Anyone would have condemned her for her behaviour — she condemned herself — but would someone who was uncaring have reacted so bitterly, have thrown such wild and wounding accusations at her?

And if he cared for her, that explained his actions last night, and his bad temper this morning: he was jealous of the attention shown her by other men. The thought was so startling, Cassandra halted in her tracks, causing Maria to trip over the edge of her pelisse.

When she thought of him with other women, it made her feel hurt and angry — and thoroughly unreasonable. Could it be that seeing Cassandra as the centre of attention, especially from his friend Stewart, was arousing jealousy in Nicholas? But he couldn't be in love with her, or surely he would have said something. . .

Cassandra wandered on, her frown of concentration making her look fierce enough to discourage the young bucks, who were out to ogle the passing young ladies.

Perhaps he hadn't realised how he felt. In novels, so she had heard, men were notoriously slow in recognising a dawning *tendresse* for the heroine. Well, if he hadn't realised, she would make him! There was no point in flirting with the younger men; Nicholas had already dismissed them as puppies. But Lord Stewart was different. His mild attentions last night had already roused Nicholas to a display of bad temper. . .if she really tried to attach Stewart, there was no knowing what he would do.

Cassandra had a momentary qualm about toying with Lord Stewart's affections, then concluded that if he were dangling after a well-connected wife, she was hardly likely to break his heart. She turned on her heel and began to walk home. If challenged now, all Nicholas would admit to was a brotherly desire to keep her out of the clutches of a well-known roué. It was up to her to make him see things differently.

That afternoon, she sat in the Blue Salon with her godmother, writing out the gold-edged invitations, while Lady Lydford reviewed the prospective guests for the ball she intended to give in honour of her goddaughter's come-out.

'I suppose I must invite Regina Cooper and that bracket-faced daughter of hers.' She paused, adding, 'I always wished for a daughter, my dear. I *am* enjoying this!'

Cassandra smiled at her. 'I fear I am very expensive, Godmama!'

'Fiddlesticks, child. I love the excuse to spend money on clothes, and I am enjoying your company. Your mind is as sharp as your mother's, and I have missed my dearest friend.' She gave herself a little shake. 'I shall be getting sentimental, and we must press on with this list. A week is short notice, but I doubt if we will be short of company.'

The pile of invitations grew steadily. Cassandra had just paused to sharpen the point of her quill when the butler announced, 'Miss Hartley, Miss Lucy Hartley, my lady.'

'Charlotte, Lucy. . .what a pleasure. You will stay for tea? Hector, the tea tray in twenty minutes.'

'We have come with a note from Mama and to thank you for the party last night,' Charlotte said. 'Are you sure we are not interrupting?'

'Not at all, sit down, both of you, and I will tell you my plans for Cassandra's coming-out ball.'

The ladies were cosily involved in a discussion of the relative merits of a string ensemble or a military band for the music, when the butler reappeared, with the tea tray and the announcement, 'Lord Stewart, my lady.'

Even Miss Hartley, newly affianced as she was, paused to pat a curl into place. Lord Stewart entered with his customary ease, despite the handicap of two large bouquets, which he presented to his hostess and Cassandra.

'With thanks for an enchanting evening, ma'am,' he swept a bow to the Dowager. 'And the enchanting company,' he added, with a warm glance at Cassandra.

She accepted the flowers with blushing confusion, not entirely unaware of the envy she was arousing in Miss Lucy's breast. Lord Stewart cut a magnificent figure with his slim, blond elegance and the faint military air which still hung about him, although he had resigned his commission the previous year.

As he sat down beside her, crossing one elegantly booted leg over the other, Cassandra reflected that if one's heart wasn't given to an infuriating, green-eyed, bad tempered Earl, one could very easily fall under the spell of this man.

Lord Stewart soon had the ladies' attention with his amusing description of the antics of his eccentric Austrian valet. He had just accepted a second cup of tea when he saw a small ink spot on Cassandra's hand and broke off to tease her about the dangers of working too hard.

It could not have been better contrived, Cassandra reflected afterwards, that Lord Stewart had taken her hand to examine the mark, just as Nicholas came into the Blue Salon. Lord Stewart retained her hand while he nodded amiably to his friend, but Cassandra laughingly withdrew her fingers.

'Tea, Nicholas?' his mother asked, as he took the seat between the two Misses Hartley.

Really, there couldn't be a better opportunity to put her plan into operation, Cassandra thought, turning with a brilliant smile to Lord Stewart. 'Do you ride much in Vienna, my lord?'

Five minutes later, while she was laughingly accepting his offer to take her riding and to lend her a horse, she risked a glance under her lashes at Nicholas.

Charlotte Hartley was deep in discussion of bride clothes with Lady Lydford, leaving Miss Lucy to Nicholas's undivided attention. Charming in peach muslin, which showed off to perfection her rounded figure and delicately flushed complexion, she was all attention as Nicholas chatted easily to her.

He was showing no interest whatsoever in Lord Stewart's attentions to Cassandra, and swallowing her chagrin, she had to admit Miss Lucy was enough to distract any man. And, of course, he must have known her in London.

It would be easier if she could dislike the young woman, but Lucy's good nature and bright intelligence had endeared her to Cassandra very quickly. She saw Lady Lydford watching the couple with an indulgent smile touching her lips, and her heart sank. Lucy Hartley, well-bred, well-behaved and exceedingly well-dowered, was every mama's dream for her son.

Beside her, Lord Stewart was describing delightful rides in the Viennese countryside and she responded with every appearance of interest, while inside her heart felt like lead. She must have been insane to have deluded herself that Nicholas felt anything for her. His behaviour last night was simply that of a rather over zealous cousin, concerned to protect the reputation of an inexperienced girl.

And his anger this morning, she thought miserably, stemmed from the discovery of her wanton behaviour, her apparent spiteful desire for revenge.

'Lydford, why do we not make up a riding party tomorrow, if the weather is good, and take the ladies to see that wonderful view you get from the western hills? Miss Hartley, Miss Lucy, would you accompany us?'

Lady Lydford added her approbation of the scheme, and suggested Miss Fox as a chaperone.

'Splendid idea, Stewart,' Nicholas agreed. 'But if I may suggest, rather than all go on horseback, it would be an excellent opportunity to give you that driving lesson I have been promising you, Miss Lucy. Come now, say you will.' His voice was warmly persuasive and Miss Lucy showed no inclination to resist.

'If mama permits,' she dimpled prettily, 'I would love to — if you think me strong enough to control your horses.'

'Don't be afraid, I'll be there all the time,' Nicholas assured her.

Cassandra ungritted her teeth with an effort: the mental picture of Miss Lucy in a dashing riding habit with the Earl's strong hands enveloping her tiny gloved ones on the reins was too much to bear.

'Unfortunately, I do not possess a riding habit,' Cassandra said tightly.

'Oh, what a pity,' Nicholas replied carelessly. 'Never mind, I expect you and Stewart can join us on another occasion.'

'Nonsense, she can borrow my habit,' Lady

Lydford said cheerfully, as the young ladies rose to make their farewells.

When their guests had left, the Dowager regarded her son and goddaughter with complacency. 'Well, what a splendid afternoon we have had. Almost all the invitations are written, Nicholas—and did you see the lovely flowers Lord Stewart brought Cassandra?'

'Very handsome,' he remarked lightly. 'Perhaps I have misjudged him. Should I enquire what his intentions are towards Cassandra, Mama?'

'A little premature, I think, but I will not deny I have hopes. Now, don't blush so, Cassandra, you seem to have quite a partiality for his lordship.'

Having effectively rendered her goddaughter speechless, she turned once more to her son. 'And as for you, Nicholas, I really am most pleased with you, I have had great hopes of your finding a suitable wife in Vienna. Miss Lucy Hartley would be ideal.'

'I will do my best not to disappoint you, Mama,' he said smoothly, opening the door to allow the Dowager to leave.

'Nicholas. . .'

He turned to Cassandra, his eyes as hard as emeralds and held up a hand. 'No, don't say anything. I have no wish to cause my mother pain, so I have decided we will say no more about Venice or what happened this morning. As far as I am concerned, the subject is closed.' The door closed behind him with the thud of finality.

CHAPTER THIRTEEN

THE Embassy ballroom blazed with light from the hundreds of candles fixed in branched wall sconces, and the great chandeliers hanging at intervals down its length. It had taken a team of workmen most of the week to lower them, polish each lustre, and hoist the great weight up again.

At the far end, chairs and music stands were being set out for the orchestra and beyond that, the double doors stood open into the long drawing-room, where supper would be set out. The Ambassador had granted permission to use the Embassy plate, as well as the ballroom and his servants, and the overall effect, Cassandra thought, was as grand as a palace.

She had slipped in on her way down to dinner for a last look at the flower arrangements she had been helping with all afternoon, and had stopped in amazement at the transformation. With the dust covers removed, the lights ablaze, and watering cans and flowerstems tidied away, the room was magical.

'It looks very fine,' said the Ambassador behind her, causing her to jump. 'I'm sorry, my dear, didn't mean to startle you.'

Cassandra bobbed a quick curtsey. 'Not at all, sir, and I must thank you for letting Godmama have the ballroom and all the servants this evening. It must have put you to a great deal of inconvenience.'

The Ambassador, a man normally unmoved by

the rather vapid charms of most debutantes, found himself smiling paternally down at this one. A taking young woman, he thought. Not conventionally pretty, but handsome, with a lively mind. She seemed to him an interesting mix of innocence and common sense, and he detected an intriguing whiff of mystery about her.

He was, by profession, too discreet to ask questions, but he pinched her cheek and told her she was looking 'very pretty, indeed.' He consulted his pocket watch, then offered her his arm. 'Time to be gathering for dinner. Will you do me the honour?'

Sweeping into the reception room on the Ambassador's arm, to be presented to the minor royal who was the guest of honour, Cassandra had to pinch herself to bring her feet back to earth. Could it truly only be ten weeks ago that she had climbed out of her bedroom window and down the apple tree to escape Lord Offley?

Never, in her wildest imaginings, had she dreamed of a night such as this, held just for her. Whatever happened in the future, whatever became of her and Nicholas, tonight would be a special memory to treasure always.

Having made her curtsey without a stumble, and exchanged stilted conversation with the somewhat plain Grand Duchess, Cassandra thanked the Ambassador and slipped away to join her godmother.

'Come and stand quietly with me, child,' Lady Lydford said kindly. 'Let me look at you.'

Her gown, her first ever silk gown, was not in white or pink like most of the debutantes, but a deep cream, trimmed with old lace around the deeply flounced hem. The bodice and tiny puffed sleeves were smocked and caught with gold knots and the high waist caught with a broad golden ribbon which matched the tiara in her hair.

Godmama's hairdresser had pomaded her chestnut curls until they gleamed and clustered around her head and, as a finishing touch, Godmama had given her a pair of gold drop earrings.

Cassandra pointed one toe to admire her new satin slippers, then smiled at her godmother who smiled back. 'You look a picture, my dear. Every man at the ball will fall in love with you!'

Cassandra was laughing off the compliment when Nicholas arrived, impeccable in knee breeches and swallow tail coat, a filigree holder of dark yellow roses in his hand. She had scarcely seen him during the last week, since the outing to the western hills with Lord Stewart and the Hartley sisters.

He had been cold, distantly polite, but she would not let herself give up hope that his behaviour proved that he cared for her. Looking at him critically, she thought he looked pale, and his face, handsome as ever, showed signs of strain.

Having kissed his mother, he turned to Cassandra with a slight bow. For one wild moment, she believed he was about to offer her the roses, they went so perfectly with her gown.

'Nicholas. . .how lovely!' she began impetuously, stepping forward, smiling, her hand already outstretched to take the flowers.

He raised a brow in apparent surprise, took the proffered hand and bowed over it, kissing the air a good half inch above her fingers. Then he turned and made his way across the salon to where Lucy

Hartley stood. She blushed prettily as Nicholas bowed over her hand and presented the flowers.

Cassandra stood cringing with embarrassment, convinced everyone in the room had witnessed the rebuff. Then the butler came in to announce that her ladyship was served.

The ball might be her come-out, but as a very junior debutante, Cassandra found herself seated well down the table, between the Ambassador's nephew and someone's aide de camp. Neither of them seemed greatly inclined to conversation, allowing Cassandra ample opportunity to watch Nicholas.

He was seated next to the Grand Duchess, nodding gravely at appropriate moments in the conversation she was dividing between him and Sir Marcus. He appeared to be managing Royalty with aplomb, but the Grand Duchess had neither the charm nor the looks to engage his total concentration.

Their eyes met as he glanced down the long polished table, and without thinking Cassandra gave him a small, conspiratorial smile. To her joy he returned it, suddenly the old Nicholas again, sharing a secret joke in some wayside inn. Then he turned back to his duty, leaving Cassandra glowing with an unexpected hope.

It was almost half past ten when the dinner party made its way through to the glittering ballroom. Cassandra took her place between Godmama and Sir Marcus at the head of the sweeping double staircase, and the next hour passed in a blur of compliments, bobbed curtseys and unfamiliar faces. Sir Marcus's diplomatic connexions and Lady Lydford's social circle had combined to produce a dazzling assembly of notabilities. Lady Lydford intended to make this ball the talking point of the Season, and already she recognised, with satisfaction, the heady buzz of a truly successful occasion.

When the receiving line thinned to a trickle, Lady Lydford dismissed Cassandra. 'Off you go into the ballroom now, child; dance with your beaux!' She looked at her goddaughter with pleasure, 'Enjoy yourself.'

Cassandra stepped into the ballroom with some trepidation: it seemed so full of unknown faces as the mass of dancers passed by in a swirl of coloured silks, a confusion of dress uniforms, and the dark elegance of male evening attire.

Then the music stopped and as couples came back to the gilt seats around the walls, she began to recognise faces. Soon she was the centre of a cluster of eager young male admirers, all clamouring for a place on her dance card. Laughing, she pencilled in names, trying to save space for Nicholas.

Surely he would come and ask her to dance soon? Surely that shared, secret smile meant something? She was clutching at straws, but to give up would break her heart. Cassandra looked around, hoping to see him, but could only catch a glimpse of the back of his head, bent to listen to a group of young ladies across the room.

'Dare I hope you are looking for me?' Lord Stewart was at her side, having displaced, with no apparent effort, a number of less effective young men.

Cassandra, her heart already engaged, was able to admire him dispassionately and realise that she was an object of considerable envy by many of the

debutantes present. Anthony, Lord Stewart, was as
blond as Nicholas was dark and nearly as tall. He
carried himself with a careless elegance that drew
the eye to the sombre magnificence of his evening
attire, moulding the breadth of his shoulders and
the length of his well-muscled legs.

The arrangement of dark Palma violets in a
filigree holder his messenger had brought earlier
was a perfect complement to the cream of her gown
and Cassandra thanked him warmly, holding the
fragrant posy up to her nose to inhale the rich scent.
Across the room, she saw Nicholas watching the
little scene. He gave a slightly mocking bow, as if in
reference to his jibe that she was trying to ensnare
Lord Stewart.

Cassandra allowed herself to be swept into the
next dance by Lord Stewart. Perhaps her wild plan,
that she might pique Nicholas into recognising feelings for her he would not admit to, could yet
succeed.

As they passed Nicholas and his partner on the
floor Cassandra was laughingly protesting, 'But
Lord Stewart, I could not possibly call you Anthony!
That would be most improper. . .'.

For a moment, she thought Nicholas was going to
ignore the provocation, then as she glanced out of
the corner of her eye, he bent towards her and
whispered in her ear, 'Minx!' Before she could make
a rejoinder to this almost affectionate scold, the
movement of the dance separated the two couples
again.

'Can I hope you will be remaining in Vienna for
the whole Season?' Anthony Stewart enquired, as

he escorted her back to her seat against the cream and gold pilasters.

'I am entirely at Godmama's disposal,' Cassandra responded demurely. 'Do you intend to remain here, too, my lord? I felt sure I had heard Nicholas say you intended to leave next week.'

'So I did,' he responded easily. 'But then Fate took a hand, and I find my plans changed.' The look he gave her was warm and full of meaning.

'How inconvenient for you,' Cassandra murmured, as she sat down and unfurled her fan.

'May I?' He sat beside her taking the fan from her hand and began to wave it gently to and fro. 'I do not find it particularly inconvenient: perhaps you can guess why?'

This was going too fast for Cassandra. If he were in earnest — and he was too accomplished a flirt for her to tell — she could not risk wounding his feelings. Loving Nicholas as she did, it would be dishonourable to accept any other gentleman's suit without telling him why she could not return his regard. And, equally, she should not be encouraging a warm flirtation from a man such as this.

The young men of her own age were safe. They were too young yet to fix their interest and think of marriage, and a flirtation was safe and enjoyable for both parties. But Lord Stewart, like Nicholas, was too old and experienced to be taken lightly.

Flustered, she moved involuntarily and the heel of her slipper caught in the lace flounces at her hem with an audible rip.

'Oh, dear!' she exclaimed, twisting to look at the damage. 'I had better go and pin it up before it tears further. If you will excuse me, my lord?'

Some of the smaller rooms off the ballroom had been set aside for just such an emergency, and Cassandra slipped quickly through the throng, holding up her skirt carefully to avoid further damage. She remembered Godmama ordering one of the ladies' maids to remain in the smaller room with pin cushion and sal volatile to attend to whatever emergency might arise, and she pushed open the door, confidently expecting to find the woman in attendance.

A screen had been set just inside the door to afford privacy to the ladies and Cassandra was just about to slip round it when she heard voices.

Lucy Hartley was saying in a voice breathless with excitement, 'But, of course, I promise! I won't breathe a word!'

Blushing with confusion to have so nearly interrupted an intimate conversation—perhaps even a declaration—Cassandra was gathering up her skirts and preparing to back silently out when she was arrested by Lucy's next words.

'Oh, Nicholas, I am so happy!'

Cassandra felt as if her heart had stopped in her chest, and she reached out blindly to grip the door frame for support. Nicholas! Nicholas and Lucy Hartley! Her worst fears had come true. . .

But there was still hope, she realised dazedly. The man had not yet spoken. . . Nicholas was not an uncommon name. Perhaps it was another man and not her Nicholas.

Between the leaves of the screen was a narrow gap. Holding her breath, Cassandra put her eye to it just as Nicholas—her Nicholas—said, 'Lucy, you *are* a darling! What you tell me makes me so happy:

you cannot believe the torment I have been through.' Through the crack, all Cassandra could see was the dark head bent towards the blonde and Lucy's white arm coming up as she reached up to his shoulder to draw down his face to hers.

Cassandra choked down a shattering sob and backed away from the screen in desperate silence. To be discovered there, to have those two feel sorry for her, pity her, was a humiliation she could never tolerate.

Every foolish hope, every foolish dream she had ever harboured, that Nicholas could feel for her as she did for him, lay shattered at her feet. All that mattered now was to escape undetected, her dignity intact. Now he was engaged to another woman, he must never guess how she felt about him. No wonder he was unwilling to talk further about Venice! What did it matter to a man who was in love, and was loved in return, by a beautiful young debutante?

Cassandra found sanctuary in the retiring room next door and sat shivering with reaction, unheeding of the abigail who pinned up the torn flounce. I must have been mad, she thought, her thoughts chasing round like a rat in a cage. How could I have mistaken his careless kindness, his protective anger, even the fleeting moments of passion for love?

How am I going to get through the coming weeks of betrothal celebrations and wedding preparations? Lucy would expect her new friend to rejoice with her and share in her plans. But what alternative was there for her now? To throw herself at Lord Stewart's head? Cassandra sensed that if she gave him enough encouragement, he would declare himself. But she could not do that to him, she liked him too well to hurt him. And to marry him without love would be to dishonour both of them.

'Miss. . .miss. . .I've finished.' The maid had obviously been trying to attract her attention for some moments. Absently, Cassandra thanked the girl and stood up. Opposite, a mirror showed her her own reflection, her eyes glistening with tears she was determined not to shed tonight. She smoothed down the cool silk of her skirts, remembering the hope with which she had dressed, then straightened her shoulders, took a deep breath and opened the door.

The first person she encountered as she crossed the passage to the ballroom was the languid figure of the Comte de Courcelles. As she stood there, unable to believe her eyes, she saw first puzzlement, then dawning recognition cross his features.

For one desperate moment, she believed he had not recognised her, then he stepped forward with both hands outstretched. 'Can it be? *Mon Dieu*, what a transformation from Paris! Just as I suspected — Cass the valet makes a very beautiful young woman.'

It was useless to deny it: speculation and mischief lit up his face. 'Guy. . .what are you doing here, of all places?'

'Why, I have just arrived in Vienna and I make it my business to have an entreé to all the most interesting entertainments. And you,' he gestured to her finery, 'you look beautiful! What a change from fustian and breeches. What are you doing here?'

'Ssh! Say nothing about that! It is my come-out.'

Cassandra put her hand on his arm and drew him back into the ballroom. 'Lady Lydford is my godmama.'

'But, of course, I remember from our conversation in the library in Paris.' There was a pause. Cassandra was aware of his scrutiny. 'You are sad, little one. Why so, on your big night?'

'It is nothing I can talk about, and in any case, it is all my own silly fault.' She gave him a watery smile. 'You are kind, Guy, but there is nothing you can do to help.'

The Count shrugged, 'Perhaps it will seem better tomorrow. . .'

He broke off as Cassandra gasped at the sight of a beautiful woman waltzing past in the arms of a cavalry officer. 'But. . .that was Mariette!' The spiteful cardplayer from the Paris party was unmistakable. 'What is she doing here?'

'I made the mistake of offering her escort from Paris.' He shook his head. 'She is as sharp as a needle. . .'

Cassandra could see the woman's gaze riveted on them now. There was recognition and malicious speculation on her kittenish face. The look boded trouble.

'Ah, Miss Weston. We have missed you, I am quite pining away, I assure you!'

Anyone less in danger of pining away than Lord Stewart wold be hard to find, Cassandra reflected. She saw, with slight alarm, the steely glint in his eye as he glanced at Guy's hand resting over hers.

'Lord Stewart. . .that silly girl took such an age to do my hem. And on my way back I met the Count. . .' Her voice trailed away. How was she to explain her familiarity with the Frenchman when she supposedly had only just come out into Society?

'An old friend of the family,' Guy supplied easily. 'Guy de Montpensier, Comte de Courcelles, at your service, *monsieur*.'

'Lord Anthony Stewart.' The two exchanged formal bows. 'Miss Weston, I came to claim my dance — I am on your card, I believe?'

'I think not, my lord,' said Cassandra, composedly. 'I have already stood up with you twice, which some might think very forward. I dare not do so again.'

'Excellent,' the Count exclaimed. 'So that means this dance is free? Please do me the honour.'

It was a waltz. Although the Count had not been presented to her as an approved partner for this daring dance, Cassandra was beyond caring. Perhaps Godmama would not notice. . .

Guy encircled her waist lightly and as the music began asked, 'Is that the one who is breaking your heart?'

'No!' Cassandra was taken aback by his perspicacity. 'I mean, no-one. . .' Across the ballroom she saw Nicholas, his face suddenly arrested as he saw her dancing past with the Count.

'Nonsense! Do you expect me to believe that? Tell me who it is and I will run him through for you.'

Cassandra could not suppress a somewhat shaky giggle.

'That is better. Now, tell me how I can help you.'

Cassandra circled in his arms, her eyes fixed on the solitaire diamond in his cravat and wished she could pour out the story to him as easily as she had told the tale of her flight, that night in the library in Paris.

'Truly, Guy, no-one can help me.' She looked up into the sympathetic brown eyes and the attractive, ugly face. 'Not even you. I have been foolish, and it hurts, but I must live with that.'

As they left the dance floor, Anthony Stewart appeared at their side as if by magic.

'You may not feel able to dance with me, Miss Weston, but surely I may claim you for supper?' He extended his arm to her, with a challenging glance at Guy.

'But surely, Cassandra, you will not abandon an old friend on his first night in Vienna?' the Count pressed in his turn.

Cassandra looked from one to the other and felt herself wilting with the heat and tension. 'Gentlemen, you must both forgive me, but the heat. . .'

'My dear Miss Weston, allow me to take you to the terrace.' Guy saw her doubtful look and hastened to reassure her. 'Several of the chaperones are already out there, and some other parties have taken their supper outside.'

'That would be wonderful.' Suddenly the hectic colour and the noise of the ballroom on top of the shocks of the evening struck a discordant note; fresh air and the cool flagstones of the terrace would be soothing.

The Count propelled her gently towards the French windows. 'Out you go, *ma petite*, and we,' he cast a resigned look at Lord Stewart, who was obviously not going to give ground, 'will fetch you some supper and a little champagne.'

The cool air struck the heated skin at her breast

and forehead as Cassandra wandered slowly across the terrace to a pillared belvedere which stood empty, looking out across the gardens. She rested her brow against a fluted column for a moment and let her mind empty. Tomorrow she would have to think, to plan, but tonight that was beyond her.

'Oh, Nicholas. . .' she whispered against the cold stone.

'Cassandra.' His voice behind her came so prompt on her words, she thought for one mad moment she had conjured him up out of her imagination

'Nicholas?' She turned and saw him, unmistakably real, the moonlight striking dark lights from his hair. She knew she had gone pale, but he did not seem to notice.

'I thought I was never going to get you alone.' He took her by the elbow and steered her further into the shadows, his voice low and serious. 'I must speak to you.'

CHAPTER FOURTEEN

'No, NICHOLAS, you have said quite enough,' Cassandra began, certain he was about to confide the news of his betrothal to Lucy to her. She needed at least a night to compose herself to hear that news with anything like an appearance of complacency. She lifted her skirts and tried to brush past him.

'Wait, please hear me out.' He took her by the shoulders, holding her back against the pillar.

Cassandra shivered as the stone struck cold through the thin silk and instinctively Nicholas drew her closer to his warmth. 'Don't be frightened of me, Cassandra—I know I've been short tempered and difficult to be with. . .' He broke off, running one hand through his hair distractedly. 'No, damn it, I've been harsh and unfair. . .'

'I understand.' And she thought she did. He must have been on tenterhooks, worried that his suit with Lucy Hartley would not prosper. It was enough to make any man short tempered, and then to discover her deceit in Venice would have been the last straw.

Nicholas stroked the back of one hand lingeringly down her cheek. 'We have both behaved badly, there are things I regret. . .'

'There is no need. The regrets are all mine,' she said thinly.

'You don't seem to realise the position we find ourselves in. I had not intended to say anything of this to you tonight, but now that Guy and that little witch Mariette are here, everything is changed.'

'But why?' Cassandra was confused. 'He was so pleased to see me, he is our friend.'

'So he is, and an indiscreet mischief-maker when he chooses, although Guy's capacity for trouble is nothing as compared to Mariette's! She bears me a grudge. One word that they met you in Paris disguised as a boy, and you are hopelessly compromised. . .ruined.'

'But Guy wouldn't betray me,' she protested indignantly. 'And surely Mariette cannot be that wicked?'

'I cannot take the risk.' He broke off and regarded her with exasperation. 'This is not at all what I intended. Please, listen to me, Cassandra, and for once in your life, don't interrupt!'

Cassandra fell silent, watching his face in the moonlight. No doubt he was irritated that he had had to take time from his newly-betrothed to speak to her.

'What I am trying to say, Cassandra, is, will you marry me?'

Cassandra stared at him, lips parted in stunned amazement. When she could find words, she stammered, 'Marry? Me — marry you? But. . .Lucy. . .'

'So you know I've spoken to her? Don't worry, Cassandra, no-one else knows, and Lucy will understand, she is entirely in my confidence.'

'Understand!' What could he say, what could any honourable gentleman say, to explain why he was breaking an engagement only hours after making it?

'I will explain everything to her. But, Cassandra, never mind about Lucy, what is your answer?'

What could she answer to a man whose lunatic concept of honour would lead him to jilt one young lady in order to protect the reputation of another he did not love!

'I thought I had seen you at your worst, Nicholas!' She stepped free of his arms, drawing herself up, anger shaking every word. 'But I did not think I would live to be so insulted by you, or to see you behave so dishonourably!' Her fury burned away every tender feeling she had ever had for him. 'Now I see how you can behave. . .'

'Cassandra, you cannot have understood me. I repeat, I wish you to become my wife — why are you acting as if I had offered you a *carte blanche*?'

'Sir, I consider your behaviour as dishonourable as if you had asked me to become your mistress! Now, let me go!' She spat the last words at him and ran across the terrace, tears burning at the back of her throat.

She managed to evade Nicholas in the maze of small passages that led off the ballroom, but one pursuer found her as she threw herself onto a heap of cushions in the window seat of the small salon, and finally burst into tears.

Someone gathered her up; for a moment, she struggled, then she saw it was Guy, not Nicholas, and capitulated, sobbing bitterly into his shirt front.

He waited patiently until the tears subsided, then found her a handkerchief and sat her back in the cushions. 'Now, do not tell me there is nothing I can do to help. I can at least listen. Speak to me, Cassandra.' Once again she found herself pouring out her story to him.

When the whole sorry tale was told, Guy was

silent for several minutes. Cassandra sat staring blankly at a vase of flowers which swam in and out of focus before her tired eyes. Confiding everything to Guy had left her drained.

'Of course,' he said thoughtfully, 'if it were only myself involved, I would go to Nicholas and assure him my lips were sealed. But there is Mariette. . .if I appeal to her good nature — which does not exist — she will know there is a scandal to be made. Yet if I say nothing, we can still be certain she will make trouble. She has no love for Nicholas: he has repulsed her too often; what he said to you shows he is aware of that danger.'

He fell back into thought. His solution, when it came, was so startling, Cassandra was jerked back to reality with a vengeance.

'You could always marry me.'

Cassandra stared at him incredulously, scarcely able to credit what she had heard. 'What? You mean elope? Guy — you don't want to marry me, how would that help either of us?'

He shrugged insouciantly. 'I have been thinking lately that perhaps I should marry, settle down. Domesticity has its charms!' He smiled at her. 'It might suit both of us very well, but, of course, I do not press you if you are unwilling. *Naturellement*, you would stay with my housekeeper and I will stay at an inn, so you can feel quite comfortable. We will announce our engagement: there will be some talk, but with my reputation. . .*c'est le vie*. That will convince Nicholas that he is free to do the honourable thing by Miss Lucy. And if you decide afterwards you do not wish to marry me, we can quietly break off the engagement.'

Cassandra rubbed one hand across her eyes, wondering if she were asleep and dreaming. She could never marry him, as he was so light-heartedly suggesting, but he was right, this would offer her a breathing space. And, more importantly, it would force Nicholas's hand.

'Do not worry, *ma petite*. You can trust me, you know.'

'I don't doubt that for a moment,' Cassandra assured him. He may be a rake, but he was a gentleman.

'So why do you hesitate?' He shrugged, 'We are friends, are we not? After a good night's sleep, this will all seem simpler. Tomorrow is another day.'

Cassandra couldn't believe she was even considering his offer. 'Guy, I can't do it! What of your reputation?'

Guy laughed. 'It could only be enhanced by your company.'

'No,' Cassandra stood up. 'I am sorry, Guy, but I cannot accept your offer, it would not be fair of me, nor honourable.' She looked up and caught his wry smile. 'But we can still be friends — can't we? You are the only one I can talk to. . .'

'Ah, *ma petite*, of course. And I will not accept this as final — my offer still stands if you change your mind.'

'I must go and find Nicholas and make sure he says nothing to Lucy to break their engagment.' She shook her head in bewilderment. 'I do not know what he was thinking of, to behave so dishourably.'

'Do not judge him too harshly. He is worried about you and he did not take the time to think this thing through. I have a reputation as an *intrigant*, but he should know I would never risk the reputation of a lady.' He raised her hand to her lips, then gave her a gentle push towards the ballroom.

Godmama and Miss Fox were sitting, heads together, on a satin covered banquette just inside the door, talking animatedly. Cassandra paused to make sure they didn't see her as she slipped past and remark her reddened eyes, then was caught by what they were saying.

'My dear Sophia,' Miss Fox exclaimed, with unusual animation. 'I do congratulate you! What an excellent match, what a charming daughter-in-law she will make.'

'Well, I must admit to some anxiety, my dear Araminta. He seemed so slow to recognise what was perfectly plain to me — that he was in love with the girl. But men can be so dense!' For a few seconds, the two ladies contemplated the frailties of the male sex, then Lady Lydford added, 'It will be such a suitable match, she has the looks, the charm, the character, to make him happy. When he told me he was going to ask her this evening, I was overjoyed — I do wish he would come and tell me he has been accepted. Where *is* he?'

As the two ladies scanned the dance floor, Cassandra slipped past behind a column and began her own search. So he had told his mother about Lucy! It was even more important now to make sure he did nothing to break the betrothal.

She found him at last on the terrace, but to her horror, not alone. Lucy Hartley sat by his side, one hand confidingly on his sleeve while she listened intently to his words. It was impossible to hear what he was saying, but the effect was clear to see.

Lucy's expression changed from concentration to one of shock and dismay. Then she fumbled in her reticule and dabbed her eyes with a delicate handkerchief, her face averted from Nicholas.

Cassandra did not wait to see anything else. It was too late to stop him now, but if she was out of the way, already ruined by some other action, then there was nothing to stop him marrying Lucy. And if she acted now, quickly, before the broken engagement became a public scandal, perhaps the gentle Miss Hartley might forgive him and take him back.

Lucy was not the sort of person who would blurt out the news of her jilting in public — she would have too much pride and sense of decorum. Cassandra thought she had until tomorrow morning at most to put things right, but she must act now and find Guy.

He was where she had left him. One look at her face as she entered the room brought him to his feet, his hands outstretched to her.

'It's too late, Guy, he's already broken off the engagement.'

'*Sacre bleu!*' Guy swore. 'So, what do you want to do now, Cassandra?'

'I don't know, I just do not know,' she cried. 'Loving Nicholas as I do, I cannot allow him to ruin his life!'

'Then come away with me,' Guy urged. 'Whatever madness is possessing him at the moment, he is an honourable man. He cannot marry both of you: by coming with me, you free him for Lucy.'

Cassandra stopped her agitated pacing in front of him and stood looking deep into his eyes. She saw the concern there, and knew she could trust him, however madcap and unconventional he seemed.

'I'll do it,' she said resolutely. 'I'll come with you, Guy.'

CHAPTER FIFTEEN

Guy took her hand and squeezed it encouragingly. 'Don't worry, things will work out.' He sounded very light-hearted about the whole business, Cassandra thought. She only wished she could share his optimism.

'I will come with you. I love Nicholas: if I cannot marry him, I will marry no-one. For his sake, he must marry Lucy, and you are right. If I am apparently engaged to you, he will believe himself free of his obligation and can follow his heart.'

Guy glanced at the determined, intelligent face. 'What is it? You have had an idea?'

'Yes! As soon as Nicholas is convinced of our intentions and the marriage to Lucy is announced, I will throw myself on Miss Fox's mercy. She will find me an eligible situation.'

It sounded a neat solution, but she had an uneasy feeling that in reality, things would not fall out so easily. That did not matter now—the important thing was to convince Nicholas she had gone beyond his reach.

As she had come to expect, Guy raised none of the objections she was so uneasily aware of. 'Very well, then, it will be as you say.'

'We must think what to do now,' Cassandra said. Having made the momentous decision to flee with Guy, she now felt stronger. 'We must act quickly so Nicholas has a chance of retrieving matters with

Lucy—and I must leave a note for Godmama telling her I am going to marry you. She wishes Nicholas to marry Lucy, so she will do everything to promote the match.'

'Is there a room where you can write without being interrupted?'

'My room would be best,' Cassandra decided quickly. 'No-one would expect to find me there now. Come,' she took him by the hand and led him through the maze of passages to her deserted bedroom.

Once she had begun to write, the words came easily from her pen. She explained that she had met the Count in Paris and fallen in love and now they had met again and seized their chance of happiness. Godmama would be deeply shocked, and the thought pained her, but at least the Dowager would feel free to wash her hands of such an erring goddaughter.

She pressed a wafer over the folded paper to seal it and slipped quietly along to Lady Lydford's bedchamber. The bed was already turned down, ready for when the Dowager finally came to bed. Cassandra heard the chime of the little clock as she laid the letter on the lace-trimmed pillow. She hesitated for a moment beside the bed, hoping her godmother would forgive her.

Once she had gone with Guy, there would be no turning back, Nicholas would be lost to her forever. Then she remembered Lucy's white arms encircling his neck so lovingly, and hardened her resolution: he was already lost.

Four o'clock already. Soon the ball would be over, carriages were even now collecting weary revellers, and the street outside was growing noisy with the rumble of coachwheels and the cries of porters summoning coachmen.

Back in her chamber, Cassandra pulled a small valise from a cupboard. 'What shall I take?' she asked.

'I know nothing about the etiquette of elopement,' Guy said drily. 'Surprisingly, given my reputation, this is not something I have undertaken before, even in pretence.' He paused, consideringly. 'It must look convincing. . . Your hairbrush and so forth,' He dismissed feminine toiletries with a wave of his hand. 'And a gown suitable for travelling.'

'Shall I change now?'

'No. If you leave here in a day dress, it will be remarked upon by the servants. In a balldress with an evening cloak and the hood pulled over your face, you will be in no way remarkable.'

He was right. Cassandra, her heart in her mouth, slipped through the throng of guests, flushed and laughing as they waited in the hall for their carriages to arrive at the front doors. No-one noticed her small, cloaked figure as she followed the Count's broad back as he made his way out.

'I will not risk drawing attention by calling my carriage. Come,' he slipped his hand under her arm. 'We will go round to the mews and find it there.'

Minutes later, they were bowling down the wide boulevard away from the Embassy towards the house on the outskirts of the city which Guy had taken for his stay in Vienna.

Cassandra sat in the shadowed coach, stealing sideways glances at the man beside her. He was not conventionally good-looking; his nose was too prominent, his expression too quizzical and sardonic, his hair unruly despite his barber's best efforts. But his personality was so warm, his infectious enthusiasm so charming, that Cassandra felt she could trust him completely. And despite his devil-may-care reputation, she believed him when he said he would look after her.

Now the excitement of the actual escape was ebbing, she felt again the cold knot of misery in her stomach. She remembered Nicholas and their journey; the moments of tenderness, of passion, of joy and laughter. They could have been so happy together — friends as well as lovers.

She knew more about him than any respectable woman should. She knew he was bad tempered in the morning and that he did not snore. She was really most improperly acquainted with the Earl and his tastes. Despite her misery, a small snort of remembered amusement escaped her lips.

'Is that amusement or hysteria?' Guy asked wryly.

'Amusement, I think. No doubt I should be having hysterics, but I seem to have lost the capacity for vapours.'

'Believe me, Cassandra,' he said with feeling, 'I would never have carried you off if I thought you were prone to the vapours!'

The sound of the wheels changed as the carriage drew off the highway into a flagged courtyard. Guy helped Cassandra down and glanced up at his coachman. 'You have not seen this lady tonight, Jacques.'

'*Bien sur, monsieur.*' The man shook the reins and drove the team on round the corner of the house towards the stables.

A sleepy porter opened the door and was swiftly

dismissed with an order to send for the count's valet. 'You can sleep here,' Guy pushed open a bedchamber door. 'It is my room; if you need anything, I will be in the dressing room next door, changing into riding clothes. I will go to an inn tonight as soon as I have spoken to the housekeeper about you.'

'Yes, of course,' Cassandra said thankfully, looking at the bed. How wonderful just to climb in and sleep for hours, forget all that had happened tonight.

As soon as the door closed behind him, Cassandra peeled off her long gloves, tossed her reticule onto the bed and began, with difficulty, to unhook her dress.

Lady Lydford reached her bedroom at four thirty and sank gratefully into a chair as her dresser unfastened her jewellery, then knelt to unlace her shoe ribbons.

'Good heavens, Siddons, I am quite exhausted, I must be getting old.'

'Not you, my lady,' the dresser said comfortably. 'Did you enjoy your evening? I hear we may be expecting happy news in the household. . .'

Siddons had been with the Dowager for many years and, while discreet, was not above enjoying a little gossip with her mistress when they were alone.

'Well, I hope so, Siddons.' The Dowager stood to let the gown fall to her feet. 'But I haven't seen my son for hours—it is too bad of him to keep me in suspense. But then,' she added thoughtfully, 'I have not seen Miss Weston for some time either. It is most improper if they are off somewhere holding hands, but then, if they are engaged, I suppose there's no harm. Besides, I'm too weary to chase after young people at this time in the morning.'

'My lady.' Siddons turned from the bed, a puzzled expression on her face, a folded paper in her hand.

'What on earth?' Lady Lydford broke the seal and scanned the contents swiftly, with a sharp intake of breath. She read it a second time, more slowly, then snapped, 'My robe, quickly. And, Siddons, not a word of this to anyone, but Miss Weston has run away.'

As Siddons helped her mistress into her robe, she said quietly, 'With your permission, I will find Miss Weston's maid and tell her to say nothing. If anyone should ask we could say she is too exhausted after the ball to leave her room.'

Lady Lydford nodded her thanks and hurried out, her long skirts sweeping behind her. She flung her son's bedroom door open even as she knocked and, to her relief, found him, apparently just retiring.

'Mother! What is wrong?'

'Read this.' She thrust the letter into his hand and waited impatiently while he read it.

Nicholas swore, then pulled on his coat again. 'The little fool! I don't believe a word of this. Although why she. . .' He broke off with a taut smile for his mother. 'Don't worry, Mama, go to bed. I will bring her back.'

'But, Nicholas, whatever did you do to drive her away and into the arms of this Comte de Courcelles, or whatever his name is?'

'I don't know, but there is some misunderstanding here,' he said grimly. 'I will get precisely what I deserve if she does marry him. Try not to worry, she may be safer than you fear: Guy is not the reprobate he likes to be thought. Or perhaps I am comforting myself. . . But there is no time for speculation now. I will bring her back.'

As he strode to the door, the Countess called, 'But how will you find him?'

'He will have signed the Embassy guest book with his name and direction. I will start there. I cannot believe she intended this madness from the start, therefore they will have to make some preparation.'

He was gone before his mother could respond and it seemed only minutes later when she heard the sound of hooves on the cobbles as he cantered off into the night.

After a considerable time, Cassandra had finally managed to free herself from her ballgown and was perched on the edge of Guy's bed, unlacing her shoe ribbons.

She sat wriggling her aching toes, almost too weary to make the effort to roll into bed. Without warning, the quiet of the mansion was shattered by a thunderous knocking at the front door, and the sound of raised voices.

'Milord! Stop! You cannot. . .my master is not receiving.'

'The devil he's not! Stand aside.'

Heavy footsteps pounded up the stairs. Guy, in his shirt sleeves and breeches, flung open the dividing door from the dressing room.

'What is happening?'

'It's Nicholas!'

'*Mon Dieu!* Events are moving faster than I thought.' He strode over and put a protective arm around her shoulders as she sat on the bed. 'Your godmother must have found your letter at once. Your Nicholas, unless I am much mistaken, is out for my blood.'

'Oh, Guy,' Cassandra clutched his hand, terrified of what Nicholas would do when he found them like this. She was acutely aware of her bare legs and shoulders, of her flimsy petticoats and Guy's own half-dressed state.

The chamber door opened with almost maddening slowness to reveal the Earl of Lydford, his face taut with anger. Through her fears, Cassandra felt her heart surge with joy at the sight of him. He was here and, for whatever motive, it seemed he cared enough to come after her.

'A very touching scene,' Nicholas remarked, eyeing the pair of them as they sat on the edge of the bed.

'Nicholas — it's not what it seems. . .' Cassandra began.

'That I can well believe,' he retorted. 'I suggest you take your arms from around Miss Weston, Count. This farce has gone quite far enough.'

'I have no intention of leaving the side of my affianced wife,' Guy said, with some panache. 'Leave my house immediately, you are distressing Miss Weston.'

'If Miss Weston is distressed, it is entirely her own fault. Cassandra, put on some clothes and wait downstairs. I will come and take you home in a minute.'

'No! I won't leave Guy! You'll challenge him to a duel or something dreadful and one of you will be killed. . .'

'Probably me,' Guy muttered, *sotto voce*.

'Undoubtedly you,' Nicholas remarked. 'Cassandra, will you do what you're told?'

'I think perhaps the time has come to tell him the truth.' Guy got off the bed and moved with studied casualness to a position nearer the dressing room door.

'How can you suggest that?' Cassandra said reproachfully. 'You know why I can't.'

'One of you had better tell me, or I will have to extract the information some other way.' Nicholas leaned one shoulder against a massive armoire. 'And my patience is not unlimited.'

Cassandra felt herself go pale. She couldn't let Nicholas fight Guy, yet nor could she betray whatever hopes there were of his honourably marrying Lucy.

Guy, however, had other ideas. 'No, really, *mon ami*. You cannot be considering fisticuffs? This evening suit has suffered enough, what with being wept down. . .'

Nicholas grinned. 'You have my sympathy.'

'Oh, stop it! Stop it, both of you!' Cassandra could stand it no longer. 'This isn't a joke. Nicholas, Guy was only trying to help. I came away with him so you would be free. . .free to marry Lucy.' There was a surprising lack of response from Nicholas, but she stumbled on. 'How could you hurt her by jilting her when you love her so? I saw you together kissing. . .how could you make her cry like that?'

Nicholas straightened up slowly, his eyes on her face. She had all his attention now, and the tolerant amusement had vanished.

'What is this about Lucy Hartley? I can make

neither head nor tail of it. What has she to do with any of this? You can't have run away because the girl kissed me on the cheek, for heaven's sake! Why should I have to marry her?'

He seemed entirely sincere. Cassandra shook her head in confusion. 'But I overheard you in the retiring room. You were making a declaration, you made her promise not to tell anyone. And then you proposed to me out of some misplaced fear you have compromised me, and say Lucy will understand. No wonder she was in tears on the terrace.'

There was a long silence while Nicholas digested this outburst, then Guy said wearily, 'I confess I do not understand how you English manage to make simple matters of the heart into such dramas. It is a wonder any of you marry at all. And if you would stop regarding me with that sinister look in your eye, I will assure you that not one word of Miss Weston's escapades in Paris or here will ever cross my lips.'

Nicholas glanced at him. 'I will take your word for it. But why you felt it necessary to interfere, and why you had to descend on us with that minx Mariette in tow. . .'

'You've spoken to her?' Guy waved a hand. 'But surely you see, one word from her and Cassandra's reputation would be ashes.'

'Ah, but she now knows I can spoil her chances here in Vienna, just as effectively as she could damage Cassandra's good name. She will keep her mouth shut.'

Nicholas looked at Cassandra. There was an expression in his eyes she had never seen before, and when he spoke, it was as though he had forgotten Guy. 'Is this all true? That you fled because you thought I was proposing to you only out of a sense of duty — and for no other reason?'

She nodded dumbly.

Nicholas turned to Guy. 'You are decidedly *de trop*, my friend. Might I suggest you leave us?'

'With pleasure, Nicholas.' He slipped from the room, closing the door silently behind him.

'Now, let us be clear. On seeing Guy and Mariette, I am supposed to have decided to jilt Lucy, and offer for you, to save your reputation?'

Cassandra nodded. 'Well, didn't you?'

'No. What you overheard was me telling Lucy of my intention to propose — not to her, but to you, Cassandra. I wanted to propose to you tomorrow, when everything was quiet and we could be alone. Then, when I saw Guy and Mariette, I felt I had to establish your position at once, beyond any doubt. But I handled it badly, my love. I am not surprised you misunderstood.

'As for Lucy, knowing how close you had become over the last few weeks, I thought she might give me some clue as to how you would receive me. Lucy is a friendly soul, I've known her for years. People keep suggesting we should marry,' he added ironically, 'and perhaps we would have done. But neither of us truly loved each other that way, and mercifully, we are friends enough to admit it. What you saw was Lucy giving me her approval with a kiss. Then when I told her how coldly you had rejected me, she was upset: hence the tears.'

Cassandra stood staring at the man she loved, wondering at how this tangle had come about, then the import of what he had said dawned on her. 'You were going to propose to me, anyway? Before you saw Guy? But why?'

He moved slowly towards her, the tension easing slowly from his face to be replaced by a wry smile. 'Can't you guess, brat?'

'But you don't love me,' she said shakily. This couldn't be happening.

'Don't I?' He was very close to her now, but still he did not touch her. 'Oh, but I do, Miss Weston. I think I've loved you ever since you braved Aunt Augusta with that pile of shirts. I just didn't realise it.'

'But why not?' she whispered, looking up into the green eyes, too afraid to believe this could be true, and not a cruel joke.

'First of all, because I thought you were a child, and I felt thoroughly guilty about the way you made me feel.' His hand came up to cup her chin gently. 'And you made me feel so very. . .' He broke off at the blush staining her cheeks.

'And when I discovered the truth about your age, I was so confused by the responsibility I felt for you, and my regret at dragging you half way across Europe, and the sheer irritation you invoked in me every time I started to feel fond of you. . .'

'Ha!' Cassandra exclaimed, suddenly, miraculously, enjoying herself. It was all going to be all right: he loved her, he had always loved her! 'I was never as irritating as you were!'

'You were enough to try the patience of a saint.' He smiled down at her. 'You still are. Cassandra . . .do you think, just possibly, you could. . .'

'Love you? Is this a declaration, my lord?' Cassandra feigned coyness. She hated to see

Nicholas, her Nicholas, deprived of his usual self-assurance.

He raked his hands through his hair. 'Yes, of course it is, you provoking woman. I love you. Do you love me? Will you marry me? Is that plain enough for you?'

She opened her mouth to say yes, then was struck by a cold fear. 'Even after what I did in Venice?'

He didn't reply, but took her hand and led her to a chaise longue. Seated beside her, he gathered up both hands in his and said quietly, 'Tell me why.'

Cassandra looked into the strong, tender face she loved so much and struggled to find the right words. 'I wanted you to see me as a woman, not a silly, troublesome girl who had spoilt your Tour. I wanted you to see that those moments when you'd seemed to want me, meant something, that we were right for each other.'

'But you could have told me.'

'I didn't think you would understand, seeing me as you did, a mixture of a boy and a child. But I loved you as a woman, although I didn't understand what that meant until that moment in Lucia's bedroom. . .'

'That woman! She led you astray. What can one expect from a. . .'

'No, that is not fair. She wanted to help me; she made me see that perhaps you cared for me. I was wrong to accept her solution.'

'Why did you run away having come so far?' he queried gently.

'I had no idea it would be like that, that I would feel so overwhelmed. I was frightened and then, I realised it would be wrong to do something that would dishonour both of us.' She lifted troubled eyes to his, 'Can you understand?'

Nicholas put his arm around her shoulder, pulling her hard against his chest. 'Why couldn't you tell me?'

Cassandra kept her face hidden in his shirtfront: the smell of clean linen and the warmth of him was achingly familiar. 'I knew you'd be angry. I couldn't bear you to think less of me. And I was afraid, I couldn't control what I had incited in you. . .'

'You have no need to be frightened, Cassie: next time it will be different, I promise you.' His voice was very husky against her hair.

'But not too different,' she ventured, daringly.

Nicholas laughed, and tipped up her chin. 'Minx! We are getting very solemn here, but while we are, let me say I never meant any of those things I said to you the other morning when I found the necklace. I was hurt and I struck out: I should have trusted my feelings for you.'

Cassandra twisted free from his arms and looked at him directly. 'Why did you not tell me how you felt when we reached Vienna?'

'Because I thought you had had enough of me!' he said wryly. 'I had scolded you, walloped you, lectured you, nearly got you drowned. You'd seen my bad temper. . . How could that compare with being courted by the likes of Lord Stewart or a horde of well-bred, amiable young men?'

'What could Lord Stewart give me that could compare with being attacked by brigands, bitten by fleas, poisoned by disgusting food and entertained by the Bulstrodes?' She regarded him from under her lashes. 'I think you must agree, Nicholas, that either I'm in love with you, or I am fit only for Bedlam.'

'I think we're both mad,' he said, with a smile. 'But tell me you love me, and will marry me.'

Cassandra looked at him, the happiness welling up inside her so she could hardly speak. 'Yes, Nicholas, I love you. I think I have loved you for years, but I only realised what it was in Nice. I will marry you, it's all I ever dreamed of. I only ran away with Guy because I saw no future without you — and I wanted you to be happy. I would never have married him — nor anyone else.'

'Little fool,' he said huskily, pulling her against his chest and kissing her with a passionate, possessive intensity. With a sigh of surrender, Cassandra responded, melting into his embrace. For the first time, she could express all the love she felt for him without reserve, without fear.

How long they would have stayed there locked in each other's arms she had no way of knowing. All she knew was that Guy tapped on the door and strolled in, a bottle of champagne in one hand, three glasses in the other.

'It seems I must play the chaperon tonight, my friends. Not a role I am used to, but then, tonight has been full of new experiences.'

Nicholas turned to him challengingly. 'How could you play such a trick on me, after all the years we have been friends?'

The Count was concentrating on setting the glasses down safely. 'I guessed Cassandra might be wrong, and if that was the case, I was sure you would come for her, as indeed you did. If I had been wrong, well, I would have done my best to help her.' He sketched a small bow, 'I am entirely at your service, my friends, and you see what risks to life and limb I am prepared to run for you!'

There was a short silence while both Nicholas and Cassandra regarded the Count, then Nicholas laughed, hugging Cassandra against his side possessively. 'It seems we must both thank you. Will you come to the wedding?'

The Count de Courcelles popped the cork and filled the glasses. 'Your health!' He raised his wine. 'To the Earl and Countess of Lydford!'